Tagging the Moon:
Fairy Tales from L.A.

Tagging the Moon:
Fairy Tales from L.A.

S. P. Somtow

Night Shade Books
San Francisco, CA
2000

Tagging the Moon: Fairy Tales from L.A.
Contents © 2000 by S. P. Somtow
Cover, cover design © 2000 by John Picacio
Interior artwork © 2000 by GAK
Photographs © 2000 by S. P. Somtow
Interior design and composition by Tim Holt

The publisher would like to thank the following people, without
whom none of this would be possible:

William K. Schafer (note the "C").
Alan Beatts, Jeremy Lassen,
and the rest of the San Francisco freak squad.
Typhoid Matt Johnson.

First Edition

Limited Edition ISBN 1-892389-05-3
Trade Edition ISBN 1-892389-06-1

Night Shade Books
560 Scott #304
San Francisco, CA 94117

Story Chronology

Gingerbread first appeared in *The Ultimate Witch,*
ed. John Betancourt and Byron Preiss, 1993.

The Ugliest Duckling first appeared in *Urban Nightmares,*
ed. Keith DeCandido and Joseph Sherman, 1997.

A Thief in the Night first appeared in *The Immortal Unicorn,*
ed. Peter S. Beagle and Janet Berliner, 1995.

The Hero's Celluloid Journey first appeared in *Weird Tales,* 1998.

Dr. Rumpole first appeared in *Realms of Fantasy,* 1998.

The Sleeping Ice Princess appears here for the first time.

Though I Walk through the Valley first appeared in
The Ultimate Zombie, ed. Byron Preiss and John Betancourt, 1992.

Mr. Death's Blue-Eyed Boy first appeared in *Phobias,*
ed. Edward Kramer, Wendy Webb, and Richard Gilliam, 1994.

A Hummingbird among Angels first appeared in altered form as
"The Voice of the Hummingbird" in *The Beast Within,*
ed. Stewart Wieck, 1994.

Tagging the Moon first appeared in
Isaac Asimov's Science Fiction Magazine, 1993.

To the Krispy Kreme Krewe

Contents

Gingerbread • 9

The Ugliest Duckling • 41

A Thief in the Night • 57

The Hero's Celluloid Journey • 75

Dr. Rumpole • 111

The Sleeping Ice Princess • 127

Though I Walk through the Valley • 145

Mr. Death's Blue-Eyed Boy • 171

A Hummingbird among Angels • 197

Tagging the Moon • 235

The Other City of Angels • 257

Gingerbread

When we went to live in Hollywood, we saw many wonderful things. We saw many cruel things. Some people touched our hearts and some people touched our bodies. We grew up much too fast, and when we were all grown we found we'd been trapped in our childhood forever.

This is me, Greta Blackburn, writing all this down so my brother Johnny will one day remember if he chooses to. I can write real good now because there are a lot of books here and they let me take as many as I want into my room and I can keep them there without signing for them or anything.

On Sundays, a screenwriter comes to the institution and tells us stories. His name is Bob, and he is unemployed. But I've never seen him panhandling for money, and he wears expensive clothes. He is nice, kind of, and he never lays a hand on us. He is a volunteer. The Writers Guild has this program where they send writers to talk to people like us. It's supposed to keep us anchored to the real world.

Bob encourages me to write and he makes me keep a diary. Every week he reads what I've written and corrects most of the grammar. He doesn't correct all of it because sometimes he thinks it's charming the way it is.

I know I am too old to listen to stories but I go because of my brother. He doesn't talk much anymore, but I think he is taking it all in. The time Bob told us the story of Hansel and Gretel, I could see that Johnny was paying attention, because he fixed on Bob with those clear blue eyes. That made me listen too. That's how I finally figured out what Titania Midnight was. I hadn't been able to put my finger on it, not until I heard Bob read us that fairy tale, but the moment I realized it, it was obvious.

Titania Midnight was a witch.

•

We didn't meet her until the second time. The first time our parents tried to dump us, they didn't succeed. That's because Johnny had snuck down to the kitchen for a Snickers bar, and he overheard them in their prayer meeting. He woke me up by banging on the ladder that goes up to the top bunk. "Greta," he said, "they're gonna take us away and … and they're gonna *ditch* us."

I was groggy and I thought he'd wet the bed again, but he just kept shaking me, and finally I crept out of bed, just so he'd calm down, and I went downstairs with him.

They were in the living room. There was a drape we used to hide behind whenever we listened to them arguing. It was a nice living room with big vinyl sofas, a mahogany piano and a painting of Jesus over the fireplace, with big kind eyes. I couldn't see Daddy but I knew he was standing right in front of that painting and drawing his authority from the Lord. "It's all settled, Martha," he was saying, "no ifs, ands or buts about it. I've prayed on it, and I've begged the Lord to take this cup from us, but he said, 'I've made up my mind, Jed, and there ain't nothing more to say about it.' And you'd best obey me, because you're my wife, and the apostle Paul says—"

"Maybe it wasn't the Lord talking to you. I mean, to abandon your own kids … maybe it was … someone else … you know … *mimicking* the Lord."

"You calling me a satanist, Martha?"

"Told you," Johnny whispered, and he gulped down his second candy bar.

"But how can we know they'll be all right?" Mom said.

"We have to trust in the Lord. They'll be provided for, long as they don't stray from the paths of righteousness."

I hugged my brother and said, "We have to make a plan."

Later, when we were settled in again, Daddy came into our bedroom. He checked to make sure Johnny was snoring. Then he sat down on the bottom bunk next to me and slowly peeled down the sheet. I half opened my eyes. In the blue glow of the Smurfs nightlight my father's face looked like the face of a demon. As usual, I pretended to be fast asleep, and I waited for it to end. But this time he didn't start right away. Instead, he began to talk, in a sweet voice full of hurting, a voice I'd never heard him use before.

Daddy said, "Forgive me, I'm not a bad man, there's just something that comes over me and I can't help myself ..." and then, "if only you knew how much I love you, baby, but I can't talk about those things. I'm just a sinner and your mother don't understand ..." and then he called me tender nicknames he would never use when I was awake. But after a while his voice grew harsh, and he said, "God damn them to hell, them ayrabs and them chinks that take away a decent Christian's job, and them usury-practicing kikes that caused this damn recession and take bread out of our mouths ... the krauts should've never let them crawl out of them ovens, damn them, damn damn damn," and he called me *bitch* and *whore* and I just squeezed my eyes tight shut and made myself very small and very far away until he was all done with me.

The next morning, after breakfast, they made sure we brushed our teeth, then we got into the station wagon and set off. Daddy had to go to a job interview first, and we waited in the car. He came out looking dour.

"God damn all them Goldbergs and Goldsteins and Goldfarbs and Gold-shitass-Satan-worshipping baby-sacrificing jewboys," he said. "A decent Christian can't get enough to feed his family, and they own half the damn country."

"Jed, please don't curse," said our mother, "not in front of the children."

They left us at some shopping mall, told us they'd pick us up in an hour, and went away. But we were prepared for that, and we had memorized every turn and every street name, and by sunset we managed to walk all the way home.

Daddy prayed on it all night. He didn't even come into our bedroom. Johnny peed the bed, but I overslept and didn't strip the sheets. They didn't notice, just fed us breakfast and told us to wait in the garage.

The second time, they locked us in the trunk and they drove and drove, and Johnny was carsick and we could hardly breathe. Johnny cried all the way. Partly it was the sugar that made him hard to deal with. I guess that's why they wanted to ditch us. Still, I was the one who took care of him most of the time. I'm a good girl.

•

When we woke up, we were in a blind alley, and it was night. There was a dumpster leaning against the wall, so I knew that we wouldn't go hungry. But it was cold and I didn't know how late it was or how long we had been there. Johnny was whimpering because he hadn't a candy bar in a long time. From beyond the wall we could hear a buzzy kind of music and there were neon lights flashing in rhythm to it. There were people chattering, too, and the sound of spiked heels on concrete, and, now and then, a police siren. But inside the alley it was all quiet and dark.

"It hurts all over," Johnny said.

"Maybe we should go back to sleep for a while," I said, because I knew that when you're asleep there is no pain. We curled up together but the pavement was damp and cold, and finally we climbed up on the dumpster and found comfy places among the trash, which was not bad; back home, Daddy sometimes made us sleep in the garbage to teach us a lesson. He'd say, "You're poor, and you're white, so you might as well be trash, too." I got a better deal because Johnny had a lot of fat on him and his butt made a pretty good cushion after I wedged it tight against the metal casing with a beer bottle.

The next time I woke up, it was still night, and I was looking into Titania Midnight's eyes. She was shining a flashlight in my face, and she was all in shadow, except for her eyes. They were sunken into a mess of wrinkles, but they were young eyes, and kind, like the painting of Jesus in our living room. "By Isis and Hecate," she said, "I've struck gold tonight."

That was when Johnny woke up and he started carrying on like he always does. "Double gold," said Titania midnight, "even though the second nugget is a little ... dare I say it ... *larded.*"

"That ain't nice," I said. "Johnny can't help being, um, *ample.* It's his glands."

"Oh, I daresay, I daresay. But within the chrysalis, something beautiful, no? You'll come with me, of course; you'll want food."

"I had pizza earlier. It was still warm even, two slices, pepperoni. But Johnny has to have his sugar fix or he'll get crazy."

"I've just the thing." She rummaged in a tote bag and gave something to Johnny. "Baked it meself. Gingerbread is best. I think it blends a lot better than brownie mix."

"Blends with what?" I said.

"Oh, oh, you innocent, wide-eyed creature. Fundamentalist parents, I'll bet. Raped you too, I wouldn't wonder. Maybe not the boy, he's so *gelatinous.* No wonder you bolted."

I didn't understand what she was talking about, but she seemed kind, like in the parable of the good Samaritan. Johnny gobbled the gingerbread cookie greedily and asked for another one.

"Oh, nonsense," she said, "you'll be stoned out of your ever-loving mind."

She asked us our names and she told us hers. I thought it was a fishy-sounding name, but I didn't want to be impolite. I'm a good girl.

"Well," she said. "Come along now. You'll be wanting to freshen up. Get a decent night's sleep and all that. No time to stand around chit-chatting. Hollywood's like the Forest of Arden. Anything can happen. Sorcery. Gender confusion. Love potions that make you see a donkey as a sex object. Whew! But it's a magic place. You'll see. Wonder piled on wonder."

I helped Johnny out of the trash and dusted him off a little bit. We followed Titania out of the alley and that's when the lights and the music hit us full blast. God, it was wild.

Posters tall as buildings with painted ladies on them and musclemen in just their underwear, and a big Chinese dragon that lit up and wall-to-wall cars and hip-hop making the pavement quake and skateboarders with long hair and one side and bald on the other and people snapping pictures everywhere and stars on the sidewalks and a dinosaur climbing up the side of one building ... oh, it was Disneyland. I held Johnny's hand tight because he gets frightened easily. But actually he didn't seem to mind even though he had never been among so many people in his life. His eyes just seemed to go all glassy. The gingerbread must have been real good.

Everyone seemed to know who Titania was. People would come up to her and she would smile at them or wave. The colors of the lights kept changing and sometimes she seemed young and sometimes she seemed old. She had a nose like a parrot's beak and her lips were red as cherries and her eyelids were all covered with gold paint. A man in a white suit came up to her and pointed at us, but she said, "Don't you touch any of my babies, you hear? They're too good for the likes of you."

And I whispered in Johnny's ear, "She's nice. She'll protect us. Maybe she's our guardian angel."

"Yeah," Johnny said, and then he giggled for no reason at all.

We turned down a side street and then another one. This was a narrow street and all dark, except for one neon sign, blinking, and it read

PSYCHIC READER AND ADVISOR
DONUTS

and I knew that there had never been any place like *that* where we came from. From the street it seemed like just a regular doughnut place and there were a couple of customers inside, including a policeman. Next to the entrance was a real narrow unpaved alley with high walls and there was a side door. Titania used three keys to let us in, and then she punched in a code on the security pad inside the doorway.

Inside there was a dingy living room. A black girl was lying on the rug watching *Murphy Brown*. The clock on the

wall said three a.m., so it must have been a videotape. She
looked up at us. "Hey," she said, "I thought you said no more
kids."

"No jealous fits, now, Laverne," said Titania, "you really
must learn to share."

"Where they gone sleep?" Laverne said. "And what about
lardass there? You could strip him and sell him for parts,
maybe, but in one piece, he wouldn't even make it round the
block." She frowned and flicked the remote to MTV. I knew
it was MTV, even though we didn't have cable back home,
because it showed Satanic stuff.

"Oh, you cruel heartless beast," Titania said, but there
was no malice in the way she said it. "Put on the light; let's
have a look at this one. Ai, ai, ai ... what are we to do with
him?"

Laverne got up and switched on a naked light bulb that
swung from the ceiling. All of a sudden the room was harshly
lit. I could see more of the room. One side of it was all drapes;
they were a tad open and I could see through to a big kitchen,
maybe where they made the doughnuts. The walls were covered with signed photographs of famous actors. The shag
carpeting was spotty ... one or two places looked like puke
stains. Titania and the black girl were leading Johnny by
the hand until he was right under the light, and they were
studying him, like dissecting a frog in school.

"You know," Titania said, "Laverne, you are too ready to
flush people down the toilet bowl of existence. This one has
possibilities. Notice the eyes, how big they are. They are the
eyes of an angel. And the flesh, well, the flesh ... even though
we are not Michelangelo, can we not see David in this block
of marble? Can we not whittle? Hone? Hollow the pudginess
so the cheekbones stand proud, even arrogant? And look at
his sullenness. The lips can be worked into a wilfull pout.
Strip him for parts indeed!" They were all poking him and
looking at his teeth and looking down his shorts and Johnny
started to cry. And Titania let go of him and made Laverne
step back, and she said, "That's it. The finishing touch. Listen to that weeping. It's like the cry of the seagulls over some
solitary isle in the bitter cold North Sea."

"I think I know what you're getting at," Laverne said slowly.

"What *is* she getting at?" I said, and I could feel my stomach curl up.

"He will be our fortune!" Titania cried, and kissed Johnny wetly on the lips, which caused him to make one of his goofy faces. They laughed. "He'll have the beautification room," Titania said. "As for ... Greta, was it? ..."

"I ain't sharing my room with no honky greenhorn," Laverne said.

"Oh, you were always selfish."

"You can tell she's not right for us!" Laverne said. "She gots a strong firm body like a who', but she don't have a who's eyes. She be needing one of your magic potions every time she goes to work."

Suddenly, for the first time, I panicked. "You can't split us up!" I said. "We've never been apart, not for one minute! And I'm the only one who can tell when his sugar's off."

That set both of them to laughing, and Johnny to carrying on still more, and I could feel a few tears brimming up in my eyes too, until it dawned on me that there would be no visit from Daddy tonight. I realized I had died and gone to heaven.

•

The beautification room was about the size of a large closet but it had a TV and a VCR. It could only be locked from the outside. The door had a little glass pane where you could look in. There was no toilet but Titania gave him a potty that she made me empty once a day. She fed him on nothing but water and little blue pills. I told her he needed sugar but she said, "It's okay, hon, this is just for a little while, the dexies will get him thinned down, bring out those dimpled cheekbones."

Titania was the only one who had the key, but you could talk to Johnny by putting your ear right on the pane to listen, and putting your lips up to the glass and talking soft enough so the sound wouldn't carry beyond the corridor. But I couldn't touch Johnny and I knew that upset him. Still, I didn't want to complain too much to my host. I was a good girl, and I had been through a lot worse times than this.

It wasn't much fun sleeping with Laverne at first though. She used to hog the thing you folded out to sleep on (she called it a futon) and she would talk about me as though I wasn't there, and even when she talked directly *to* me she made it sound like I was stupid. But a lot of the time she was gone all night, and I could sleep by myself, which was great because it was a tiny room, the size of a large bathroom maybe, with no windows.

When Laverne got home—it didn't matter how late it was—she kicked me out of the futon so I was at least half-way on the floor. She would turn on the television and smoke cigarettes.

She was addicted to the Jeffrey Dahmer case, which was on the late, late news every day. "I *love* Jeff," she would say. "I think he's beautiful. He eats people alive. He's the Grim Reaper."

I didn't know if that was a satanic thing to say or not. I shut up about it mostly. But no matter how late she came in, she would always go flick, flick, flick with the cable controller until she found some piece of news about him. It was scary how obsessed she was. The third night, even though I was afraid she'd bully me and tell me to shut up, I just came out and asked her why she didn't watch something more pleasant. She only said, "Sometimes I wish he'd carve *me* up."

"But why would you say that?" I said. "Aren't you happy here?"

"Sure," she said, "sure, Laverne happy."

In the dark room all I could see were her eyes, large and round and full of disappointment. I thought she was just contrary. Things were good for us girls. We had a lot to eat. And even though Titania didn't let Johnny eat anything at all, it was true that Johnny was shedding his rolls of fat. By the third day, looking at him through the pane in the door, I could see what Titania meant. Johnny was beautiful, and I cussed myself out because I, his own sister, hadn't seen fit to notice a plain fact like that, right under my very own nose.

His eyes were getting more and more like the eyes of the Jesus that hung in our living room over the fireplace.

"Titania," I said over dinner, "you must know magic or something."

"I do," she said. "Finish your corn muffins and take Johnny his pills. And empty his chamberpot and weigh him and get dolled up, because we're going into Beverly Hills."

I used to watch *Beverly Hills 90210* every week, of course, so naturally this was the most exciting moment for me since we arrived in Hollywood. Titania made me borrow some of Laverne's clothes. They were tight and skimpy but Titania kept telling me I looked beautiful. Then she made me put on makeup so I looked like a painted whore of Babylon. I guess I did anyway, because though I had never been to Babylon I'd heard Daddy talking about them often enough, and I knew they weren't good girls like me. But I was afraid not to do what Titania said because she had been so good to me. And then again I thought of Johnny, locked up in the beautification room, with the ugliness melting away from him with the pills and the starvation, and I knew that what Titania was doing was a dark mystery … like the changing of water into wine. If Titania could really work miracles, she had to be connected to the Holy Spirit somehow, because Daddy told me that Satan can't *really* do miracles; he can only deal in illusion.

And when I looked in the little hand mirror Titania gave me, I really was beautiful. It wasn't an illusion. I looked like, I don't know, Julia Roberts. It sure made me happy to know I could be beautiful even though I had never been in a movie.

Titania came out of her room and she was wearing a long black gown, studded with rhinestones. She wore so much makeup she seemed to have no wrinkles at all. In the harsh light of the living room her face seemed to be made of porcelain. Laverne came in for a moment and when she saw me dressed that way she turned her nose up at me.

"Bitch," she said.

"Now don't you carry on," Titania said. "You can be *so* immature sometimes, Laverne."

But I was sorry because I figured Laverne was a little envious because she wasn't coming with us, and I said, "Why can't we bring her along?"

Laverne said, "She taking you 'cause you white."

"Now you know very well that that simply isn't true," said Titania. "Each of us has his appointed place in the cosmos. You have yours, and Greta will have hers ... and a splendid place it will be," she added, handing me a gingerbread cookie out of her clutch. I nibbled it as she went on, "Come on, now, Greta. It's time you learned the ropes. And really, dear, we must do a little better than *Greta*. So *plain*, so, I don't know, *teutonic!* What about Anastasia? Or Renée? Carina? Perhaps some advice, Laverne? You people always have such unusual names."

"I hate you," Laverne said. "Gimme one of them cookies."

"In time," said Titania, and it seemed that her porcelain face grew taut and brittle, "but now, get your black ass back out on the street and don't come back until you've made your quota for the night." She didn't sound like the same woman at all; she had a scary voice, like those women who sometimes get possessed and have to have the devil cast out of them in church. Then Titania turned on the charm again and said to me, "Honey, we're off."

•

A limo picked us up and we went onto the freeway. Actually we went way past Beverly Hills—I got a chance to look at all the posh houses—and then down a winding road that hugged the ocean. I watched television and Titania fussed with my hair. I flick-flick-flicked until I saw the image of Jeffrey Dahmer on the television screen. He was being tried and his face filled the whole TV screen. I didn't think he was beautiful at all, and I sure didn't want to get cut into pieces and eaten. I wondered what it could be that made Laverne think that way. After all, life is a precious gift.

The limo drove past solitary beach houses. There was a house shaped like Darth Vader's face, peering from the side of a cliff. There was a house that seemed to be made of vines, and another all glass, and another all chrome. It was gloomy and you could hear the ocean sighing even through the closed windows of the limo. Titania was putting on more makeup. For the first time since I'd known her, she seemed nervous, tapping the armrest with her tapered fingernails, smudging and redoing her lipstick over and over. When she thought she was all done, she said to me, "Now, Anastasia, I'm going to introduce you to a *very important* person. He can really change your life if you're good to him. I want you to do what he says, even if it seems a tad peculiar to you ... do you understand?"

I nodded as I watched on television that they weren't going to send Dahmer to the electric chair after all, since they don't that kind of thing in Milwaukee. That was strange to me, that you could kill all those people and not be killed yourself. It went against the Bible. But I had been thinking less and less about the Bible these days.

Where the party was there was a long wooden deck that ran on stilts beside the sea. The house was wooden and all white. There were maids in black uniforms and all the guests wore black even though it wasn't a funeral. Inside the house there were big splotchy paintings and sculptures made of wire and the guests sat in small groups, drinking and sniffing some kind of Nutrasweet into their noses. I was scared and stood in a shadowed corner, but Titania just plowed right into the crowd, screaming out endearments like "darling" and "honey" to people even though I could tell she didn't care about them at all.

"Titania Midnight!" said a woman who was wearing enough jewelry to sink a ship. "You have just *got* to do a reading for me."

"Well," said Titania, "the moon is full and the night is bright." She blinked her gold-lidded eyes and her lashes *rippled*, I don't know how to describe it except once, in school, before my parents took us out because they'd been teaching about evolution, I saw a paramecium-thingy in a microscope, and it had those little legs, *cilia* they call them, and they were just like Titania's eyelashes. "Come, Anastasia," she said, and it took me a minute to remember it was me, and we went out to the deck, to a private place that was surrounded by potted plants.

Titania sat on the redwood planks, in front of one of those electric waterfalls where the water comes down all beads, and she pulled a deck of cards out of her clutch, and she handed them to me. The woman squatted across from us and I realized I had seen her before, in *All my Children* maybe. Titania shuffled and the movie star woman shuffled and then they handed me the deck and whenever Titania held out her hand I was to give her one of the cards, face down. And Titania would turn it up and lay it down on the deck in a cross kind of pattern, which reminded me of the Lord's crucifixion. Then she closed her eyes and mumbled to herself ... I guess she was praying in tongues ... and she said things like, "Oh, no, oh, no. You won't want to hear this, honey, but ... the other one ... he is darker, isn't he? I think, a swarthy man, hairy also, and ... wearing a gold chain: thick."

"Oh, my God," said the movie person, "I can't wait until I totally tell all my friends ... this is, oh God, *uncanny*. Well, it's a platinum chain actually, Herbie's, you know, *allergic* to gold and all. Can you relate?" she added, turning to me, but I don't think I was supposed to answer.

Then I looked up and saw the blond beautiful man with long hair. He was wearing a black suit and he had an earring in the shape of a scythe, dangling all the way down to his shoulder. He wore mirror shades. Maybe Laverne was in love with Jeff Dahmer, but she'd probably think again if she saw *this* man. He had a little stubble, like Jeff did in the courtroom, and the clearest eyes; I couldn't decide if they were more like Jeff's or more like Jesus's.

"You old witch," he said to Titania. "What have you conjured up today?"

Titania saw that I was staring at him with my mouth wide open. She said to me, "Anastasia," and she nudged the base of my skull so I'd look more demure, with downcast eyes, "this is your host and mine, Dana Harrington. I think you had better call him Mr. Harrington."

"But what about the dark hairy man with the platinum chain?" said the movie star woman. "Do we get to, you know, like, *do* it?"

"Hold your horses, hon," said Titania, taking the next card and flipping it through the air, "you have the Death card. I think you should wait until after the divorce. Or else ..." She made a throat-slitting gesture.

"*Shit,*" said the movie person, "the fucking trust fund. The palimony. I'd better lay in a supply of Seconals."

"Go with Mr. Harrington," Titania said to me.

I followed Mr. Harrington through the party crowd, which parted for him like the sea. We reached a bedroom that was all white and didn't even have a television in it. There were toys on the white carpet ... boy's toys, but the kind that are a few years out of date, I mean, Transformers, TMNT action figures, and stuff. Above the bed there was an huge painting in a gold frame, and it was a picture of a boy. He was a thin boy with big eyes, but in a strange kind of way he reminded me of Johnny. I couldn't help thinking of Johnny at that moment, wondering what his was doing and whether he had wet himself yet. There was a tray of chocolates next to the bed and he offered them to me. I had one. There was a weird liquid in the middle, which tasted the way Daddy's breath used to smell some nights. It made me feel a bit woozy, but part of that was from the gingerbread I'd had earlier. I had a few more chocolates.

"How old are you, Anastasia?" said the blond beautiful man.

"Fourteen. And my name's really Greta."

I said I was older than I really was. Later I found out you can get more money if you say you're younger.

"Do you like the chocolate liqueurs? Have some more." He smiled. He was nice. I wondered if he would start calling me names, like Daddy. But he just made me sit next to him on the bed and he toyed with my hair. I was scared my hair would get messed up and Titania would be mad at me so I just sat there, all stiff, eating the chocolates.

"I want you to know that I'm not a bad man," said Mr. Harrington. "I do have ... *weaknesses* ... but I'm in therapy now. You really needn't worry about me hurting you or anything like that. I'm the last person in the world who would do that."

"I know you're a good man, Mr. Harrington," I said.

"I'm an important man," said Mr. Harrington. "Maybe I could do something for you one day."

"I got everything I need," I said. "You don't have to worry about me, Mr. Harrington." But he had already slipped a hundred dollar bill into my hand. "You sure got a lot of art here."

"I'm a collector. I only have the most beautiful things in the world here. Like you. I have an insatiable appetite for beauty. I eat it up. I consume it and afterwards I'm still hungry. You know. The Chinese food syndrome." I wasn't sure what was so great about some of those splotchy paintings, but I was too good of a girl to point that out to him. Mr. Harrington took off his shades.

"Who's that?" I said. I pointed to the portrait that reminded me so much of Johnny ... not fat little Johnny but the Johnny that Titania was squeezing out of Johnny's flesh ... the ideal Johnny, Johnny Angel.

"It's my son," he said.

"He looks nice."

"He's dead."

"I wish I'd of known him."

"You would have liked him. Everyone did. He was everybody's favorite Hollywood kid. He was precocious but not obnoxious. He was bright enough to be witty but not enough to be an egghead." Mr. Harrington looked away from me, remembering.

"How did he ... I mean ..." I knew I shouldn't have said that. Because Mr. Harrington turned to me and he was so full of rage I was afraid he was going to slap my face.

"Don't!" I said and I shrank back, and that left him kind of dazed, staring at his hand.

"Violently," he said at last. "He died violently." I saw a tear in the corner of one eye form slowly, like a drop of condensation on a glass of soda, and slide down his cheek. I wondered whether, right now, Daddy was crying over me. Probably not, I thought. Mr. Harrington was a very special kind of man, blond, beautiful, and caring. He wiped his eye on a sleeve, and he smiled a little, and put his mirror shades back on again so I couldn't see his eyes anymore.

Then he fucked me.

•

Titania Midnight allowed me to keep ten dollars out of the hundred and things got better for me after that night. I did parties and dates every night except Sunday, when I helped out in the doughnut shop, stirring the big vat of batter and putting the croissants into the monster oven in batches, a hundred at a time. Sometimes I made as much as a hundred dollars a week. I became good at makeup. I became more beautiful. And so did Johnny. But when I went into his little room to take him his pills and empty his potty, I tried not to look at him too much. He would mumble things I didn't understand. I think it was because of all the videotapes he watched. He didn't have anything to do but look at television. It was lucky there were a lot of tapes: musical comedies, slasher movies, pornos, and even some that weren't in English.

Johnny's skin had a shine to it now, like a polished vase. It glowed as though there were a candle burning inside him, and I could see what Titania meant about his cheekbones. But I'd clear out of the room as quickly as I could, every morning. I felt guilty, I suppose. I knew that somehow I had betrayed him. Once in a while I'd slip him a piece of gingerbread.

Titania had taught me how to make it, from sautéing the dried marijuana in butter beforehand to kill the taste, to rolling the dough and fashioning it into flat little men with raisin eyes, noses and mouths. "Creating life in the laboratory," Titania called it, sipping her coffee and wolfing down three or four powdered doughnuts, her favorite. It sure seemed to give Johnny life because he'd just wolf that thing down. He was always sad and that was part of what made him beautiful.

Titania even showed me the larder where she kept all the fixings for her special treats. There was a jar full of white powder, and mortar and pestle, and dried toadstools, and a big brown envelope full of marijuana. There was a corrugated brown box marked *Valium.* And a whole lot of other stuff that you could use in baking to get unusual results.

The best times of all were when it was real late at night, and Titania would let me sit in on her readings. They were in a big room way in back, and it was hung with black velvet drapes and there would always be music playing there, the kind of music where you can't quite catch the melodies even though they are almost the same thing, over and over, twisting around one or two notes. I would sit in shadow and hand her the cards. Sometimes she told them I was a mute, or retarded, because they were afraid I would betray their secrets. They would look at me and say, "Poor thing," and stuff, and I had to pretend I couldn't understand.

After the last customer left, Titania would show me how it all worked. Every card, she said, is a window into another world. There's what you see and there's what you don't see. Look at this one: what are the wolves howling at that's just beyond the edge of the picture, the thing that we can't see? Is that a lobster or is it a scorpion in the water? When you open yourself up, she told me, you can hear what the wolves are saying. And more. You can hear the voices that speak from all over that hidden world. You can hear the weeping of the moon. Listen. Listen. Turn over another card.

Tonight the card was Death.

The first time I'd flipped up Death had been at Mr. Harrington's party. Death was a bent old skeleton-man with a scythe, grinning. Mr. Harrington had a scythe hanging from his left ear. The ground was strewn with severed heads. Jeffrey Dahmer had heads in his refrigerator, apartment 213, the same number as our area code in Hollywood. Looking at the card this time made me all shivery and I wanted to cover it with another card.

Laverne poked her head in the doorway. "Eww," she said, "someone gone die tonight."

Titania took both my hands in hers and said, "Dear, dear, dear! The first lesson for the good clairvoyant is this: *Though shalt not kill the goose that layeth the golden eggs!* Imagine, honey, the horror of telling some Hollywood fashion plate, 'Eww, someone gone die!' You'd never survive a fortnight in the biz."

"But what if I get the feeling that someone *is* going to die?" I said. "I have to tell the truth, don't I? Ain't that what the gift of prophecy is all about?"

"Laverne, go check on the chocolate dips, there's a dear." Laverne threw a roll of twenties on the floor, slammed the door, stalked off down the hall. The money crossed the Death card and all you could see was the tip of the scythe. Titania flicked the money out of the way and whispered, "Now, my dear dear dear disciple, now we come to the greatest mystery of them all. Death is not death. Death is transformation."

"Oh, I get it. Like the death and resurrection of the Lord."

"Bingo! Aren't you the clever one."

"So if I draw the Death card, I have to tell the questioner that ..."

"There will be a transformation. No, no, there is no death. Chrysalis and butterfly, corpse and maggot, life rolls over into life, death is a tango through eternal night. Look at your little brother ... how he has shed his fleshy self ... how he is translated into the ethereal! Ai, ai, ai, Johnny Angel indeed!"

I stared and stared at that card, but I couldn't figure it out.

•

In the morning, Johnny moaned and carried on, and he was mumbling and muttering and he had a fever. His skin was all translucent and you could see the veins. I mopped up his sweat with a dish towel and he tossed and turned in my arms, but I couldn't understand anything he was saying, until, looking straight past me, he said, "The man with the big curvy sword."

The room became all cold. I thought I felt someone breathing on my neck. Johnny seemed to see someone, standing behind me, swallowing both of us in his shadow. Maybe it was the fever, or maybe he really could see something; he's gifted that way; in church, he always used to know when someone was possessed.

After the blast of icy breath died away, I couldn't feel anything anymore. But Johnny could still see whatever it was he saw. I knew it was terrifying him because he started to piss himself, which he normally only does in his sleep.

I fed him gingerbread men until he dozed off. Then Titania came in with a Polaroid camera, and she made me lay him down, very carefully, like a dead body on a bier, and she took three or four snapshots of him all lying there, asleep with his eyes wide open.

•

I have a lot of men inside me now. I've sucked little pieces of them into myself. One day the little pieces will dissolve and I'll be able to piss them away and become all clean again inside.

They liked it when I called them Daddy. Maybe they didn't have daughters of their own. Sometimes when she sent me out to work, Titania brewed me what Laverne used to call her magic potion. The potion made me crazy. I learned how to buck and heave and make those little panting noises. But oftentimes they liked it better when I played dead, closed my eyes, pretended to be asleep. That was the easiest to do, because I learned it from home. It was different from home, though. Because sometimes they told me jokes, bought me little gifts, tried to treat me like a real person. They didn't call me names. And they gave me money, so that I wasn't worthless anymore.

I'll hardly ever watch television or go to the movies these days. You never know when one of them's going to appear. And then I'll feel all queasy inside and I have to excuse myself to go to the bathroom.

After a while, maybe because she wasn't Titania's favorite anymore, Laverne kind of drifted away from us, and sometimes she'd stay out all night. One day they were yelling at each other and Titania screamed, "Go away, get what you want, I dare you," and sent Laverne sulking into the neon night, and Laverne never came back.

I saw one evening on *A Current Affair* how Jeff Dahmer had his own groupies who used to hang around the courtroom waiting for a glimpse of him. You'd think they would all be a bunch of fat wannabes but no, some of them were good-looking, not the kind of people who needed to get a life. I had this idea that Laverne had maybe taken the bus out to Milwaukee to become one of the groupies. Since the verdict, Jeff had not come on television as often anymore, so that was probably why I had not seen Laverne on TV. Maybe in a year or two, if they ever had one of those "What ever happened to—?" type shows, I could see Laverne, hovering outside the walls of a bleak gray prison, and she'd still be calling out to him, "Come and get me too, because I love you."

I did see Laverne on television, but it wasn't how I imagined it. They were pulling her body out of a dumpster. I think it was the same one Johnny and I had slept in, that first night in Hollywood.

Later Titania and I went down to the morgue to identify the body, because we were all the kin Laverne had. She was in pieces, but it was her alright. Her hands had been cut off and strung around her neck with a length of her own intestine, and one of her feet was poking up out of her, you know, down there. Her skin was just like Johnny's, translucent. She had never been that black but now she was almost yellow. Her eyes stared past me the way Johnny's stared that time, seeing someone I could not see. It still seemed to me that she was sneering at me, even now that she had been shuffled and redealt.

In the pocket of her jeans, they had found a Jeffrey Dahmer trading card. I knew then that this death had been the death she'd prayed for. It was hard to believe that a man in a prison far away could have reached out, heard her wishes, and granted them, maybe by sending down some divine ambassador to wield the scythe that had sliced her into thirteen pieces. After all, Daddy had always told me that only God can do things like that. But he also said God can be anyone, anywhere, anytime.

Maybe even inside a serial killer.

It made me sick, and later I asked Titania how she could still say to me, "There is no death."

But all she would say was, "You have to look past those things." And she took a sip of the hospital cafeteria coffee.

Sure, she'd said, *sure, Laverne happy.*

Now I couldn't get any of them out of my head: the bone man swinging the scythe and Dahmer and the head in the refrigerator and Mr. Harrington and the dead boy who'd died violently, *violently,* and my brother transforming into an angel inside that beautification room. "God, why'd you have to bring me here?" I screamed at her. "Did you make this happen when you told her she would get what she'd always wanted? Is this another one of your magic spells?"

"Temper, temper," she said. "I have to open all the doors in the dark castle, dear; you have to gaze at the searing face of the deity; yes! Oh, Anastasia, oh, Renée, you have looked the demon in the eye and know him to be yourself!"

It was then that I knew Titania Midnight was crazy. Only Johnny could know if she was sick in the head or whether some devil had taken possession of her body. I was half crazy myself, because I loved the old woman, because she was what I had to cling to in the madness that whirled around me. The city of night had given me a thousand fathers, but only one mother. I cried then, and I hugged her and told her it would all come out all right in the end.

After all, she still had me, and I could do double the work to keep us all afloat. And I did.

•

There was another party at the Harrington place. It was another Harrington place, actually, not the one in Malibu, but the one actually *in* Beverly Hills. The house was different but the room was the same. It was uncanny. The room was a kind of shrine I guess. There was probably one like it in every house the beautiful blond man owned.

The bed, the portrait of Mr. Harrington's son, even the outdated toys that were scattered on the rug in exactly the same places. Mr. Harrington gave me two hundred dollars this time because by now he had found out my real age, plus now I was real good at behaving just the way he wanted. Right after it was over I fell into a deep sleep because it was the best way to stop feeling the pain.

When I woke up, Titania Midnight was in the room, and so was Mr. Harrington, fully dressed now in his tuxedo, ready to go to some premiere. They were sitting on the edge of the bed.

"Can we talk? She won't wake up, will she?" said Mr. Harrington.

"Not if she drained that Valium cocktail to the last drop."

Mr. Harrington said, "You've been very good to me, Titania. In accommodating, well, my tastes. But there was something else you were going to look for ... I don't know how much progress you've made."

"A lot. I want you to see some polaroids," Titania said. I kept my eyes closed because I didn't want them to know I could hear them. I could hear Titania rummaging in her purse, could hear papers rustling, and then I heard Mr. Harrington sigh. "The eyes. The sadness. The crisp hard curl of a lower lip that can't quite twist into a smile. He's so beautiful you could eat him up."

"No poetry, Titania," said Mr. Harrington. And he sighed again.

"No poetry? But how can you say that when you see these pictures? But it gets better. No papers. No dental records. No milk cartons. No television appeals. He does not exist. Not until you spring him, fully-formed, into the world. Come for him tomorrow midnight."

"I'll have the cash."

They didn't talk for a long time. It took time for the weight of what they were saying to settle in. I pretended to sleep until they left the room. Then I got up and prowled around. I didn't go back down to the party because then they might know I'd overheard them. I tiptoed across the toy-strewn rug. Titania had left her purse on the dresser. I was sure she'd been showing Mr. Harrington the polaroids of Johnny and I was right. That's what they were. I held one of them up to the lava lamp and I glanced up at the portrait of Mr. Harrington's son. Titania had caught the look exactly. Somehow, she had turned Johnny into this dead boy. It was like Johnny's body was an empty glass and you could pour in any soul you wanted. Maybe the pills did more than melt away his fat. And Mr. Harrington was a collector, he'd told me. Was he planning to collect Johnny? I became real frightened and I guess my hand was trembling because I knocked the purse onto the floor.

A lot of stuff fell out: a key ring, a packet of Dunhills, a driver's license. I knelt down and tried to put everything back in. I looked at the license too. It showed Titania's picture, but the name on it was Amelia Goldberg. Hadn't Daddy said something about Goldsteins and Goldfarbs … sacrificing babies and taking away his job? It didn't seem possible that Titania Midnight could be one of those people. She didn't even know who my father was, so how could she take his job? And it wasn't *her* who had killed Laverne.

Or was it?

I didn't want to think such terrible things about the woman who had taken me in, given me a job with decent wages, and tried to share so much of her wisdom with me. But it sure made me think. There was more to all this than I had ever dreamed. It really scared me.

Especially when I finally put my clothes back on and I went back down to the party, and I saw Dana Harrington gliding through the thick of the crowd, smiling a little, in a world of his own, and the scythe in his ear catching the light from the crystal chandelier. He moved among the chatter, and the clinking of cocktail glasses, but he himself seemed to be inside his own private silence.

•

That night I dreamed about the beautiful blond man, and the scythe swinging and people screaming and their heads flying through the air like bloody soccer balls. When I woke up I wished Laverne would be lying on the futon next to me, even if she would kick me half onto the floor. It was real late and I knew that even Titania would be asleep by now, either in her bedroom or in the reading room, slumped over a deck of tarot cards, or in the easy chair in the big kitchen among the unbaked doughnuts.

I had a feeling I had to see Johnny. It was Johnny who had spied on Daddy's prayer meeting and who had had the presence of mind to come and warn me. It was only fair I should tell him about things I overheard. So I pulled on a long *Beverly Hills 90210* teeshirt, and I crept down the corridor to the beautification room.

I looked at my brother. He was leaning against the wall, staring at the television. He didn't seem to see me. I put my lips to the pane and whispered his name a couple of times, but he didn't look up. Then I tried the door. It was unlatched. I wondered how many times it had been unlatched in the past, how many times we could have escaped. Except where would we have escaped to? Titania had fed us ... me, anyway ... loved us, for all I could tell. I slipped into the room and I was almost touching him before he seemed to notice me. "Johnny," I said, "Johnny, I think they want to do something to you, I don't know what."

Johnny said, "I don't like the pornos that much. I seen all that stuff before, at home. Westerns are cool. The horror movies are the best. I love Freddy Krueger's fingernails."

"Johnny, can't you hear me?"

"When I close my eyes the movie still goes on. The man with the curvy sword is dancing in the street. Under the neon lights. The flashing Mann's Chinese sign makes a dragon on his face because his face is like a mirror."

God, I thought, thinking of Mr. Harrington's shades as he moved up and down, up and down, seeing my face get big and small, big and small. "Johnny," I said, "are there mirrors over his eyes? Is the curvy sword dangling from his ear? Is he a beautiful blond man dressed in black?"

Johnny giggled. But that was because of something on the television. "You have to tell me," I said, "it's real important."

But Johnny began to babble in tongues. He was always a lot closer to the Lord than I could ever be. He carried on for a while, waving his arms and making his eyes roll up in their sockets, but without the gift of interpretation I couldn't understand what he meant. But finally he switched back to English and he said, "The skull." And pointed straight at the television screen. But all I could see was a Madonna video.

"Come on, Johnny. Let's run away. I don't think this place is safe anymore. I think they're gonna do something really bad to you. Look, I got a couple hundred bucks saved up, tips and stuff. I know we don't remember how we got here, but maybe we can find a better daddy and mommy. I met a hundred new daddies here and most of them were pretty nice to me. You could have all the candy bars you wanted. You wouldn't have to be this way."

Johnny turned to me at last. The room was dark except for the pool of gray light in front of the television. He sat up. He was wearing only a pair of yellowing BVDs and his whole body was shiny, like the TV screen, and his eyes were haunted and deep. His hair was as pale as the hair of the blond beautiful man, and his fingers tapped at the empty air. "We can't go," he said softly. "You can't run away from the man with the curvy sword."

I hugged Johnny and said, "I got a plan, Johnny. We'll be okay." I didn't know what the plan would be yet, but my mind was racing. We'd use my money to buy a bus ticket to Disneyland. We'd find a mommy and a daddy and a tract house in a green, green suburb. We'd overdose on gingerbread and fly into the sky.

I tugged at Johnny. He started to budge, then I heard the key turn in the latch of the prison door. I looked up sharply and saw Titania's face in the television's ghostly light. She must have just come back from a Beverly Hills reading, because her face was powdered to a chalky whiteness, and her lips painted the crimson of fresh blood, and there were charcoal circles around her eyes. She sniffed like a hungry she-wolf, and her lips twisted into a sharp-toothed smile. Then she faded into shadow.

Titania Midnight was more than mad. She was evil.

I held Johnny in my arms the whole night long, and didn't sleep until dawn.

•

The blond beautiful man with long hair was coming at midnight. I knew that from overhearing that conversation. I didn't have that long to do what I had to do. I went to Titania's secret larder and pulled out about forty Valium, and ground them up with the mortar and pestle, and I folded and sifted them with a half cup of powdered sugar. I poured the mixture into an envelope, tucked it in my jeans, and went out to work.

Work was not too bad that day. All my dates were regulars, and I already knew how they all liked it. So I didn't really have to concentrate very hard. I just let myself drift, and I swallowed just enough gingerbread to loosen up my soul, and not enough to cut the kite string that held me to the real world. Everyone was pleased with me and I got a lot of extra money, which was good because maybe me and Johnny would need it later.

I stayed out as late as I dared. When I came home it was already an hour before midnight. I found Titania in the kitchen of the doughnut shop. She had turned off the neon and pulled down all the shades and hung up a sign on the door that read ON VACATION—CLOSED. She had a whole pot of coffee out and, even though she wasn't going out anywhere, was dressed to the teeth. She had on a long black robe embroidered with suns and moons and stars. Her eyelids were painted in rainbow glitter, and her lips were midnight blue. When she saw me she became all agitated and she started to cackle.

"Tonight's the night, my baby Anastasia," she said. "No more slaving over a hot kitchen for you! No more blowjobs in BMW's. You're going to be a princess now, and Titania's going to be queen of the wood. Be a dear and do me up some powdered doughnuts. Mama Titania'll be back in a few minutes."

I fetched the doughnuts and dipped them in the Valium powder. She was gone for a long time and I became more and more nervous. I took the croissants out of the oven and stacked them up. I wondered why she was still baking if we were supposed to be on vacation ... and rich besides.

When Titania came back, she had Johnny with her. He was wearing a brand new blue suit with crisp, sharply creased short pants. Titania had moussed his hair and brushed it. It was hard for Johnny to stand in the light. He kept blinking and he seemed not to know where he was.

Titania said, "Things will be different now, Johnny. You'll be able to eat anything you want. Would you like some candy? Would you care for a doughnut?" She snatched one from the plate I had so carefully arranged and handed it to him. Then she stuffed one into her own mouth. While she was busy chewing I pried the doughnut loose from Johnny's fist and gave him something else, a chocolate éclair. He sucked on it, savoring the cream.

"My two little darlings," said Titania Midnight, "tonight Mr. Harrington is going to come for you. Well, the deal is only for Johnny, but I think we can manage to get Anastasia thrown into the package ... oh, my angels, how I slaved to make you ready for this moment! But tomorrow it's curtains for Titania Midnight, reader, advisor, pimp, and doughnut manufacturer extraordinaire ... and now ... for my next transformation ... enter Amelia Goldberg ... rich bitch from Encino ... estate broker... millionairess ...queen of the glitterati ... oh, it'll be splendid, splendid, splendid, my honey babies!"

I said, "There's a picture on Mr. Harrington's wall. He says it's his son. He says his son died violently."

"I know," said Titania. "So sad, isn't it? Torn to pieces by a mad slasher. Time, indeed, for a new son."

"You're lying!" I said. "You made Johnny into an angel so Mr. Harrington could kill him! He's the man with the big curvy sword, the grim reaper, the Jeffrey Dahmer man!" How could I have been so stupid before? Daddy always told me that people like her liked to sacrifice babies. He said they shouldn't have let them crawl out of the ovens. Titania had sent Laverne out to die with a single sentence. She had said that death and transformation were the same thing, and now she was telling us to get ready for transformation. Right. For death.

He's so beautiful you could eat him up.

Wasn't that why the oven was still on?

"We ain't going where you tell us any more," I said. "We ain't going to die for you. It's too much to ask."

Her face started to transform then. There really was a demon inside. I could tell by the way her eyes burned and her fingernails raked the air.

"Whore!" she screamed. "I take you in ... you *nothings* ... I make something of you, I see the chance to pull all of us out of the gutter ... and you dare defy me ..." She lunged at me, but that was when the Valium kicked in and she sort of folded up and then I pushed her with all my might. Right into the oven. She slid in easy. I slammed the door but that didn't keep out the stench. And then fumes began pouring into the kitchen. There was a smell like burning plastic, maybe from her clothes, and another smell, like barbecuing lamb, that made my mouth water in spite of what I knew it was.

I started coughing. The smoke detector went off and the alarm screeched and I could hear clanging and buzzing and a siren in the distance, and I stood there for a long time, too numbed to move, until I realized that the fire was going to eat all of us up unless I took Johnny by the hand and steered him out of the doughnut shop.

There was smoke all over the street and the whole place was burning up. There was a Rolls Royce parked in the alley and the blond beautiful man was standing there, all dressed in black, with the scythe dangling from his ear.

"Get away from him," I said to Johnny. "He'll cut you in pieces."

But Johnny just stared at him, and he kind of smiled. And he began walking toward him. I ran after him, trying to pull him back, crying out, "No, Johnny, no!" but he wouldn't listen.

Mr. Harrington took off his mirror shades. He was just staring at Johnny as though he was looking at a man from Mars. Then he started to weep.

"He does look just like him," he said softly. "Titania was right." He started to reach forward to touch Johnny and that was when I lost control.

"I killed Titania! Now you can get out of our lives too!" I screamed. And I pumeled his black silk jacket with my fists. But he was hard and strong and hollow.

"She's dead?"

"I shoved her in the oven," I said. "God damned baby-sacrificing kike."

"Oh, my God," said Mr. Harrington. "Where did you learn to say such hateful things?"

"From Daddy," I said.

"You killed her." He started to back away from us. "She wasn't an evil woman. In her way she did try to help you. It's true that she trafficked in young flesh ... but ... no one is so evil they deserve to be ..." The odor of burning meat wafted across the alley. "Poor Titania."

"Poor Titania? She was gonna give Johnny to you ... so you'd kill him and cut him in pieces and eat him ... like Jeffrey Dahmer."

"She didn't tell you? I was going to adopt him. Both of you, probably. You could have lived in Beverly Hills with me and had everything you ever wanted. For years I've wanted a new son ... and Titania knew the dark country where you live, the forgotten, the abandoned children. I promised to pay her well to find me a kid who looked so much like ... like...."

"Don't give me that bullshit. You fucked me."

He winced. "I wish you wouldn't use that language."

The smoke blended right into the smog of night. I just glared at Mr. Harrington. I think he saw my anger for the first time. Maybe I shouldn't have lain there, leaving my body behind while my mind drifted far away. Maybe I should have looked him straight in the eye and shown him all my rage, all my frustration at being so weak and powerless. Then maybe he wouldn't have done it to me. But it was too late now. I could see now that the powerful emotion that had shaken him when he first saw us might have been the beginning of love. But it was fading now.

"I'm not a bad man," he said. "I'm ... a weak man. I would have been good to you."

Johnny said softly, "I'm gonna pee my pants."

"But of course I can't adopt either of you now. My reputation ... the scandal ... you know how it is. I'd better go." Now I could see that he thought of us as slimy things ... cockroaches ... vermin. "I'll call 911 from the car."

He kissed Johnny on the forehead and touched my hair. Then he got back in his Rolls Royce and drove away, and we stood in front of the burning doughnut shop, waiting for the fire department.

•

Sometimes I see the blond beautiful man on television. But I change the channel. In a few months the court will send us to a foster home, if they can find one. But it might be hard since I'm a murderer.

After Bob read the last entry in my diary, the one where I talked about the fire at the doughnut shop, he told me that it made him cry. I don't know why. *I* never cry. I don't have time because I have to look after Johnny.

After he read *Hansel and Gretel* to us, I told Bob my witch theory, and he shook his head slowly and said, "Greta, there's only one kind of magic in the world. You made magic when you wrote the words that made me cry. Words can be black magic and they can be white magic, but they are the only things that can transform us. Even a movie starts with just words on a page, a screenplay."

That's why I go on writing it all down. If I write enough words down, maybe we can still have the things we long for … the tract house, the mommy and daddy, the green, green suburb far away. But so far nothing has come true.

I guess I'm not that good at witchcraft.

The Ugliest Duckling

But you know, he wasn't ugly exactly; in some ways he was the most beautiful of all those changelings of the twilight who blend in with the shadows of dumpsters, who flit from alley to alley, who lurk in the doorway of an all-night grocery store till, with a reticent half-smile, they find their mark and move in for the kill.

I know them well; I have been a conoisseur since I first started coming to the all-night coffee shop, thirty or forty years ago; it was still there then, though not yet owned by Greeks. I moonlighted—they way it is with me, moonlighting is the only way I *can* work—as a photographer. Exactly. *That* kind of photographer. And this part of town was the best place to find subjects for my peculiar branch of the art.

My studio was a bungalow, a guest house with a private entrance, up in the hills, ten minutes' drive from the alley with the back door of the coffee shop; that door was always locked in the '60s, but now the new owners always leave it open; it gives the homeless somewhere, inconspicuously, to go to the bathroom; Stavros the manager, son of a Thai prostitute and an Athenian bookmaker, feels that it's the compassionate thing to do.

These days, I am called Estelle de Vries; the French first name, the Dutch surname, I suppose that makes me Belgian. I appear to be in my mid-to-late forties, but in the right light I can appear ageless, and when you really look deep into my eyes, you can't help knowing my real age, give or take a millennium.

"Estelle," Stavros said to me, as he poured me coffee, knowing I would never drink, "you see him too, don't you?"

"Efkharistô," I said, putting one hand over my cup. "You know I never drink ... coffee."

"I am sorry," he said, as he always says, "force of habit."

"Who did you mean?" I said.

"Over there," he said, and pointed with his lips.

Across the street, in the window of a doughnut shop owned by Cambodian refugees, is where they tend to gather. The light is more flattering there. There are more boys than girls, but you can hardly tell them apart. They are colored the same: dirtied by the grime of the streets, sickly in the radiance of the lime-neon store sign. That night, though, there was one who stood apart.

"His name is Luke," said Stavros, who always knows everyone's name. "I know, I know, he's beautiful."

Human beings are nothing if not shallow. How can they be otherwise? They barely live before they are consumed by darkness. Youth is a flash, adulthood an instantaneous decay. Attractiveness, for them, is telegraphed by a few simple signals: wealth, beauty, and a frenetic pheromonal hyperactivity which they call love. The boy had at least one of the three attributes; and even through the window of the coffee shop and the tang of pollution in the night air I could smell a faint taint of another. With two out of three, it should have been easy to acquire the third.

Cars cruised the boulevard. Now and then, one stopped. None stopped for Luke. Stavros and I talked of many things. We talked about how blue the sky is in Greece. I told him how I used to sit beneath the stars in Syntagma Square ... ride the steep highway past Arakhova to the oracle at Delphi ... stand on Parnassus and look down at the gray-green valley. I did not tell him that it was long before he was born; I did not tell him that it was not a car I drove to Mount Parnassus; that would have confused him too much. Now and then, Stavros would try to pour me coffee. I do eat there, sometimes; you have to keep up the pretense. Tonight I didn't eat, though the special, lamb souvlaki, rare and dripping with blood and brine and lemon juice, was one of the few dishes my delicate appetites could stand. I just wanted to watch.

"There goes Gloria," Stavros said. "She finally found a regular; he's an Indian john, I mean from India or Bangladesh or something; he pays her with one-ounce gold bars."

I had photographed her before. She wasn't that pretty, but with a chiaroscuro kind of lighting effect she achieved a certain voluptuousness. I sold the photographs to *Busty Bitches* magazine for three hundred bucks. Only paid her fifty. You get what you pay for. I was glad she'd found a steady source of income.

I watched the others as they loitered, but in my peripheral vision there was always Luke. By four in the morning there was only Luke, steadfastly staring at the street, his blond hair haloed by the blinking neon, his eyes flecked with trepidation.

"In fifteen minutes," said Stavros, "he will come into the coffee shop and I will be forced to feed him."

"What do the owners say about that?"

"Oh no, scraps, leftovers, doggie-bag food really; he can get it here, he can find it in the dumpster in the morning; might as well get it while it's still 'luke'-warm, no?"

The doughnut sign fizzed; the bulb was going bad I supposed; one day there would be no alien glow for the street kids to stand in; I didn't think they'd fix it. Things do not get fixed on this street corner.

We talked about the way the water glistens in the Isthmus of Corinth. How dazzling-white the houses are on Mykonos. How the Aegean sparkles beneath extinct Thera. I did not tell him I can no longer see such things except in the cinema of the mind; I did not tell of my curious allergy to sunlight. I wonder how much he knows. Probably nothing; human beings are notoriously unperceptive; but Stavros is intelligent.

Then Luke is standing behind him. Stavros doesn't see him, can't possibly smell him—humans just aren't that sensitive—but somehow he happens to slip away at just that moment—a waitress calling for his attention, perhaps.

Luke says: "You take pictures, don't you?"

"Yeah. My name's—"

"Estelle. I know. He told me."

"Are you hungry?"

He grinned. *"Fucking* hungry," he said. "Thanks." He turned, winked at Stavros, who was now puttering around with the coffee machine; gave him a thumbs-up sign. It had been a conspiracy of sorts, I suppose. Luke sat down in the booth across from me.

He was thin. I don't think he'd changed his clothes in a month. Through the holes in the sleeves of his beat-up Bulls jacket I saw scars: cigarette burns, needle marks; he put his hands on the table and I saw deep, white gouges in his wrists.

"Where are you from, Luke?" I said, expecting the usual: Oklahoma, Michigan, the Hollywood dream, the Greyhound, the disenchantment.

"I'm from Encino," Luke said.

"Oh. Then what about—"

"My parents? Fuck 'em."

"But you do have a—"

"Yeah. I'm not *totally* homeless. Don't make no difference."

"You don't talk like you're from Encino."

"Sometimes I do," he said. "When I forget I'm living on the street." His accent has shifted, almost imperceptibly, over the hill, toward the nouveau-riche valley of the valley girls.

He hadn't ordered anything, but a waitress brought Luke a plate of French fries and two slices of Boston cream pie. Luke ate both at the same time, stuffing them alternately into opposite sides of his mouth. The waitress didn't stay long, exchanged no pleasantries, hustled away as though Luke had the plague.

Which, of course, he did. I knew. Because I, unlike the others who share my world, have a sense of smell. Everyone's blood smells different, and every disease has a different taint to it, a different bouquet.

"Don't worry about it," he said. "I'm used to it."

"Are you on anything for it?" I asked him. "AZT, maybe, or one of the new experimental drugs?"

He laughed. "Need insurance for that." He went on eating, and didn't volunteer any more until both plates were completely consumed. He was beautiful. Breathtaking, except that I don't breathe. The eyes were wide, clear, blue as that same Aegean sky I may no longer look on; his skin had a familiar pallor even though I could hear his heartbeat, hear the blood sing in his arteries, sense the Brownian motion of dust-motes in the air between us as he exhaled. "I know you don't wanna fuck me," he said. "Nobody does no more. They all know somehow. Everyone talks to everyone else on the boulevard. But you could take my photograph. I'll let you take my picture for twenty, no, ten bucks, cause you bought me dinner."

"I think you're pricing yourself way too low."

"Maybe. But you're a nice lady. Who gives a shit anyways? I'll be dead soon. Ten will keep me going for another day. One day at a time." Sufficient unto the day is the evil thereof, as a wise young rabbi once told me; on the other hand, they crucified him.

"Okay, Luke. I'll take your picture and I'll give you ten bucks. I wouldn't be able to sell them anyway; you're too young."

"Older'n I look."

Me too, I thought. "But these days, we have to have proof of age on file; otherwise, we can get busted."

"Fuck 'em," he said softly. But when he said it, he sounded curiously tender, vulnerable even; he was only playing at toughness, hiding a lifetime of pain.

•

We cruised around for a while in my '66 Impala. It impressed him that someone like me would have a cholo car. Actually it was bequeathed to me by an ... acquaintance of mine. Not entirely voluntarily.

I was getting hungry now. It would be dawn in only a couple of hours. I had no intentions on young Luke. I am finicky about picking fruit before it ripens. A boy should have a chance at being a man, even if that chance was a flimsy as Luke's.

"Tell me about the dude who gave you the car," Luke said.

We turned up Highland, drove past Sunset and Holly-wood, up toward the hills on the other side of which lay the life he had rejected.

"I don't know that much about him," I said. "We didn't know each other long."

"But you were, you know, intimate."

"Yeah."

The *War of the Worlds* church loomed above a Chevron station, just beneath the Hollywood Bowl. Intimate in a sense. Alfonso had tried to rape me in an alley. Thought I was just some white bitch walking around in the wrong 'hood, chased me down the alley in the Impala, thought he had me trapped between the front end and the graffiti; didn't know that I can't be squashed; I can make myself as insubstantial as a puff of smoke.

We were intimate for about five minutes, and I had a new car; no one really missed Alfonso; luckily, the sticker had eleven months to go. Alfonso may have been young, but he had certainly ripened enough to pluck; his existence was a dead end; I had no qualms.

"What's it like?" said Luke. I decided to eschew the free-way and go uphill toward Mulholland. The streets were nar-row and twisty, the houses cramped and overpriced.

"What's what like?"

"Being intimate."

"You don't know? I thought you—"

"Nah," he said. "I look like a hustler but I don't have what it takes to kill my own kind."

"But you have—"

"Born with it," he told me. "Mom was an intravenous drug user."

"In Encino?"

"Yeah. Sucks, don't it?" Oh, I thought to myself, such innocence.

By the time we turned onto Mulholland Drive, my hun-ger had become noisome in its persistence. But I knew where we were going, and I knew that the boy was in no danger. Here in the hills, we were above the smog. You could even see the occasional star; but the stars were almost drowned out in the lights of the city; to my right, the valley sparkled like a Christmas tree carpet; to my left, more subdued, were smears of rainbow radiance that were Hollywood, West Hollywood, even, like a wispy distant galaxy, Bel Air.

"Cool," the boy said. "But there's no stars."

"One or two," I said. Some joker had altered the speed signs from 30 to 80.

"Yeah, there's one."

We rounded a sharp bend. "Actually, I think that's a satellite."

"And then there's you. Estelle means star, I think."

"You knew that?"

"Had a book once. What to name your baby. George means 'farmer'. David means 'beloved'. Never looked up my own name, though."

"Okay. We have to stop for a moment."

After another hairpin came a lookout popular with lovers. I pulled into the lot; as I suspected, there were other cars parked here. There were couples, lost in each other's arms, eyes, saliva; in a convertible, a man leaned back against black leather and a tousled head bobbed up and down; above us hung the moon, huge and purplish in the alien L.A. light. No one noticed us, a middleaged woman and a boy; why would they? That would be almost the least perverse sexual combination in town.

"I've never been up here before," Luke said. "Saw it in a movie though. I think it was *E.T.*"

I ignored him for a moment. Above the parking area there was an earthy rise; a fence discouraged tourists from seeing the real view; but I knew there would be someone on the other side. Luke followed me at a distance; I could smell him. I stood awhile in the bushes, carefully listening for signs of trouble. There was always trouble on a Saturday night. The chill air sweated booze and indica fumes.

I saw trouble in a clump of oleander, a little way down the slope; I was downwind and caught a whiff of the pheromone of fear; I blended into the cold hill's side, shifted with the breeze until I was right on them. It was a woman, bound and gagged with gaffer's tape—how very Hollywood—and bruised all over; the moon made her blood all quicksilver and black. Hunched over her was one of the many serial killers who ply their trade in this town; I had had my eye on him since the last full moon, when I'd found a victim of his, dying, in an auto graveyard in Sepulveda, and sniffed him scurrying away. It was too late to save the woman, and so, regretfully, I fed. But this time, I could hunt prize quarry, hunt the human hunter of humans.

The woman saw me. She was so close to death that she could penetrate the veil of shadow I had cloaked myself with. I smiled at her. I don't know what she saw; perhaps I was a good Samaritan, perhaps an avenging angel with a flaming sword. Enough of this. I turned to the serial killer, who had just removed a hacksaw from a battered tackle box. I attenuated myself, engulfed him, sucked out all the blood in one quick whoosh through every pore in his skin so that he wrinkled up, all at once, like a dried shiitake mushroom, then broke in a thousand pieces, brittle as brickle. It happened so fast. I don't know what the victim saw; I flicked the gag off her and coagulated back into my human shape, and, sated, climbed uphill to where Luke stood.

Presently, I heard the woman screaming, screaming, screaming; she had held in that scream so long, and now she could not stop.

"I saw that," Luke said. "Dude. You're a—"

I shushed him with a finger on his lips. He smarted; always and forever, my touch has the coldness of the grave about it. "There's no need to say the things we both know," I said. "Listen. Listen. You people never listen; you fill your lives with your own noise, drowning out the music that fills the space between spaces. Listen, Luke, listen."

The purr of a passing Porsche. The breeze. The screams of the woman gradually subsiding, subsiding ... footsteps, tennis shoes on gravel on dirt, lovers breaking off their bracketed entanglement, curiosity getting the better of passion ... I thought to myself: I know he hears these things, but can he also hear a different music? Can he hear what songs the veiled stars sing beyond the city's mist and smog? I wonder. No. Surely not. He is mortal. Beautiful and mortal.

We got back in the car. Luke was not afraid. That was strange. Perhaps not so strange; he believed himself doomed; he knew no possible redemption.

We drove a little further down Mulholland; and then I turned on Beverly Glen, took a sharp slide down Coy, heading for my bungalow. He didn't speak much. Even I became a little nervous. Usually they can't stop talking. They can't help themselves. I'm so alien to them, so scary, so mythically familiar. We reached the house; I had a private entrance round the back; the main house belonged to some big-name screenwriter, who had put on so many additions, turrets, minarets, and balconies, that the whole resembled a kind of Arabian nightmare.

•

My own humble dwelling was dingy and unkempt. Gorged, I went to the coffin—it doubles as a coffee table—and sat on the lid for a moment, letting the blood slow to a sluggish crawl, resetting my metabolism. When I looked up, Luke had already taken off his clothes.

He stood, unselfconscious, in the swath of light from the open doorway of the bathroom, against a kitchenette counter stacked with pristine coffee cups.

"I guess I forgot to ask," he said. "The pictures. You want me naked, I guess."

"Oh, yeah. The pictures. I forgot. Ten bucks."

I reached into my purse.

"Not right now," he said. "The money. I mean like, I'll take the money but, I mean, dude, I mean … not everything's about money. I mean, maybe I'd like to think you were just all taking my picture, just to, you know, take my picture. Like a mom would. Yeah I mean, I guess you will end up selling them to someone but, I would have done it anyway. 'Cause you're a nice lady."

Nobody loved him. Nobody cared.

He stood there and sure, he had no clothes on, but he wore over his scarred body so sublime an aura of purity that he seemed innocent of all those human pecadilloes they call sin. I took pictures, dozens of pictures. I used the 1600 film so I wouldn't have to use the big lights; I posed him in the chiaroscuro of the light from the bathroom door and the dark of the kitchenette. He was a natural. He was one of those models who stares right out of the picture, out of the printed page, whose eyes seem to have something special to say to you alone; but one of the ways you do that is to have your eyes be wide, vacant, reflective, so that the viewer can fill the void with his own fixations, his own private delusions; perhaps that's all love really is, the art of polishing the mirrors in your eyes until you are the beloved's reflection reflected, back and forth, toward an infinite intensity.

Luke had that look. I speak of his eyes only because they drew the viewer's attention so intently that one barely saw the rest of him; the scars, the self-inflicted stigmata, the flat, firm pubis coyly figleafed by a slender hand that I had not the heart to move out of the way of my camera's uncompromising eye.

And this is what he said as he stood in the half-light. "Can you really be intimate, Estelle? I know what you are now. Can you, like, love us? Or do you only hunt us down?"

I said, "There are some things I love. The night. The dark. The cold. The first sip of blood as it gushes up from a freshly severed artery. The cadent decrescendo of a heart as it pumps its last; oh, that's a kind of music. I wish that you could hear it."

"So," he said, "do I."

He kissed me; not in an erotic way, but as a child who seeks comfort in a comfortless world.

"Be careful what you wish for," I said.

"How fucking careful do I have to be?" he screamed. "I'm gonna die, ain't I? What difference does it make?"

I didn't answer him. I just put down my camera, went over to the refrigerator, fixed him a sandwich and a Coke, and waited for him to calm down.

It was an hour till dawn; my blood was beginning to run cold.

"Do you want me to go?" Luke said. "You have time to drop me off, before, you know, the sun...."

"Don't take those myths too seriously," I said. "But yeah, the sun; I don't like the sun too much."

"Or do you want me to stay?"

•

That was not my decision; it never could be. Not every ugly duckling is a swan. Most ugly ducklings are precisely that. To embrace eternity is a kind of destiny; it comes only to those who hear the music. I could not tell, really, if Luke could hear it.

I said to him, "Wait awhile. I'll have to retire soon. If you feel like staying, stay; otherwise you can always take the Impala."

"But how will I give it back?—I mean, I don't know if I can even find this place again."

"For me," I said, "there'll always be other cars, other rewards, other ... intimate moments."

"Thanks," he said softly.

"Hey," I added, "you can probably sell it for a couple of thousand, make a deposit on a place, have a real roof over you head for a while; even, I don't know, get a job; there's a law that says they *have* to hire you, they can't discriminate. Who knows, you might be able to hang on till they find the cure. And I'll still be here if you need me."

"I'll think about it," he said angrily.

I opened up the coffin. It was crush velvet inside, deep purple, with a pretty pillow of Chantilly lace; and a velvet pouch full of soil from a place so far away and so long ago I'd just as soon forget it. I went into the back and got into, as they say, something comfortable; a nightie, a shroud, whatever you want to call it. I lay myself down in the coffin; I didn't close the lid yet. I wanted my last image of the day to be the boy; they are beautiful, you know, these humans, beautiful mostly because they are so ephemeral, because they dare not cross the river to the cold dark shore; oh, he was beautiful. Even with the dirty air between us I could feel the warmth of his skin. I could hear the trickle of his blood. I could smell all his emotions: his terror, his dread, his hope.

"In a moment," I said, "I'm going to close the coffin lid. Be a good boy, Luke. In the kitchen, in the cookie jar, there's a little more money. If you need a hundred or so, help yourself; I trust you."

He seized me by the wrists. I didn't know a human could grip so hard. His pulse pounded against my dead flesh. "Take me with you," he said.

"You don't know what you're—"

"Yes," he said, "I do. You don't know what it's like to be this way. I'm sick without even looking sick, without acting sick; I ain't come down with nothing, nothing wrong with me on the outside, everyone says I'm beautiful and then, then they find out, and then I'm like, they can't look at me, can't touch me, can't even breathe the same air as me cause they think they're gonna die too. I'm nothing in this world, the world's like a fucking candy store window and I'm just standing out there in the cold with my nose pressed to the glass, I'm all craving all that sweetness and all that chocolate but I know I'm gonna die before I can taste it. Fucking Jesus, I want to *be* someone, something—like you. The world grows up, grows old, drops dead, and you just go on and on, dude, I want to be like you."

"But you don't even like killing your own kind—"

"They won't *be* my own kind anymore, Estelle."

"If only you knew," I said.

"I don't need to know," he said. "Right now I'm as good as dead. I feel too many things. I want to give up feeling. I want to be cold and hard. Dead is real. Dead has meaning. Dead is alive."

"But you're beautiful the way you are," I said. "Beautiful is brief. Beautiful is fleeting. Beautiful is transience."

"I love you," he cried out. "You're my hope, my future, my star."

He threw myself on top of me, slammed the lid shut, and now there were two of us in that cramped space and he was hugging me, making love to me, trying to force my lips wide so that he could pierce his skin with my razor canines; oh, he wrapped his legs around me, thrust against me, his death wish stronger than any sex drive; he jabbed his wrists against my teeth and forced his blood down my throat, and inside the coffin's confinement the air was drenched in the perfume of his lust and fear; oh god, but he was beautiful. Even, as my tongue swelled at the touch of the warm fluid, even, as my sated innards gorged, even, as the heat shot through my jaded veins, even dying, he was beautiful. I wrapped my arms around his perfect body, squeezing out his half-life and sending him to a new half-death; we were intimate, for the first and only time, for such intimacy is too searing ever to be repeated. True love is as painful as it is transcendent; that's why mortals can't feel it; it would burn them up alive. But Luke had immortality in him, even though his disease bespoke mortality. That was why he would not be consumed by this love.

I knew then that he had heard the music; that he knew what song the stars sang.

So I embraced him, and I drank myself into the stupor of daylight; and at sunset I awoke, and found him still in my arms, dead yet not dead; the ugly duckling had, indeed, become a swan.

•

We went by the coffee shop one night, Luke and I, many days later. Stavros tried to give us both coffee; and Luke would not touch his French fries or his pie. Stavros smiled a little. He did not step back in revulsion when Luke touched him, lightly, on the arm, to ask him some trifling question— the name of a new kid who had only just started working the block. The waitress, taking away his plates, looked him in the eye and was as civil to him as she ever is to anyone.

I thought: Stavros knows more than he lets on, I suspect. He set this up, somehow. I wonder if he's dropping a subtle hint. I wonder if he wants to be a swan, too.

A country 'n' western love song crooned from the jukebox. How strange that humans are so obsessed with love when they can experience it only once before they die ... or metamorphose into us.

We spoke of the sky in Greece: how blue, how clear, how bright. Luke spoke of the dawn in Hollywood: purpled by pollution, tie-dyed by clouds of smog, spectacular; already there was a twinge of the eternal longing. And Stavros tried to pour coffee, and I knew he was bursting with repressed envy.

"You people," he said to me, "you people."

"We people," I said.

"So full of passion," said Stavros, "so full of life. One day you'll drift away from here, and I'll be an old man minding a decaying coffee shop in West Hollywood, staring through the glass at a new crop of street kids, waiting for death."

Luke looked up at him. Touched him gently on the back of his hand. Stavros didn't flinch, even though the cold must have startled him. "Don't worry, dude," Luke said softly. "I'll send you a picture." And smiled, the subtle, sensual smile of the beautiful and the damned.

A Thief in the Night

It's tough to be the Antichrist. Nobody ever feels for the villain.

Without the eternal dark, they can never shine, those messiahs with their gentle smiles and their compassionate eyes and their profound and stirring messages.

Without me, they have no purpose.

And I'm older than they are; I'm the thing that was before the billion-stranded web of falsehoods that they call the cosmos was even a flicker in some god's imagining ... some *dark* god's.

In a house by the sea in Venice Beach, California, I wait for the second coming. Not really the second, of course; there have been many more than one. But the millennium is drawing near, and one tends to make use of the tropes of the culture one has immersed oneself in; ergo: in a house, a white house, by the sea, a placid but polluted sea, I wait, by a sliding glass door that opens to a redwood deck with shiny steps that leads down to the beach, for the second coming.

A unicorn led me here.

I can tell that the unicorn is very near. I can't see him directly, of course; I don't have the kind of stultifying purity that allows that. But we've achieved a kind of symbiosis over the eons. He works for me. What he does for me is very obvious, and very concrete. He leads me to purity so that I can destroy it.

What *he* gets out of this I do not know.

Today, a summer day, a cloudless sky, an endless parade of rollerbladers down the concrete strip that runs beneath my window, I feel him more than ever. When they breathe, there's a kind of tingling in the air. Sometimes you see the air waver, as in a heat-haze. Today the shimmering hangs beside the refrigerator as I pour myself a shot of cheap Chardonay.

"Where is he?" I ask the air.

I hear him pawing the carpet. I turn in his direction. But already, he's just beyond my peripheral vision. I don't know how he manages it. One day I'll be too quick for him. But it hasn't happened in three billion years.

I hear him again. To my right. I slide the doors open. I squat against the redwood railings. I look to my right.

Against the slender trunk of a palm tree, the sharp shadow of a horn. Only a moment, but it is disquieting. A shadow is all I can normally see, or sometimes a hoofprint in the sand, or sometimes a piercing aroma that is neither horse nor man. The one who is purity personified is very close. Like an arrow on the freeway, the horn's shadow points me home.

He is a youth with long blond hair. He is rollerblading up and down the pathway. He wears only cutoffs and shades. I've seen many messiahs. This one does not seem that promising.

Sex is usually their downfall. I think that's how it's going to be this time. I go to my closet and pick out what I'm going to wear. I'm going to be as much like him as I can. His type. I select a skimpy halter top, and as I slip into it my breasts start morphing to strain against the cotton; I squeeze myself into Spandex leggings, strategically ripped; in the back of the closet, which after all does stretch all the way to the beginning of time, I find a pair of rollerblades.

In the mirror, I am beautiful. Too beautiful to be true. I am California herself. The sandy beaches are in my hair. The redwoods are my supple arms and torso. My breasts are the mountain lakes and in my eyes is a hint of the snow on the summits of the Sierras. My scent is the sea, the forest, and the sage. I am ready to go to the new messiah and fuck him into oblivion.

Outside: I follow the hoofprints which linger but a moment before dissolving in the fabric of reality. I glide along concrete. The wind gathers my hair into a golden sail. I pass him. I don't think he recognizes me. His eyes are childlike, curious, wide. I whip around a palm tree, cross paths with him again; he looks longer, wondering if he's ever met before, perhaps; then, a three-sixty around the public toilets, a quick whiff of old piss and semen, passing him for the third time, calling out to him with my mind, stop, stop, stop, at the palm tree tottering, slipping, slamming down hard against the pavement, have to make it look good now, me, the mother of all illusion.

I look up. Shade my eyes. The shadow of the unicorn crosses his face. You can tell; the sun is blazing, there's no shade, but his countenance darkens and then, moving up and down his face, the telltale stripe that shows the unicorn is standing between us somewhere, bobbing his head up and down, pawing at the sand perhaps, for there's a flurry of yellow dust about his heels.

Oh, he is beautiful.

Now, sensing something wrong, he shimmies across the concrete, smooth as the wind.

Bends over me. I groan.

"Are you hurt?"

"Only a scratch."

I look up with what I know to be a dazzling smile, one that has toppled empires. It is not a glad smile; it's a smile that knows all the sadness of the world. But he counters my smile with a smile of his own, a smile like sunlight, a smile like the sea. Takes off his shades, lets them dangle around his neck on a gold chain.

"Let me heal you," he says softly.

"Nothing can heal me," I say.

"It's a gift," he says.

He touches me where it hurts. I have made sure to be hurt only in the most strategic places; where he touches, I murmur arousal. He only smiles again. His hand wavers over my breast, just scabbing over, and the wound closes in on itself.

"How did you do that?" I ask him.

"It can only be temporary," he says. I know now that he must be the one I'm seeking. He has the long view. He really knows that the cosmos will crumble to nothing one day, and it grieves him. He has compassion.

I moan again. "What's your name?" I say.

"I don't know," he says, "I just live here."

"On the beach?"

"Mostly. Don't remember how I got here."

"You just popped into existence?"

"No, I do remember some things. Parents kind of a blur, I guess. Social worker talked to me once, took me to McDonald's. I ordered a bag of fries. Everyone had some. It was cool how long those fries lasted, you coulda sworn there was five thousand people in that restaurant. Okay, so the social worker, she's totally trying to dig some kind of trauma out of me, you know, drugs, molested by daddy, whatever, but she made me remember a couple of things."

"Like?"

"Dunno like, pieces of a jigsaw. Can't see the whole picture. There's a dove over my head. Keep thinking it's going to shit. That's good luck, isn't it? My mother ... I only remember her a little. Kissing me goodbye at the bus station. I don't know who my dad is."

"Do you sometimes think he came down from above?"

"Oh, like an alien? Sure. But that don't make sense either, bad genetics. I ain't so dumb."

"I feel a lot better." The air is chill; it's the unicorn breathing down our necks. He's impatient, maybe. He doesn't like to work for me that much. He is a slave, in a way. His shadow crosses the boy's face.

How old? I still can't tell. So blond, you don't know if there's hair in his pits. "Old enough," he says, "if that's what you're thinking."

I'm thinking: what are you telling me, you stupid beast? After all these eons, you're coming down with Alzheimer's? This is the purest heart in the world, and he's staring at me with knowing eyes, and his smile turns into an earthy grin and I don't think he's any stranger to sexuality? I remember the one that got away, two thousand years ago. Now there was purity. Is this the best you can do? I cry to the unicorn in my mind; but though he hears me, he seldom answers.

But I might as well see this through. The Antichrist can leave no stone unturned.

"You've made me feel, I don't know, so *healed,*" I tell him. "All warm and tingly." I'm not even lying. "Is there something I can do for you?"

"Is that your condo over there?"

"Yeah."

"Maybe Coke?"

"I'm all out. I might have enough for a couple lines."

"You're so funny. I mean Coke as in pop."

A smidgin of purity at least. I laugh. "Come on over," I say. There are possibilities in this after all.

So we're standing in the room by the glass door that leads to the deck with the stairway down to the sand and he has his soda in his hand and then, always smiling, he sort of drifts over to where I'm standing, almost as if he still has his rollerblades on, that's how he moves. He kisses me; his lips are very sweet as if they've been brushed with cherry lip gloss; his kiss draws pain from me, each nugget of pain almost more painful to pluck out than it was when it lay festering inside me. I feel myself respond. It's a strange thing. I don't feel passion over what I do, but now, oddly, I'm vibrating like a tuning fork, and he hasn't even taken off his clothes, although I have, of course, temptress that I am, and yeah, there's a dick down there somewhere straining against those frayed cutoffs. But what's happening to me? Aren't I supposed to be sucking his purity out of him? Aren't I the vampire darkness that encircles, poisons, and consumes? I bite into sweat and sand. He laughs. It's like hugging a tree. I yank down on the denim, no underwear, pull him into the jungle chaos that seethes inside, and his eyes are closed and I think yes, yes, yes, you see now, I am killing the god-child in you, killing the future, closing the circle of the world, shoving the serpent's tail into his jaws. Oh, I cry out in an ecstasy of conquest. I exult. One more that didn't get away. It's child's play, I tell myself, as I let him empty himself into me.

I feel a fire down there. I've never felt that before. It's never been so good to destroy.

But then he opens his eyes and I know something has gone wrong. Because he doesn't seem to have lost his purity at all. What I see is not the dullness of a flame extinguished. I see compassion. We're still standing there, flesh to flesh. Perhaps the flame that raged through me was not victory. Perhaps I was not detached enough. Perhaps he has actually caused me to have an orgasm. I am not sure. My thighs are throbbing.

Gently he leads me to the futon. It's black, naturally, L.A.'s most fashionable color. The pine frame is glazed black, too. He sits me down. And he says, very softly, "Sex is a beautiful thing, you know. Sometimes, when I'm with a stranger, I feel I'm giving away all of myself, and yet there always seems to be more to give."

I stare at him dumbly. Have men evolved that much, then? Have I given them too much freedom of thought? It has only been the blink of an eye since St. Augustine equated original sin with filthy sexuality. In his purity, this boy is completely innocent of such an idea. To me, what has transpired has been a wanton raveling in flesh and fluids; to him, I realize in astonishment, it has been an act of love, even though it was consummated with a stranger.

"You needed me," he says. "I heal people."

And turns away from me, and whistles, and I see the pointed shadow on the wall, and he walks away in his cutoffs with his blades slung over his shoulder, and the shadow follows him, and I wonder who the unicorn works for, and what he is getting out of all this, after all.

At the sliding door he says, "Oh, later. And I'm Jess. I don't know *his* name." He can see that creature as clearly as I see him, and he assumes everyone else can. A sure sign of a prophet, the ability to see such things. In the '90s they also call it schizophrenia.

I don't look up. I hear him slipping the blades black on and thudding down the wooden stairs.

I work myself into a frenzy. He has to be destroyed. I sit by the sliding door and gaze down onto the sand, and I see him whooshing past, a can of soda in his hand, and his hair streaming.

Sex is still the answer, I tell myself. That's still what the Garden of Eden thing means, isn't it? Though he seems to have found a way out of the Augustinian dilemma. He's found a way of imbuing sex with the attributes of divinity. There's deep theology here somewhere, but what do I know of theology? I am not God. The rules of the game keep changing. How was I to know you could have sex and still retain your purity?

Sex. But somehow it's got to be made more potent. And keep love out of it. And make it so I can't be healed.

I think I have an idea.

Evening.

It's easier to follow the unicorn in the night, in a crowded wharf, on a narrow walkway crammed with vendors of beachwear and hot dogs and incense and sunglasses and car shades. In a sea of faces, an equine shadow stands out. Practice it sometime. Watch the dark patches that ripple across walls, past people's gray complexions.

I follow. But I'm not a beautiful woman anymore. I'm a man old before my time. Too thin for the wrinkled Armani that sags on my skin and bones.

He's squatting between two trash cans; above his head, two dope dealers are squabbling. He looks up at me; I'm not sure if he recognizes me or not. He's mumbling something to the unicorn. The crack dealers hunch together over him and I realize that, shoulder to shoulder, they make the outline of a unicorn.

But the moment the image gels in my mind, the two men break apart. The one with the mohawk that seemed to be the horn of the beast, that one goes north while the other goes south, toward a hot dog stand. All that remains of the unicorn is the shadow of a torso in a pile of trash, flickering between the moonlight and the strident neon of a coffee house.

Does he recognize me? I think not.

"Hi," I say.

"You forgot 'sailor'," he says.

"Am I that obvious?"

"Do you need to be healed?"

"No."

"I think maybe you do."

"A drink somewhere?"

"A drink? But you're dying."

"Is it that obvious?"

"Yes," he says.

We go to a bar. It's a leather bar, sleazy as shit. I have a glass of Scotch, and he asks for a glass of Evian. "Nothing stronger?" I say.

"It's as strong as it feels," he says, and waves a hand over the long-stemmed goblet. I wonder if he's turned it into wine. "Do I know you? You remind me of someone I met once."

"I remind a lot of people of people."

The waiter leers at us. And why not? A dirty old man and a beautiful youth. Actually I thought he was going to get carded. But no. We sit on leatherette stools, swimming in smoke. It's grim. I'll be waiting forever if I don't charge ahead. "Do you know what I want?" I ask him.

I make my eyes still and cold. The way people imagine a serial killer's eyes to be, though in reality they are sad people, lost on the fringes of fantasy. "You want to fuck me?" he says. Ingenuous. He smiles again as if to say, sure, anything, because I'm here to make you whole, I'm the caulk that will bind your soul.

"I want to kill you," I say. "I've got it. You know."

"I know." Still the smile. He always knew and yet he followed me. Was that a swizzle stick in the bartender's tray, or was it the horn of the unicorn? The smoke swirls like the tail of the beast.

"I'm riddled with Kaposi's. I have lesions on my lesions. If I fuck you, you will die. But I don't want to play safe. I'm bitter. I'm angry. I want to kill the world. I want to kill God."

If sex is not enough, I think, then sex and death together should do it. They are the twin pillars of the human condition. The error in making the Word flesh is that flesh is necessarily flesh.

"Will it be enough," he says, "to kill me?"

"I don't know. I'm raging. I don't know if you'll be enough. I could pretend you're the world. I could pretend you're God. Maybe that's what it will take."

"I don't like to say that I'm God."

"Are you?"

"People have said it."

"What people?"

"The little girl that the one-eyed man was pimping said it. I healed her up inside, totally. She closed her eyes and said, *God, God.* The social worker found her on the beach. She was staring up at the sun. I think she's blind now. But when I visit her in the group home, she says she can see. I don't know what kind of seeing it is because she's always walking into walls and tripping over coffee tables. I know she sees me okay, she never bumps into me. Except when she needs to be held."

"Is that a parable?"

"You mean, did it really happen? When I say a thing, somehow it gets to be true. But I've never said who my father is."

He is a profound enigma, this youth with the flowing hair and the deep, unfathomable eyes. "But you mean it," I say. "You *will* consent to die." I know that he cannot lie to me. "You will yourself to die."

"If that's what it takes to heal your rage."

I take his cup from him. I drink it in one gulp. It *is* wine, one of the faceless California whites.

I take Jess back to where I found him earlier, the trash cans, the sea; now there is no one there at all. Behind us, the unicorn canters; I can hear the hoofclacks on the concrete, not a clippety-clop of an ironshod horse, but a softer sound. It is almost the sound of raindrops on the leaves of a banana tree. And then, with alarming suddenness, it *is* the sound of rain.

He bends over, spreads his arms across the garbage can lids, and I pull down his cutoffs. There is no love here. There is no compassion.

There is no desire save the need to kill. There is no passion except fury. The rain is our only lubricant. I am the battering ram with the horned head. I am all anger. I squeeze the disease into him, a billion viruses in every spurt of semen. If I can't suck the purity out of you, I think, I'll fill you to bursting with my own impurity. I'll soil you with sin. Sex may no longer be the ultimate crime, but surely I have tricked him in seeking out death, and that is a mortal sin. Surely, surely. The rules of the universe do not change that much.

The rain pours down. I feel the exultation of victory. I pull away, kick the trash cans, send them rolling down the pavement and Jess slumping to the concrete, facing the sea. I didn't just give him AIDS, it's a kind of mega-AIDS and it works right away. The lesions sprout up in a hundred places on that bronzed flesh, and they spread with every raindrop; he blackens; he shits blood; he vomits; he writhes; he is in utmost torment.

He crumbles. The rain washes him down to the sand and sea.

I go back to the condo and make myself a double espresso.

In three days, he is back.

It's not by the sea I see him, but down in Beverly Center, uppermost level, food court, me coming out of one of those artsy Zhang Yimao movies, iced capuccino in hand. He's standing in the window of Waldenbooks, at the foot of the escalator I'm about to go down. Rollerblades slung across the shoulder, black tee shirt blazoned with the logo of some gothic band.

Why hasn't he gone away?

He's coming up and I'm going down, we're crossing paths, I look at him, he looks at me, perhaps he knows me; I reach over, a glancing, electric touch of hand on hand for a split second, and I say, "Aren't you supposed to be dead?"

And he says, "I heard a rumor about that."

And passes out of earshot.

I go back up the escalator. I catch him coming down again, this time in more of a hurry. "I know you," he says, grabbing onto me; I am not sure who he sees, because I have not had time to change my shape. I run down the escalator the wrong way. We reach Waldenbooks, and the unicorn's shadow crosses the entrance. "But I don't seem to know anything else anymore."

I stop. I'm getting an idea. "You lost your memory?"

"It's more than that. Sure, like, I wandered into a home-less shelter this morning and I didn't know my own name. They thought it was maybe I was off my medication. But they didn't have anyone with authority to dole out Xanax or whatever it is, flavor of the week. So like, I'm here."

"I can tell you who you are."

"Do I want to know?"

"You know the answer to that."

He looks at me. He is disoriented. I have no shape, and he has just awoken from the sleep from which there is no awaking. But behind his confusion I can see that that demon compassion is about to come to life. I don't have much time. I have to do it soon, or it will be like that fiasco in Jerusalem. But I need to prepare myself.

I tell him I'll pick him up where Venice meets the sea, tonight, Friday the thirteenth.

Moonrise. I go to him as myself. I can hear the unicorn's breath above the whisper of the Pacific. His rollerblades are stashed against the wall of the public men's room, and he is squatting on an old recycle bin, speaking to a withered hooker. For a while, I stand beyond the periphery of his vision, listening to what he has to say.

"Tell you a story," he's saying to her. "Because you think you've thrown away your youth, lost your beauty, and now you're this mangy old bitch yapping at tourists for a ten-dollar handjob. I knew this rich dude back east, and one day his daughter runs away from home, and she ends up somewhere around Sunset and Cahuenga, turning tricks, not cheap tricks at first, but later when she's totally lost her looks and been around the block too many times to count, they do get cheap and like, she's doing crack and everything. And she starts to miss her dad, so one day when she's completely bottomed out, she checks out of the women's shelter and hitches all the way back. And thirty-nine blowjobs later she walks in the front gate of the estate, and her dad's all sitting at the dining room table with her brothers and sisters, and her mom's dishing out this pudding which is all flaming in brandy, because it's Christmas. And everyone's crying and saying, you walked out on us, see how much you made us suffer, what did we ever do to make you do this to us." I can't help smiling. The homespun stories never change. He goes on, "But the dad says, it's okay, honey. I'm not going to ask what you've been through. I'm just going to say I love you, and welcome you home." He plants a chaste kiss on the prostitute's brow, and says, "That's what you have to do, babe. Go home to your dad."

"My dad's dead."

"There's a dad in your heart. That's the dad you have to go home to."

She weeps, and I interrupt them. "Another true story?" I ask him. She takes one look at me, stifles a scream, scurries away across the sand. He looks at me too. I don't know if he is afraid; if he is, he hides it well.

"True story?" he says.

"Oh, I remember now. When you say a thing, somehow it gets to be true."

"That sounds familiar."

"This morning, before the sun came up, Jess, you were still dead."

"I knew it had to be something like that! I woke up and it was like I'd been in a dark place, fighting monsters. The whole place was on fire but the fire gave no light. Was that hell?"

"Yes, Jess. You harrowed hell."

"No kidding."

"I tell stories too, you know. You'll have to tell me if you think they're true. I've been called the father of lies, but that's kind of a sexist thing to say; I'd rather be the mother of invention."

The tide is coming in.

"You keep changing the rules on me," I tell him. "First I thought sex would do the trick; it's worked every time for a couple of thousand years. And then there was death. I was sure death would work, because to seek death is the ultimate sin. Death and sex together. But you screwed me over by letting your death purge me of the cancerous anger that I'd worked up inside myself."

"I don't remember," Jess says. "I can't even see you too clearly. I look at you and all I see is a void. I know you're there because I can hear you inside my head. Does that mean I'm a schizophrenic?"

"Most people like you are."

"Don't I know it."

"All right. Are you hungry? I'll take you out somewhere."

We go to a Mongolian barbecue on Wilshire because he seems a bit hungry. It's a no shirt no shoe no service kind of a place but I happen to have an old lumberjack shirt in the backseat of the Porsche that seems to have my name written on it in the Venice Beach parking lot, don't ask me how, probably just another of this world's whimsical illusions.

Jess eats a lot: a lot of meat, a lot of vegetables, about five ladles of each sauce, and a triple side order of rice. I watch him. Sipping my water, I detect a hint of the vintner; it's still him all right, and he's still full of the power that comes from his ultimate innocence.

"I'm starting to remember a bit more," he says. "I guess seeing you was, what do they call it, a catalyst."

"What do you remember?"

"I'm a healer."

"How do you heal?"

"Sometimes with love. Sometimes by letting the world fuck me. Sometimes by telling stories. The stories just come to me, but I know they are true. I've got a direct line to the source of the world's dreams. Don't I? That's who I am."

He's starting to know. He's coming out of living dead mode. I toy with a piece of celery, flicking it up and down the side of the bowl with my chopsticks. "Did the unicorn tell you this?" I say, not looking into his eyes.

"No," he said, "we don't talk much. He doesn't, you know. He's not people. I do all the talking."

The shadow of the chopstick; the horn of the beast. In the distance, waitresses gibber in Chinese. But maybe it's Spanish. I say, "There is something you really need to know. You're dying to know. But you can't know it because you're not fully human. The thing that you want to know is a wall that separates you from the human race."

After sex and after death, there is only knowledge.

Knowledge is the greatest of all tempters.

"You know," he says, "you're right. Maybe."

He smiles. Is he humoring me, or does it already see it? The breath of the unicorn hangs in the air; it's not cigarette smoke, because it's illegal to smoke in restaurants in L.A. For a moment, his eyes lose that I-will-heal-you look. "But if I tell you what it is," I say, "then everything's going to change."

"How?" he says. "You might be lying. Tomorrow you'll still find me rollerblading up and down the beach, pulling lost souls out of the fire. One day I'll rescue every soul in the whole world, and everyone'll shine like the sun, and the sea will part for us and we'll go into it and we'll see a crystal stairway and it'll lead all the into the arms of our father."

"Whose father?"

Your father is not my father, I think. I pop a wafer-thin slice of lamb into my mouth.

"So tell me your story," he says.

But first he gets up, fills up a third bowl with goodies, and hands it to them to cook. The restaurant has emptied out. When he comes back, I can see the doorman switching the sign to *closed,* but they don't seem to be kicking us out. Jess waits.

"Once upon a time," I say, "there was a perfect place."

"Like Paradise?"

"Kind of. You can imagine it as a garden if you want, but I'd like to think of it as a big mansion with hundreds of rooms. Super Nintendo. Videos. Edutainment. Rollercoasters. Discovery and laughter everywhere you turned. And there were two children who lived in the house, a boy and a girl. They were like brother and sister. Their father was a weird old man with a long white beard, and he lived on the top floor, and he had a lab where he experimented with creating life. Every time he made a new creature, the kids got to name it. Every day was an adventure, but the estate was surrounded by a stone wall, and there was no gate. The father loved them so much that he wanted them to stay with him forever. He knew that there was only one thing that would cause them to leave. He shut that thing up in a room in the basement of the house. They weren't allowed to go into that room. Not that it was locked or anything. That would have been too easy.

"The kids played in the house for a million years. It wasn't boring. It wasn't that they lacked things to do. But somehow they started to get fidgety. It was time for me to come to them. And I did. 'Adam,' I said, 'why haven't you gone into that room yet?' And he said, 'It's against the rules.' And I said, 'If your father had really wanted you not to go into that room, he would have locked it and thrown away the key.' So the boy talked it over with his sister for a long time, and eventually I took them all the way down there, slithering down the clammy stone steps, and I watched them go in, and I watched the door close behind them, and I waited.

"Sex and death were in that room, Jess."

"I remember now!" He's exhilarated. "They were kicked out of the house, and I've come to fetch them home."

"Oh, Jess," I said, "that's the illusion I've come to strip away; that's the one piece of knowledge in *your* dark basement room—we all have them, those basement rooms—and I've come to give it to you."

"Oh," says the boy, and the light begins to drain from his eyes.

"You see, the boy and the girl went upstairs to tell their father they'd broken the rule. The old man was very sad. He said, 'You can stay if you want. We can work this out. I don't want to lose you.' Adam and Eve looked at each other. Strange and grand new feelings were surging through their bodies. At last, Eve said, 'We have to go, Dad. You know we do. That's why you didn't lock the door.' And the old man said, 'Yes. You're human beings. You can't be children for ever. You have to break the rules. It's human to defy your parents. It's human to strive, to seek new worlds, to leave the nest, earn a living, make love and babies, filter back into the earth so that it can nourish more human beings. You're dust and you must turn into dust again one day. It's a sad thing. But it's not without joy. Look how dust dances in the light. You are beautiful because you are not immortal. I'm the one who can't change. I'm the one who has to go on for ever. Pity me, children. Pity your poor old father.'

"The knowledge the children gained was the gateway through the stone walls and into the world outside. They lived in the real world after that. Not always happily, and not ever after.

"And Paradise became an empty nest, and the old man realized that the perfect place he had built was a private hell from which he would never escape."

Jess doesn't speak for a long time. They are turning out the lights, but a different light suffuses us, the light from the unicorn's eyes. At last he screams out, "Oh, God! Why did you send me here? Fuck you—you told me I was here to love them and redeem them and really you want me to chain them up and throw the key into the ocean and—"

"You're talking to the unicorn?"

"Sometimes I think the unicorn is my father."

That's never occurred to me in all those years.

"Goodbye," Jess says softly, and he's not speaking to me. I've robbed him of his innocence at last. And now, for a few brief seconds, it is I who am pure: I am all the goodness that was once in the boy, I am his hopes and dreams, I am his sacrifice, I am his redeeming love. Only in that moment, as his vision leaves him, do I see the unicorn.

The restaurant has dissolved into thin air and the great beast is running toward the waves. The sea splashes against his moon-sheened withers. His horn glistens. The wind from the Pacific whips Jess's hair across his bare shoulders. He looks down at the sand. "I'm naked," he says at last. "Can't you hold me?"

The unicorn has dissipated into mist.

I cradle Jess in my arms, and he weeps. In that embrace, without sex and without death, I drain the last dregs of divinity from him. We love each other.

Maybe God *is* their father. But they are my children too, and I'm a lot older than God. Because darkness is the mother of light.

I love them just as much as he does. More. My nest is empty too. But *he* just won't learn to let go. He just won't let them be. He always wants to meddle in their affairs. But he always lets me have my three temptations.

They think they want to live forever. They think they want eternal bliss. But what they really want is to love and to die. That is their real nature. That is the truth that God can never face, and that's why this little war has to go on, why there'll always be an Antichrist.

Yesterday he was the savior of the world, but today, Jess is just another lost boy. Tomorrow I'll give him the keys to the Porsche and the title deed to the house by the sea, so at least he can go rollerblading to his heart's content, and have somewhere to come home to when he falls in love and raises a family and forgets that he ever had the power to mend broken souls.

I'm not the villain in this war.

Tomorrow I'll go someplace far away and I'll sit and wait for a hundred years until one day I'll hear the leaves rustling and see the darting shadow and the hoofprints in the sand, or the snow, or the forest floor. It's always been this way and it always will be. World without end. Amen.

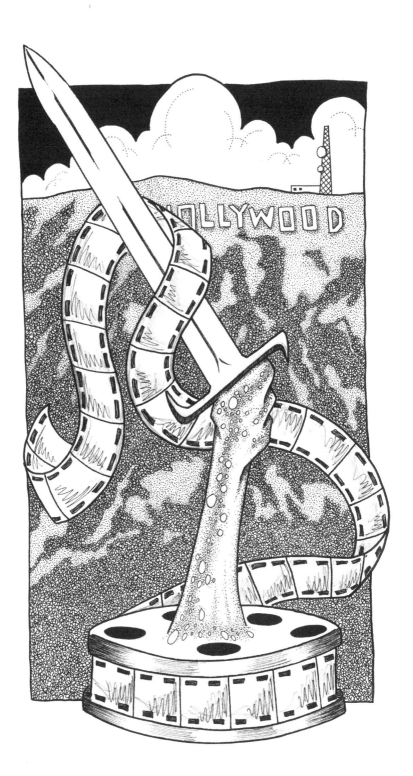

The Hero's Celluloid Journey

The first time I saw the Lady of the Lake was at the Steinfelds' party. A lavish do, they have it every year; the extravagance of the bash is directly proportional to the tax write-off their accountant has told them they need to bring them down one bracket. Hate their parties, I really do; they rarely have anyone useful at them, just your usual Z-grade starlets, predatory agents, out-of-work screenwriters, dealers, pimps, and parasites. Not my kind of people. The only thing the Steinfelds and I have in common is the support group. Matilda Steinfeld (maybe you saw her on Oprah) is recovering from persistent memories, perhaps falsely implanted by her previous therapist, of satanic childhood abuse; I am recovering from something far more mundane—my wife was hacked to pieces by a serial killer while I, tied to a chair, did nothing.

The Steinfelds' gazebo was hidden behind a wall of oleander; unless you knew your way around the estate, there was tendency to miss it. I had every reason to believe I was alone—alone, that is, save for my double Black Label on the rocks—when I hung up my shorts and lowered my shopworn, ample body into the hot tub. I just wanted to get away from these loathsome people long enough to clear my head. The cocktail canapés had not agreed with me. At first, I mistook the tickling sensation in my abdomen for some incipient digestive problem. Then, looking down into the water, tastelessly illuminated as it was by a shaft of pink light and a shaft of blue, I saw a mass of some kelplike growth undulating somewhere in the depths. Perhaps the pool man hadn't been in that week? But that was so unlike the Steinfelds— each of their house's fourteen bathrooms had color—coordinated toilet paper, for God's sake!—and it occurred to me that perhaps I should be getting frightened.

Perhaps I should even scream.

But I couldn't, you see. That's why I'm in the support group. I don't feel terror anymore. I freeze up. I just flash back to being tied up in that chair, the *Three Stooges* necktie cutting into my wrists, my wife's wadded-up bra rammed into my mouth, choking me ... and that madman slicing her, slowly, methodically, like a deli chef ... like a slow-motion ginsu infomercial ... grinning from ear to ear.

In any case, it was just as well I didn't. The mass of reddish seaweed churned about in the bubbles for a while; then— as the timer buzzed and the water went suddenly clear—I saw that it was human hair—a *lot* of human hair. It was attached to one of those pale, pre-Raphaelite faces: a thin, delicate nose, lips red as a coral snake; her hair was so long it formed a kind of robe around her nude body, though now and then a plump, firm breast went peek-a-boo; but I have not yet mentioned the eyes. They were as wide and vacuous as a Japanese cartoon's; they lent her a dreamlike quality which, had I been capable of fear, should have exacerbated it. Instead, I got out of it by cracking jokes, as usual.

"Well, well," I said, "if it isn't the Lady of the Lake. Got a sword for me, babe?"

She sat up, looked me over, and said, "Indeed, you're not quite the way I imagined you."

"Like the accent ... what is it, Irish?"

"No, it's more Welsh than Irish; something in between, indeed." Now that she was sitting up, I realized she was startlingly beautiful—wet-dream beautiful, in fact. I was glad that I was no longer prone to penile embarrassments.

"The Steinfelds sent you over, didn't they?" I said. "But you know, I'm not much in the business anymore. I seem to have a sort of negative Midas touch. You wouldn't believe that *Home Alone* meets *Jurassic Park* could bomb, would you? But mine did. Sure, they still let me keep an office on the lot ... I'm down the hall from Harry Gittes ... but nobody takes me seriously anymore. I go in one day a week. The rest of the time I'm down at USC, teaching *The Hero's Celluloid Journey: Carl Jung, Joseph Campbell, and the Contemporary Filmmaker* to first-year film students. It's a wildly popular course. I like to think it's because I'm a grand old man, I mean, middle-aged of course, who used to hang out with all those '60s legends, but really I know it's because I'm the Greg Hoffman who was falsely imprisoned for the axe-murder of his own wife in the big scandal that was on *Hard Copy* and *A Current Affair;* it's *that* that makes me an icon, not a few second-rate thrillers from the '70s."

Mostly, by the time I'm about halfway through this speech, my audience has begun to twiddle its thumbs. I've perfected the spiel as a way of keeping my distance from people. It usually takes about five minutes to alienate a total stranger; but this woman listened to me raptly, her gaze never leaving my face. Was it the hair weave? No, she was staring straight into my eyes, seeing past the barriers, past the bullshit, into places I myself no longer dared look.

And because she would not look away from me, I could not look away from her; and the more I looked, the more I knew she could not be real; beauty such as hers is a virtual beauty, spawned by persistence of vision in the dark gaps between the lit frames of a motion picture.

I said, "What's your name?"

"Bridget," she said, which is the name of a Celtic goddess.

"You don't look like a Bridget. You ought to have some poetic, foreign-sounding name like, I don't know, Anastasia, Arabella, Antigone."

"We'll never get to the Bs at this rate, Greg."

"Wait! You know my name! The Steinfelds *did* send you after all. Haven't I seen you before somewhere? Cover of *Vanity Fair?* Or dancing with Madonna, cheek to cheek, tongue to tongue, that raunchy new video, can't remember the title? Bridget *who?* Oh, but of course, that's not your stage name."

Steam hung in the air. She shook her head, clouding the water. "There's no need to talk," she said. "You're not really saying anything."

I took a deep slug of the Black Label, then reached behind me to hit the timer switch again; leaned back to receive the full pressure of the jets against my back.

"You know why I'm here," she said.

"No idea. Some kind of casting couch deal, maybe."

"No, you *do* know. You said it when you first laid eyes on me, indeed. I've come to give you that sword."

"Yeah, right. Excalibur."

She laughed. "You *are* the one! Thank the Old Ones; I've been searching right long enough, let me tell you. You've named the quest, you've named the sword."

"Well, of course I have. I have to teach this shit to freshmen who all think they're going to be the next Martin Scorsese."

"You are the hero who does not know the meaning of fear."

Well, that was true enough, in a way. If being so traumatized that you can't feel any emotion whatsoever qualifies as not knowing the meaning of fear, she had me there.

"And you've kept yourself pure for seven years."

"Pure? I'm impotent. I haven't been able to get it up since, you know, the ..."

And I still couldn't bring myself to say it aloud.

"Others have wronged you grievously, yet you have not spoken ill of them."

"You're just like that fucking state prosecutor," I said. "You've already made up your mind. Now you're twisting everything about me into your crackpot theory that I'm the next King Arthur."

She smiled at me. In the water, I could see the glint of metal. The pink and blue lights lanced the clouds of steam. A pommel was rising from the froth. I looked away. "I think I should be getting back to the party," I said. "It's been good talking to you."

"But I have to give you this sword."

"Hey, give me a break. I do the Arthurian mythos three days a week, 4 to 6 p.m. The rest of the time, it's strictly reality. If you find your fantasy world bleeding into real life, I know a good support group you can join."

•

I got dressed and waddled through the crowd that thronged the lanai, staggered over to the valet parking without even bothering to say goodbye to the Steinfelds. The place was madness. They let *anyone* here. I even noticed one of my pupils, Angel Serafino, a pre-med who was just doing my class for kicks. "Hi, Mr. Hoffman," he said, and waved at me. He was one of the bronzed young Californians who belong on the covers of cheap romance novels; his date, bedraggled and bespectacled, seemed an improbable match. They were both bearing down on me, but I was in no mood to discuss movies, and I knew that that was all Angel ever thought about. Horror in particular. Ordinarily I would have exchanged a word or two, but there was something in the air—some fragrance—that just made me want to flee.

Not now, I gestured, and managed to sneak through some French doors, down a corridor, and out toward the valet parking.

I climbed into my Ferrari—I'd been thinking of having it altered to accommodate my girth—and whizzed back over the hill to Tarzana. I can't afford Bel Air anymore, but I don't give out my new address much.

At home, I poured myself another drink, and then another. But I still couldn't stop thinking about Bridget. It was hard to escape the notion that I had had some kind of archetypal encounter. It all made perfect sense. From a Jungian point of view, Bridget would have been the earth-mother in her positive, nurturing aspect; a Freudian could easily see that the proffering of the sword referred to the possibility of curing my impotence, though my refusal to accept it might point to some, ah, bone of contention between my superego and my id.

The psychiatric resonances were so perfect that by my third Scotch I knew that the whole thing had been a dream. In fact, I was looking forward to telling a suitably embroidered version of it at the next support group.

Presented for your consideration: Gregory Hoffman, producer without a past, neuroses in the nth degree. Aspects of my emotional dysfunction: no pictures of my children to be found anywhere in the condo. (I knew, of course, that I had two grown children, Roseanne and Mortimer; but I had no memory of them.) Moreover, I had forgotten what my brother Joshua looked like. (Surely not like me. We were adopted.) There were no pictures of family members at all. Especially not Jennifer.

Looked at from the mythopoeic viewpoint, I certainly fit the profile of the lonely hero who did not know his origins.

I curled up on the sofa, turned on the gavel-to-gavel coverage of the Menendez trial, and slugged down another double shot.

It occurred to me that my two-bedroom condo in Tarzana was not substantially different from my cell on death row— the one they'd kept me in until somebody bothered to analyse the sperm stains on Jennifer's shredded pantyhouse. Of course, by then, the serial killer had done away with a few more women, and *Hard Copy* had done that episode that showed me sobbing, protesting my innocence, and one of those true crime writers—not Ann Rule, some second-string clone— had already churned out a big fat fantasy novel characterizable as nonfiction only by dint of its 2,647 uses of the word *allegedly.*

I mean, I was in jail. I counted them. Nothing else to do.

The studio had to give me my old job back, of course. It was the right thing to do. Even when *Me and My Velociraptor* bombed, they were kind. I got to keep the secretary from Brooklyn with the *faux* North London accent.

I couldn't remember that much about Jennifer's death, or the trial, or the months on death row. I had had a lot of time to think about it all—seven years in all—five since they took me off Xanax and got me on Prozac. In the support group, I sometimes made up whole incidents—worked myself into a good cry—I was one of the group's star performers, second only to Matilda Steinfeld. But you know, that evening after my encounter with the naked woman who claimed to be a Celtic goddess, sitting in a near-fetal position on a Southwestern-style sofa in an unassuming condominium, with too much alcohol in my bloodstream and too much bewilderment in my brain, I realized that I only had three clear memories of that entire year, and this is what they were:

One. The serial killer had a certain smell. Sometimes, in my memories, he had a chainsaw, sometimes an axe, sometimes some sci-fi contraption; sometimes he had a hockey mask, like Jason, sometimes a red-and-green-striped shirt like Freddy, and sometimes, like Mrs. Bates, he appeared in my memory as the drag queen from hell. But he always had that smell—it was a particular cologne. The cologne was called *Oscuridad.* Darkness. It smelled of autumn leaves— bittersweet and with a hint of decay, mortality. All right. It was *my* cologne. I used to mail-order it from Honduras. The lab said it was all over the body. Coincidence? In court, I swore I had no memory of killing my wife.

Two. I remember my brother Joshua calling me up in jail. He said, "You're free. I'm coming down to pick you up. By the way, Dad's dead and you've been disinherited—he shot himself before we found out you didn't do it. And Mom's Alzheimer's is a lot worse. I've had her put away. Oh, and they gave me and Morgan custody of your kids. You're not allowed to see them. I know the governor's signed the pardon and all that, but it's gonna take a while for the paperwork to go through on those kids, and ... well ... you know. They went through a lot of teasing at school. They're both in therapy now. I think you'd better stay away from them at least for now. So as far as family's concerned, it's just you and me for the time being. But hey, I'm here for you."

That was when I realized for the first time that everyone, even my closest relatives, thought that I'd actually done it. Since the day my brother picked me up and dropped me off in front of the Beverly Hills Hotel, I had still not spoken to any of them. I could tell that they thought that this whole semen sample thing had been some brilliant legalistic sleight of hand by that Halperin guy, my attorney. And who could blame them? Because—and this was the third thing that was crystal-clear in my mind, drugs or no drugs—I hated Jennifer's guts. She was an insatiable, controlling, petty, gold-digging, vacuous, self-centered whore. I had married her for

her beauty, which was legendary; I could not divorce her for
fear of losing the house, which I lost anyway.

I had always wanted her dead.

When her throat was slit and that noise like a broken air
conditioner came whistling through her severed windpipe
and I knew for sure she was going to die, I came in my pants.

Seven years later, I had still not had another orgasm.

•

Four-thirty or so in the morning: I had the worst hangover imaginable, but I was used to that. I staggered to the
bathroom to take a leak. I had barely unzipped my fly, though,
when the mist began roiling up from the Stygian depths of
the toilet bowl. Anxiously, I searched for my asthma medication.

The pommel thrust up through the tendriling fog. I recognized the hand that clasped it, but I was really too far
gone to care, I began to piss, noisily and carelessly, not even
bothering to lift up the seat. By now the entire hilt had come
through, and I saw that it was cunningly sculpted in the
shape of a many-coiled dragon whose eyes were cabochon
star sapphires. It was all some kind of strange metal, too,
not steel or bronze but something weirdly iridescent, like
that titanium costume jewelry they sell down in Venice along
the beach ... it looked like the work of some second-rate op-
tical effects house. It's virtual reality! I told myself. The studio had been doing a top-secret VR project. Maybe I was the
guinea pig or the butt of some executive prank. Or—yes! a
diabolical plot to drive me insane so that I would voluntarily
void my contract and check into Cedars Sinai for observation!—but I was all too familiar with that plot. I had even
produced it once. Even so, it did explain things in an almost
rational way.

Then the toilet bowl shattered and *she* emerged. Carrying the sword, her hands raised above her head, clasping the
hilt, the swordpoint hovering strategically over that zone
which, if exposed, would have reduced the vision from art to
pornography. As she moved to proffer the sword, she shook
her head and her fiery hair fell across those unseen pubes; it

was clear that the entrance to her a womb was a thing of unimaginable power, that it was not vouchsafed a man like me to gaze upon it and live.

"But this isn't very dignified," I said. "Somehow one doesn't expect goddesses to come busting up out of toilets."

"This is the '90s, Greg," she said. "And you know as well as I do that Los Angeles is a desert, and all its water brought here from distant reservoirs; this city is an artificial flower."

"Well, I didn't mean to, uh …" I found myself more sober than I wanted to be. Why couldn't the hangover come back? But my head seemed clear, preternaturally clear.

"I don't mind being pissed on, really I don't," said Bridget. "You have to understand that I don't share your civilized repudiation of bodily functions. Once, men shat directly into the earth; now, there is a porcelain conduit that hides from you the fact that you are earth; what you eat is of the earth; what you void—even that final voiding into wormy oblivion— goes into the earth to be reborn. I am the mother, I am the earth; I swallow your shit and transform it into new life; I am woman, that greatest mystery of the universe; I am one, I am many, I am all creation, creatrix, the self-created."

Wow. She sure knew her Joseph Campbell.

"Care for a drink?"

"Indeed! Grasshopper. Frappé, if you've got a blender."

"Okay. But put that thing away; it makes me nervous."

"How can I? *You* must take it from me. It is your destiny."

"But first, I must agonize." I knew that from my own course material. "I have to come to terms with my hero's nature. You know how it is." I knew she couldn't argue with that.

"All right," she said, wandering out into the living room as I followed her (I had an irrational fear that she might try to steal something, like my stereo or my soul) and staring with undisguised curiosity at the trophies of my past lives— the David Hockney over the fake fireplace, my dead wife's Oscar, my leatherbound, unopened complete works of C.G. Jung—"I'll leave it someplace where only you can get it." She cast about the room for a suitable hiding spot.

"There's a broom closet right by the hallway," I said, "right next to the teakwood elephants."

But she made straight for the Southwestern three-seater—and then, with a Valkyriesque screech, plunged the whole thing, all the way up to the hilt, into the plump pink-and-gray sofa back.

"Jesus, take that thing out—you know how much that thing cost? Don't expect me to have industry parties with a great big sword stuck in my sofa."

"You haven't entertained in years, Greg. And anyway, I can't take it out; only you can."

"I see. *The Sword in the Sofa.* I love it. Classic Disney meets *The Big Chill.* It's a winner."

"Don't be flippant, Greg. You can joke all you want, but you know as well as I do that all men are fated to live out some low-budget remake of the hero's quest. You're not exempt from that. You think you're not a man; you think there's no emotion left inside you, no fear, no grief; you think you can get rid of all your inner longings by slugging down Scotch and barfing up your silly little witticisms. Well, you're not just a shell of a man. There's no such thing as that. Inside every paunchy, mediocre studio executive with a dark past there's always a real human being crying to be set free. Do you think I'd really come to you if you were really the nonentity you say you are? And I'm still waiting for that grasshopper."

She followed me to the bar. My hands were shaking as I poured the crème de menthe. I could see, past the étagère with the Hopi vases, that sword buried in my couch. I turned on the blender and stared at Excalibur. Well, anyone could see that pulling that thing out of there would be no challenge except maybe to an eight-year-old. But it did look mighty hip, in a way; the jewel in the pommel gave a soft, pinkish glow that was quite color-coordinated with the rose, flesh and earth tones of the couch. That three-seater needed something anyway. Of course, I'd had it reupholstered after it became clear that it would be impossible to extract every molecule of Jennifer from the fabric; the killer had done a *very* thorough job.

We sat down with our drinks—I sorely missed my hangover and felt impelled to try to reinstate it—and watched Court TV for a while, they were replaying a bit of Lyle Menendez's testimony while two experts argued about childhood traumas. It was getting on to five-thirty now. I gazed at the hypnotic *verismo* on the little screen. My trial had been televised too, but that was before Court TV; it had aired on CNN, midnight to five, interspersed with excerpts from the New Bedford rape trial. Watching Lyle, weeping and carrying on, I wished I had had my trial to do over. I wished I had been able to weep. I wished I had remembered those vivid details that could make television more real than the world. Then, perhaps, I would not have been on the cover of *People* magazine with the caption, *The Stone-faced Killer.*

"You should get some sleep," said Bridget. "You've a lot of work ahead of you."

"What about you? Is this going to be one of those 'just when you thought it was safe to go back into the water' situations? Am I going to be looking behind my shoulder every time I try to take a shower?"

"You movie people," she said, sighing, "you always think about how it's going to look on the trailer ... but you are right. I'm going to have to stick around for a bit, until you grasp your destiny firmly in your hands and hold it up high and go charging off against the armies of darkness. But I'm a nurturing goddess."

"Which is another way of telling me you're the yenta from hell."

"Go to bed."

"See what I mean?"

But I *was* tired ... it was an almost supernatural kind of drowsiness, as though a sleeping spell had been spoken over me. I found myself lumbering in the direction of the bedroom. As I flopped down on the waterbed, however, I realized she had beat me to it. She was sprawled all over the left side, her thigh-length hair wrapped firmly about her hips. "Why are you in here?" I said.

"Any *other* large bodies of water in this dump?"

"You can't sleep here! Aren't you some kind of mother goddess? It's incest!"

"So what are you going to do about it?" she said, arching her back and clasping one of the bedposts between her fingers much as one might grip a sword handle, or an erect penis.

I knew the traditional answer to that one. Siegfried, sent by Gunther to capture Brünnhilde from the cave surrounded by impenetrable fire, had placed his magic sword Nothung between them as they slept so as not to violate the ex-Valkyrie's chastity. There was a sword stuck in a sofa right in the next room. All I had to do was—

"That's a trick question," I said. "I'm not pulling that thing out of the couch. Because if I do—"

"It means you accept everything I've been telling you; that you, indeed, are some kind of hero with some kind of destiny; that you're going to have to mate with your anima and wrestle with your shadow; that you're going to have to set out on a quest, slay dragons, salve the honor of beautiful princesses, perhaps even glimpse the holy grail; and you're going to have to accept that these things are possible, not in some Jungian never-never-land, but in a place as false and feelingless as Tarzana, in a milieu as hollow as Hollywood, in a time as tawdry as today."

Okay. The things she said were all commonplaces of the course I teach; in fact, my last lecture had used some of those very phrases. Perhaps it was their familiarity; perhaps it was the lilt and resonance of her voice; perhaps, after all these years, I still longed to be sung to sleep. But I began to drift; and in my slumber I floated through half-remembered images of childhood; I suckled at some mountainous breast that oozed forth blood and gall.

•

I got up mid-morning to take a piss, and the toilet was once more whole, and again I began to entertain the thought that I was having the acid flashback to end all flashbacks, thirty years too late. But the sword was still stuck in the couch, and Bridget was in the kitchen fixing eggs, lox, and bagels.

And the sword was still stuck in the sofa.

Stuck in the sofa.

I put my hand on the hilt. Gave it a little tug, enough to realize that there was nothing to it at all; it would glide out as smoothly as a well-lubricated penis. Then I saw her coming, so I hastily pushed it back in.

"Temptation?" she said. She had a demitasse of espresso and no clothes. In the daylight I saw that there was about her person a delicate mist, through which a school of tasseled rainbows darted; even in the concrete desert she could not be too far from water; she wrung what little moisture there was out of the air. Sipping the coffee, I watched her dancelike movements as she brought in the tray of bagels; the lox, like the ruby in the pommel, matched her hair. Uncanny. I bit into the fish. The sensation was indescribable. Yes, there was something of a woman's scent about that salmon. For a moment, I almost thought that my long-lost manhood was beginning to stiffen. Then I remembered. I was a self-made eunuch.

I also remembered something else. "You can't stay," I said. "Really, you can't, this time. It's the support group. They're meeting here this afternoon. Barbecue first, then therapy."

"Indeed, I'm sure I'll like your friends very much."

"But you haven't got any clothes!"

"I'm a size 8," she told me.

I went to the Galleria, told the sales clerk at the Benetton store to pick out something nice—managed to get away with under four figures for three items—and when I returned to the condo, Bridget was already hard at work cleaning trout. There was a basin of peeled, deveined scampi in the sink, and a bucket of oysters waiting to be shucked. Clearly, she had not gone to the store—at least, I hoped she had not, in her current state of déshabillé—and it occurred to me that I hadn't had any smoked salmon in the fridge the previous night, either.

I fetched myself a Bacardi and Diet Coke, and she pulled a plump, wriggling sea bass out of the disposal.

Oh yes. Though the weather report had put the humidity at less than one percent, the air in the condo was positively lubricious with feminine moisture.

"Are you becoming at least a *little* convinced," she asked me, "that I am nothing more or less than who I say I am?"

I didn't answer. I just took a couple of Valium and sacked out in an armchair in front of the Menendez trial, waiting for my fellow journeyers to arrive.

•

When I came to, they had all eaten, and the support group was in full swing. In fact, the Lady of the Lake appeared to be the life of the party, and she still hadn't put on any clothes.

Matilda Steinfeld was holding forth at the moment. "I was in sort of an iron cage," she said, "suspended from the roof. Well, it was more like a cave, not a room. There was an altar and there was a man with horns and a great big dildo with metal spikes. They made me kill my little brother, you know. I had to eat his heart. And he was screaming the whole time."

"Screaming?" it was a voice I didn't recognize. Still bleary-eyed, I thought it was Jennifer for a moment, but it was someone considerably younger. She wasn't extravagantly overdressed like the others. She had on a pair of stupefying spectacles. After a moment, I remembered where I'd last seen her—at the Steinfelds party, coming at me with that Serafino boy. "Your little brother was screaming *while you were eating his heart?* Oh, Matilda, surely you must realize that there's an element of fantasy here."

"Not at all," Bridget said. "I do it all the time."

She got a big laugh. I realized that the reason no one minded her nakedness was twofold; first, it fit in perfectly with the purpose of the support group; second, it became her.

But the plain-looking woman persisted. "But surely you've checked the hospital records ... you've figured out by now that you never had a little brother."

"I know you're new here—" I began.

"Rachel," she said. "Rachel Goldberg."

"Rachel, but they must have told you the rules. When you're within the circle of this support group, you are allowed to state any fantasy you wish as fact. You are allowed to *live* your fantasy, without restrictions, without boundaries, and absolutely without any judgmental comments."

"Sorry," Rachel said.

"No need," said Mike Lazar, our therapist, who did not generally interrupt, "I should perhaps explain, Greg, since you've *finally* woken up, that the particular fantasy that Rachel is seeking help with is the delusion that everything in the universe has a rational explanation."

More applause. Was I being made the butt of some joke? What had been going on while they slept? What was in that trout? Had my fellow travelers ingested the Christian *ichthys,* which every mythographer knows is actually the lost phallus of the dead-and-resurrected Osiris, for which the mother-goddess Isis nightly scours the depths of the Nile ... and was not Isis but a somewhat more exotic manifestation of Bridget, who had come to me out of the waters of the Steinfelds' Jacuzzi? I turned to Mike Lazar, who was still basking in the others' applause. Only the mousy Rachel wasn't buying it. Suddenly I realized that I liked her.

And now they were raptly listening to Bridget's fantasy, which was, of course, that she was the Lady of the Lake who had planted Excalibur within the rocky confines of my sofa, who was now daring them all to draw out the sword and prove that they, not I, were the *kvisatz ha-derach* of the week. Lazar was the first. Laughing, he tugged, and tugged, and tugged, and then he shrugged, as if to say, Well, well, I've played along enough already, back to reality now! Then, of course, Matilda had to have a go, even though she found the whole thing ineffably satanic; her husband, not strictly speaking a member of the group, tried it and actually budged it a notch or so, being the long-suffering saint that he was; Célestine, the lesbian transsexual, refused to try at all, citing silly machismo rituals, the Brady Bill, and political correctness; and as for Rachel, she really did try; I could tell; she was straining every muscle in her body, and I caught, mingled with the sweat odor of her efforts, a whiff of *Oscuridad* ... and then Bridget turned to me with a sort of *voilà* gesture and I said, "Oh no. You're not getting me this way. I'm not into peer pressure."

But that *Oscuridad*—

Oh, it opened the floodgates. Those fucking memories came welling up. Not the killing of Jennifer so much, but God, there were details, nauseating details ... I distinctly remembered now that her trachea had taken three hacks of the razorblade to slit all the way through ... remembered the spritzing blood ... remembered a lot more of the killer, too, remembered him muttering, "Love, death, love, death, love, death" with each swing of the ginsu knife, remembered the way he laughed. It was a curiously high-pitched laugh, like a teenager playing at villainy.

Then I suddenly remembered the first time I had ever met Jennifer. I had come upon her and my brother Joshua *in flagrante* behind the oleander bushes ... not at the Steinfelds' gazebo. I believe it was the Rabinoviches' cabana.

"Hey, Greg," Joshua had shouted to me. "Come and join us."

I always envied Josh his ability to copulate with women in odd locations, and in those days we always shared everything. I wasn't fat then, either. "Are you sure?" I said.

"Fuck yeah," he said. "She's just a shikseh anyway."

Jennifer giggled. She was a good giggler, one of those "'cause I'm a blonde" kind of girls. We all had sex. It was uninhibited, '70s-style pre-AIDS sex. We never thought we'd see her again. But a year later, she was an Oscar nominee. That made being a shikseh acceptable.

It was, come to think of it, Thanksgiving, and it was the Rabinoviches' turn, and Jennifer was junior scream queen over at Stupendous Studios, having just debuted in *East of Amityville*—hardly Oscar material. Rabinovich is every three years, so that would have made it the year before we were married, which ... suddenly I realized why Josh had wanted custody of my kids so badly, even before the family decided I was a serial killer. "That fucker," I said softly. "I'm a cuckold!"

"Not a word one hears much these days," Lazar said.

"So I read books," I said. "Not *every* producer is illiterate."

"That's good, that's very good, you venting your hostility like that; you're making great progress today, Greg. Maybe next week, at the Ben Davids, we can actually begin your descent into the private darkness that you fear so much."

Darkness! *Oscuridad!*

I caught another lungful of that cologne, and I started to go *really* wild. The scene of the crime ... it was *true,* the hockey mask, the Freddy sweater, the Mrs. Bates wig ... I hadn't made up any of those things ... I could see the killer right in front of me, an amalgam of every slasher in the celluloid world ... I heard that curious high-pitched laugh, could almost imitate it, knew it for a parody of my own laugh ... knew that the killer was drenched in *my* Honduras cologne ... had it been me after all? ... no, no ... "Who gave you *Oscuridad?"* I screamed. "Someone with a high-pitched laugh, who traipses around in a dress and wears a hockey mask and slices women in two?"

"Well," Rachel said, "my friend *does* sometimes borrow my pantyhose, but I hardly think—"

"God almighty, woman, your life is in danger! They never caught him, you know. The trail got cold after they put *me* away. Now I know what I'm supposed to use this sword for." I grabbed the hilt and it slid out easily. I brandished it as my guests dived under coffee tables and behind utility carts. "Finally I understand! I'm the one who's got to go after the man who stalked and killed my wife. I'm the one who—" The sword felt good in my hands. Somehow the gnarled hilt seemed moulded to the rills and indentations of my fists. "That's the quest that's going to restore my manhood ... you're the princess I'm supposed to rescue ... and the faceless killer is the dragon that's lusting to devour your—wait. I bet you're a virgin, aren't you?"

Hesitantly, Rachel nodded. I guess maybe she thought the others would laugh at her, but no one did.

In fact, the entire group was in shock. It was as though they had sat through the entire *Ring* cycle. I put the sword down gingerly and they crawled back to their places. Then they started clapping. In our support group, it was traditional to applaud a good self-revelation.

•

Afterwards, they all clustered around Bridget like fireflies; perhaps it was the glamour of what Lazar called "the most sophisticated Autotheistic-Delusional Disorder I've ever encountered." This "ADD" was the good doctor's personal contribution to the jargon of the neurosis-of-the-month club, and he was proud to have a prime specimen on hand.

I found myself alone with Rachel, in the kitchen, rinsing off the fishbones and stacking the dishwasher. My nostrils were full of that autumnal odor. It was the one scent capable of drowning out the fishy smell left by Bridget's conjurations. "Listen, Rachel," I said, "we can't fuck around. When I said you were in danger I meant it. Who gave you that Honduran *eau de toilette?* I'm obviously meant to track this guy down and kill him with Excalibur." It was just as I had feared. I had pulled the sword out of the sofa and now I had bought into the whole damn fantasy.

"A friend," she told me.

"What sort of friend?"

"Obviously not *that* intimate, since you were kind enough to broadcast my virginity in front of the whole gang."

"Can I meet him?"

"You see him every week. He's in that class of yours."

"He's in *The Hero's Celluloid Journey: Carl Jung, Joseph Campbell, and the Contemporary Filmmaker?*"

"That's the one."

"Which one is he?" Was it the pustulant-faced, beady-browed Elan Rosenberg, or the swarthy Levon Jihanian? Or was I succumbing too much to cinematic stereotyping? Perhaps it was someone who looked completely trustworthy ... the leading man type ... like the Matt Dillonesque Angel Serafino who always sat in the front row, taking copious notes and asking intelligent questions. The one who always reminded me of *me* as a young man. "It's not Serafino, is it?"

Rachel smiled. "Serendipity," she said, "*another* Jungian concept."

"But if Angel Serafino is the dragon, and you're the maiden to be rescued, shouldn't I be attracted to you?"

"You mean you're not?"

"Well ... perhaps in a platonic sense ... but ... well, I'm incapable of, you know."

"Yeah. I read about that in *People*. I was little, then, though."

Alone with her in the kitchen, breathing in the fragrance that brought back not only the horror that held me captive but also the last outpouring of my last manhood, I realized that I did feel something. Not lust as such. It was the lust for lust. Lust in the second degree. "I don't know if it's you," I said. "Maybe it's just the scent of love and death that you exude."

"I'm told the impotence is all in the mind."

"That's all very well, but that's also true of reality."

"Screw this! Can't we just fuck?"

"In the kitchen? Surrounded by the carcasses of trout?"

She flung her arms around me. "I need you," she said. "I need to be filled up with something larger than myself. I need passion. I need enchantment." She thrust her tongue into my mouth and I attempted to respond in kind despite the limpness of my sword. She placed my hand upon her left breast and I gave it a tentative squeeze, at which she shuddered all over; she began shaking, and weeping, and she was forced to withdraw her tongue so that I could wipe her tears away with a paper towel. "Oh, I love you, I love you, I've always loved you," she said, which was hard for me to believe since I had just met her; then, as if worried that she had said too much, she retreated to the far corner of the kitchen, next to the electric pasta maker, and stared into the wall.

I felt an overwhelming need to love her, to protect her, a feeling so powerful it seemed to derive from some forgotten wellspring of my past.

"All right," I said. "I *do* love you. I *think* that's what this is."

"Thank you," she said, and kissed me on the cheek. But chastely, so so chastely. Then, Helen Keller fashion, she wrote her phone number on my hand.

•

That night I lay down on a waterbed that held a slumbering goddess. Bridget's snores made tidal waves; the pillows pitched and yawed; the airc onditioner squalled and howled; gradually it began to seem that I was thrashing on some intemperate sea, and that the goddess's form had become a piece of driftwood to which I clung in desperation—perhaps the sculpted prow of my wrecked ship.

I don't know how awake I was. I think this was one of those lucid dreams that I had often alluded to in the Jungian portion of my class, a sending from the collective unconscious. I was surprised that an ordinary person like me could be visited by such a dream. The sky was black and the water brackish. Excalibur, wedged between the timbers, served merely as a clothes horse for my rusted armor. From cloud to cloud, a dove flitted, and I wondered whether I had fallen overboard from Noah's ark. A voice cried, *This is my beloved son, in whom I am well pleased;* but was it referring to me? Was it proper to take up arms against a sea of troubles, or would that be mixing my metaphors?

Then, in the distance, I saw the maëlstrom. My raft was coming apart. We had gone from *Jason and the Argonauts* to *Journey to the Center of the Earth.* What movie was next? Would the Kraken wake? Would *Jaws 3-D* come hurtling through the waves?

Get a grip! I told myself. These celluloid allusions were just my fevered conscious mind desperately trying to trivialize the sending. I stood up, breasted the big wind, ignored the fact that we were swirling down the toilet bowl at the end of the universe. I took the armor from its stand. It fitted easily over my jockey shorts and yellowing undershirt. The tempest began to sand away the rust. I gleamed. In the ocean without sunlight, I myself became the sun-king that must die and be reborn to redeem the world. I seized the sword-hilt in both hands. The sword made a bright arc in the air. Lightning lanced the darkness.

But was that land I glimpsed on the far horizon, a black ribbon betwixt sea and sky? I plunged my sword into the waters like an oar. The swordpoint struck something hard. The waters parted. The naked goddess-wooden prow I clung to began plummeting into an abyss, a well whose walls were the ocean; we had gone from epic fantasy to the opening of *Alice in Wonderland.* As we fell, Bridget grew. At first it was

only in the hips; they widened and widened until she resembled one of those Neolithic fertility icons. Then her breasts
began to bloat; rivulets of milk burst from the nipples; she
sighed and she heaved and her skin began to buckle into
mountain ranges, and her red hair was now the red of autumn, a billowing mass of dead leaves, and still she grew
and grew and grew until I saw that she *was* the sea bed
walled by towering water, that every pore of her was a volcano or a sulphurous geyser; that the earth was young and
bursting with reproductive energy.

In the midst of the goddess, who now stretched from horizon to horizon, the goddess who had been the prow who
had been the raft who had been the woman who had sprung
from the spa at the Steinfelds' annual bash, there was me:
Gregory Hoffman, decrepit studio executive and sometime
college professor, my wrists bound to a kitchen chair by a
Three Stooges necktie, and a bra crammed into my mouth.

On the sofa—the custom sofa which was the only link between my Beverly Hills past and my Tarzana present—there
was my wife; above her, the ginsu-brandishing killer. The air
was full of smells: the *Oscuridad,* the fresh blood, the fear—I
was choking—straining against the necktie. The killer was
raping and slicing. A shredded aureola whistled through the
air. Yes, I watched it all with a certain detachment. He wore
the hockey mask over the Freddy mask (they advertise them
in *Fangoria* magazine) and topped it all with the Mrs. Bates
wig. Every inch of him was covered—he even wore white
gloves, like a cartoon animal—except for the penis that, glistening, protruded from a pair of oversized Bugle Boys. Softly
he murmured, "Bitch, bitch, bitch," and his voice, distorted by
some kind of electronic thing strapped to his Adam's apple,
sounded so oddly familiar—and there was a kind of love in
the way he said it—and it put me in mind of the things I
wished I'd done to Jennifer, the things I should have done,
because of the things she did to the children and—

I fell into a dream within a dream now, strapped to the
same chair, restrained not with a necktie but with my own
terror, saw my wife, hair in disarray, storming through the
kitchen, popping pills with one hand and gripping the lit
cigarette with the other, stabbing first Mort's left palm then

Mort's right, and the two-year-old screaming from the smoking stigmata and Jennifer's yelling, *Christ killer Christ killer I want to be a Christ killer too,* and little Roseanne is shrieking at the top of her lungs and—

Now a dream within a dream within a dream and it's my wife and Matilda Steinfeld laughing together at the kitchen table exchanging anecdotes about fake satanic child abuse and comparing notes on the HBO special they'd had debunking it all and—

And a dream within a dream within a dream within a dream and I'm making love to my wife on an inflatable raft, drifting along in the pool beneath the dry California sky, and she herself is the goddess, she herself is the dragon, she herself is the earth, and—

Snap! Matilda and Jennifer, coupling in the king-sized waterbed, with the children, hold hands at the bed's edge, watching *Bart Simpson* on the forty-inch monitor and—

Snap! Trying to get up out of the chair, shrieking at my wife to stop this witchery, and she smiles and me and sends me flying back into my seat and—

Snap! She's dead. Her windpipe whistles. Her killer's come dribbles across the sofa's custom fabric. He turns to look at me. My wife's blood isn't seeping in thanks to the Scotchgard; it's in small puddles on the sofa and the carpet, and it's already starting to congeal.

My jockey shorts are stained with the piss of terror and the semen of arousal. I rip the *Three Stooges* tie, bound up from the chair, hurl myself on my lady's murderer. My wife is the earth I'm standing on. The earth is spilling its blood into the sea. I have Excalibur. I slash at the air. My enemy, *the* enemy, the personification of darkness, runs at me with his ginsu-chainsaw-axe upraised. Weapon clangs against weapon. My enemy taunts me with his high-pitched laugh. He roars, he breathes flame; mother earth arches her back and fills the sky with fiery strands of hair.

He chases me. Trapped against the wall of water, I have to turn and fight. I thrust. He parries. From behind the hockey mask, his eyes glow. The chainsaw buzzes and I see woman after woman chained to the wall of ocean, everyone dead or dying. I know I should be frightened, but am I not the hero who knows no fear? Suddenly I hear Rachel call out to me. "Daddy, Daddy," she says. I see her chained to the water-wall beside me.

"I'm not your father," I whisper.

We fight some more. Finally I stab him and he stabs me. He's weakened, maybe even dying. I stagger towards him. I strip away his mask. He is the person I knew it would be.

At last the fear, which I have kept frozen in place like the wall of water that surrounds me, visits me at last ... just a few pinpricks of terror, then, all at once, deluging me with the explosive force of an orgasm, as the waters themselves crash down over the ocean floor, as the land contracts once more into the mortal form of Bridget, mutating back and forth from timber-prow to flesh ... and now I'm adrift again ... and the sea is calm ... once more I'm clinging to the wood, swallowing great gulps of brine, gasping for air ... and the sunlight is streaming down. I am bleeding from a deep cut in my side. I am mortally wounded.

I see my enemy bobbing up and down nearby. I paddle toward him with my sword. "Help me," he cries. "I think you've killed me."

"Help you?" I managed to croak. "You've killed me too."

"Yes," said the enemy, "but it's not my fault, it's neither of us's fault ... we were just fulfilling our various destinies ... c'mon, man, give me a break ... hold my hand or something, man."

In the distance, now fettered to a phallic mast, I see Rachel; behind her, the white sail is unfurling; she seems to have transformed from a geek to something very like an angel.

"Gimme a hand, man," the killer says, "I don't want to die, not right away."

I hold out the sword; he grasps the honed edge, though it cuts his hands and the salt water makes him wince. He climbs on board the raft that is also the goddess, and we float on the sea that is also the goddess, catching the goddess's breath in our sails.

Our goddess-ship drifts toward Rachel. Behind Rachel is the sun, and above her head there hovers the dove of peace.

•

When I woke up from the seven-tiered dream, I realized I had become sober. It was an unfamiliar sensation. I had not experienced it for many years.

I lay on the waterbed with the sword between myself and the sleeping goddess. I got out of bed carefully, afraid that Excalibur would cause the bed to spring a leak.

I went to the bathroom to check for wounds. My side bore a faint, jagged bruise, hardly the death wound from the dream. I turned my palms over, searching for stigmata. There were none.

Then I went into the kitchen and poured myself coffee from the auto-timer espresso machine.

The first person I called that morning was my brother Joshua. The phone rang and rang; I barely recognized his voice when he finally picked up. "I'm taking back my life," I said.

"What life?" said Joshua.

"The life that's starting to come back to me, piece by piece."

"So! That support group of yours has finally gotten to you. What reeking dirty linen have you managed to dredge up out of your childhood? I saw Matilda on Oprah last year, hear she's doing a book; the buzz is Meryl Streep wants to play her."

"Don't change the subject."

"But I'm not. I've heard that satanic child abuse memories come in clusters; one person in the support group infects the others; pretty soon they've all come down with it. Saw the HBO special."

I said, "Joshua, you screwed my wife!"

He said, "Of course I did. You were there."

"But afterwards. You went on doing it, behind my back."

"Of course I did. You hated her. Remember?"

"Of course I hated her. She was cheating on me."

"No, no, she was cheating on you because you hated her. Who cares anyway? You killed her. Enjoyed it too, judging by the wad in your BVDs."

"You know as well as I do that I'm innocent."

"But in your heart, you killed her. That's the same thing."

"In my *heart?* What, you convert to Catholicism while I wasn't looking?"

"I had to. My latest shikseh is a stickler. Besides, one can always use more guilt."

"Yeah, Joshua, yeah. But there's one thing you have to tell me. It's true, you're right, I've been having these dreams, memories maybe. About Jennifer and the children. You know, violent stuff."

"Serves you right for falling asleep in front of the Menendez trial every night."

"I do *not*—" But he was right, of course. Even though I hadn't spoken to him in seven years, he still knew me inside out. "I don't know if the memories are real, Joshua," I said. "My past is in bits and pieces. I need an independent observer. What about *our* childhood? Why don't I seem to remember any of it? I know we were adopted, but why? Were we babies? Were we like, abused kids from an orphanage? Was I a changeling, deposited on the Hoffmans' doorstep by a horde of gothic-punk fairies? I need a childhood desperately, any childhood."

"Maybe you didn't have one."

He hung up abruptly.

With searing clarity I saw that my life had been, not a steady progression of events, birth, self-awareness, childhood, puberty, youthful exuberance, middle-aged mediocrity ... it had not had this algebraic arc I had always assumed it must have. It had been more like a series of unedited film clips. There were sequences that implied other sequences, scenes that promised dozens of possible outcomes. Sometimes there was more than one take; sometimes, where logic demanded that piece of exposition or a plot point, there was just blackness. That was why I did not feel like a whole person. That was why I could still receive visitations from mythic figures. It was part of the editing process. I had to take the jumbled fragments, pick out the shots, make a life out of the pieces.

It was the dream within the dream within the dream within the dream within the dream that made me realize that what I had thought of as my life might in fact be the final dream from which it was still necessary to wake before I could surface in the real world.

Of course, if I finally forced myself awake, there would be no more magic. No more goddesses. No more swords. I had to consider whether it was worth giving up those things.

•

I delivered my last lecture of the semester.

"Let's talk about good and evil today," I said. "Today, in the '90s, they are not fashionable concepts. We suffer from a collective delusion of rationality. We know that there is a *how* for everything and because of that we have come to believe that there must also be a *why*. If someone is depressed, they must have a chemical imbalance, or they must have been incorrectly potty-trained at the age of two; if someone is a brilliant artist, or a malevolent criminal, or even a second-rate, aging, balding studio executive such as myself, he must be that way because of a myriad variables that can be known and quantified: I mean his genes, his education, the traumas of his childhood, the chemistry of his blood. And even if we don't know why *yet,* we feel that if only we had an infinite amount of time, and an infinite number of books, CD-Roms, and therapist records, we could ultimately solve every equation, unravel every enigma.

"But is this true?

"Just because the rational universe is *our* universe, does that make it the *real* universe?"

I get to this point every year in the course. Then I usually pause for a while, allow the students to try to grasp these cosmic notions. Some of the students are shrooming, stoned, or on acid. There used to be many more like that; today there was just the stoner's corner, the upper left-hand segment of the lecture hall, which was perpetually shrouded in shadow. The acidheads were usually the only ones who could fully grasp the transcendent nature of what I was saying.

I noticed, though, that Angel Serafino, sitting in the front row, also seemed to understand. He watched me intently. It was as though no one else was present in the class; as though all the others were but props, computer-generated extras seamlessly matted into our private scene to lend it verisimilitude. And so, speaking directly to him, I said: "What if the question *why* were not only unanswerable—as we all know it must be—be also irrelevant? What if the archetypal situations we've explored in all the films we've covered this semester—*Chinatown, The Empire Strikes Back, Shane,* and *The Seventh Seal*—are simply the way things are, the irreducible building blocks of reality, the up, down, strange, charmed quarks of our existence? What if a madman is a madman simply because he is mad? What if a hero kills dragons and rescues virgins simply because a hero kills dragons and rescues virgins? What if the word 'because' is simply a crutch, a delusional clothes hanger for the hollow raiment of reality?

"That, my friends, is the final question we must ponder as we recall the celluloid journeys we have taken. What if the very fabric of reason were as fabricated as a schizophrenic's delusions? What if the truth is simply this: that knights are pure, that dragons breathe fire, that for each of us a sword lies buried in a stone ... and that to the degree that each of us, inside his individual consciousnesses, deviates from these ancient truths, to that degree he is but a shadow, reflection, afterimage of that truth?

"For my next trick...."

Huffing and puffing, two freshmen lugged in the sofa from my condominium. Excalibur, buried once more in the upholstery, glowed like a Hollywood neon sign.

"This," I said, "is Excalibur, brought to me by the Lady of the Lake a few nights ago while I was trying to enjoy a late-night soak in the Steinfelds' hot tub. Anyone who can pull the sword out of the couch will receive an automatic A+ even if they don't hand in their *Citizen Kane* and *Oedipus Rex* comparison sheet."

For the rest of the lecture hour, the undergraduates heaved, grunted, sweated, murmured mantras and yelled karate power words. I only took it for about ten minutes; I left them at it and went down the hall for a Clearly Canadian and a bagel. It came as not too much of a shock when, out of the frosted glass I removed from the refrigerator in the lounge, the image of a redhaired woman started to form.

She was very small, no bigger than an ice-cube, but she was perfectly formed, and still draped in her hair. She looked up at me with those cartoony eyes, and she said, "Well done, my child, it's all coming to a climax; you're starting to find yourself again."

"Your child?" I said, incredulous at being so addressed by this R-rated Thumbelina.

Solemnly, she said to me, "The lake is the mother of all things."

I poured the Clearly Canadian (peach, I believe) over the shag carpeting as though it were a blood-libation to the earth; but before the liquid hit the floor it blurred, shuddered, grew into the familiar Bridget.

"That's better," I said, never having liked *I Dream of Jeannie.*

"I'm glad you've figured it all out," she said at last. "We will only meet once more, in the place where the waters meet the sky, in the place where the sun dissolves into the mist. You've been a good king, really; no complaints."

"What about Rachel?" I asked her. It was the piece of the puzzle whose solution I didn't want to accept. "Can't I—I mean, I'm not even going to get to—"

"Oh, indeed you'll screw, Greg," said Bridget. "You know the golden rule of cinematic art: if there's a loaded penis on the wall in Act One, it had damn well better go off in Act Three."

When I returned, the class was over; the room was empty save for Angel Serafino, who had not, apparently, stirred from his seat at the front of the class, had not even attempted to pull the sword from the sofa. Angel was wearing the Honduran *Oscuridad.* The reek of it was overpowering. More bitter and less sweet, less fragrant, more putrescent. It was the smell of love and death.

It was late afternoon now. In fifteen minutes, the traffic over the hill would become unbearable, and I would be stuck downtown until after dinner. How typically Angeleno of me to worry about the freeways when the entire universe was at stake! I sat down on the couch. Slugged down the dregs of the Clearly Canadian, put down the glass.

I knew who Angel Serafino was; I knew who Rachel Goldberg was; I no longer turned their pictures to the wall of memory.

"Hi, Dad," said Angel Serafino.

I waited.

"You do remember me now, don't you?"

I did. I had ripped the hockey mask from his face.

"You took the rap for me, didn't you?" he said. "You let them think you'd killed her. Why, Dad, why?"

"Because there had to be a reason for you to turn into a monster. I loved you, Mort ... I can't bring myself to call you Angel ... I never hurt you, never reproached you, never molested you, never warped your mind with cults or politics ... there *had* to be something. You know. Bizarre rituals in the basement with your mother in black robes and a spiked dildo. Look at Matilda Steinfeld. All the things that happened to her. In the *Enquirer,* on Oprah."

"Dad, you know she made that stuff up. You think reality is like the Menendez trial, but it's not. There is absolutely nothing you could have done to prevent me from wanting to rape and kill women who happen to remind me of my mother. The fact is, I'm just another axe-murdering motherfucker."

I supposed that double-entendre to be deliberate, but I didn't find it funny.

"Why didn't you tell, Dad? You could have stopped me, man. Had me put away. I was only a boy. I had only killed one mother. I never quite got it right, and I could never quite find another mother to try it out on; oh, they looked a lot like her, even smelled like her sometimes, but the high just got less and less compelling. I murdered a woman in Houston a year later. I killed another one in Greece; no one ever found out, though; it was on one of those tourist islands. I got her good. Did you see on CNN, the one with the meathooks in the caves at Lascaux? That was me. And I'm going to keep doing it. I'm even going to kill Rachel—Roseanne—one of these days, when she starts to sag a little, like Mom was starting to; women are like balloons; if they start to sag you have to pop them, or the bang won't be as big."

"Does your sister know?" I said.

"Dunno. This meeting was her idea, really. She's the one who missed you desperately, tried to kill herself four times; she fucked some lawyer on your case so he'd give her access to the psych files, and that's how she knew you'd completely blocked us from your memory. Then she thought of the cologne I always used to steal from your bathroom ... she wondered if the smell might be able to trigger, you know, all the repressed bullshit in your life."

"You're saying I couldn't face the fact that my son was a serial killer ... so I repressed it ... and that's how I ended up on fucking death row?"

"Hey, Dad, you *love* me. You couldn't reconcile your love with the idea that I'd sprung from your loins. Right? But you shouldn't have looked for a *because*. Enough *becauses*. You say so yourself. I don't belong here. I don't see things in the 16.7 million halftones that the rest of the world sees. I see things in black and white. I am evil. You should have killed me. And now that you have the sword, you will."

Now I knew why he had listened so raptly in my classes. For years I had harangued these college kids about other universes, other perceptual systems, but I had only been playing games, juggling with words. My son understood. He had always belonged to the world of absolutes.

And now I too belonged, and I could not go back.

I pulled the sword from the couch, knowing full well that in slaying my son I also slew myself.

He stood up from the desk. He knelt down in front of me, like Isaac before Abraham. We were about to step irrevocably into that world of absolutes.

But there was something pulling me back. It was seductive, this world where reason ruled and where nothing was eternal. I hesitated. "Before we go through with this," I said, "isn't there something we could have done together, father and son ... you know, quality time?" I had searched through the raw footage of his childhood and found only a few fleeting scenes.

"You could have taken me places. Lunch at the Hard Rock Café, dinner at Dominicks, the rollercoasters at Magic Mountain, even the Universal tour."

I knew that I would kill him by sunset. But I wanted to savor the last few hours of our relationship in some human way. I didn't want to just act out the timeless sitcom of our destinies like a robot, like a shadow puppet. So I said, "All right; we'll go cruising for a while, then I'll do it."

•

Around sunset, we did end up at Universal Studios. It was off-season, so the tours had ended for the day; luckily, one of the older guards still recognized me from the time I produced *Stranded in Eternity,* and we snuck into the back lot. I drove the Ferrari along the tramway in the gathering twilight; Mort and I shared the frisson of the *Psycho* house. We stood in silent awe in before the *Leave it to Beaver* residence; we couldn't get into the *Battlestar Galactica* and *Earthquake* and all the mechanical stuff, of course, but at length I parked on a side street, in front of a building (in which Jennifer had been murdered, not once but three times, in the film *Three Times a Zombie)*—and we walked along, past deserted brownstone shells, through ghost towns and Mediaeval villages, seemigly without aim ... though I knew where we were headed. It was the Martha's Vineyard set, with the little lake that had often stood in for the Atlantic Ocean in *Jaws.*

We stood at the edge of the tramway, watching the sun set on the artificial sea. We pretended we were a loving father and son with genuine lives that stretched in non-disjunctive lines from birth to death. Because we'd grown up in show business, we knew all about the method; we convinced even ourselves. I held in my hand the hand that had dismembered the woman I both loved and hated. The simulated warmth between us was so poignant, so puissant, I almost wanted to turn back; yet I could not. There was still a final dream to awaken from.

We shared a strawberry ice cream cone, and then I plunged Excalibur deep into my son's chest. He did not groan. He slid forward along the sword as though to embrace me, drenching my Armani suit with gore. As he died, I felt a searing pain in my own side; blood gushed from wounds that tore spontaneously through my two palms; and I knew that I too would be leaving this universe, that I would wake up for the final time.

I drew the sword from my son's heart, and flung it into the celluloid ocean. To the grinding music of double-basses, a shark fin rose from the water; it was Bruce, the tourist shark, somehow still circling even though the power had been turned off. When the shark had gone by, there was a woman walking on the waves; it was Rachel Goldberg. She was transformed. She was all woman, and still my little girl. She came to me across the water until she stood right next to me. The air was ripe with the autumnal scent of Darkness. Her feet floated an inch or two above the water, and she reached out and touched my wounded side. I winced.

"Daddy," she said.

"I can't," I said, and tried to push her away. Pictures flooded my mind: the naked little girl in the bathtub, giggling, the coy thirteen-year-old at her high society bat mitzvah, the adolescent who screamed "It wasn't my Dad" at Connie Chung before they dragged her away. Could these be buried memories? And yet they were still frames from a montage ... there was no thread of a relationship running through those images.

She tossed her glasses onto the pavement and they shattered, and then she put her arms around me, across the body of her dead brother, and murmured, "Love you, love you, love you."

"But you're my daughter," I said.

"Oh, bullshit," she said, "you know as well as I do that I'm really Uncle Joshua's daughter, that you're both adopted, that I'm no real kin to you; but you can have all the titillation of breaking the incest taboo that you want ..."

"You mean, like Woody and Soon Yi?"

"Oh, Daddy, forget all that nonsense. It isn't real. When the gods mate, it is always incest." And she pulled me over the edge. My feet slid over the pool of blood and the corpse that was already starting to melt into thin air. In fact, the corpse was slowly melding into the naked body of my daughter. Perhaps they had always been one, their binary quality another figment of a dishonest memory.

As my shoes hit the lake, both they and the blood began to swirl away from my feet, marbling the water with liquid red and black.

I looked back at the *Welcome to Amity* sign with its alluring, bikinied sunbather and the row of quaint New England shop façades. I knew at last that the world and all its denizens are façades, celluloid within celluloid. I was a shadow who loved another shadow. Those lips, breasts, hips, eyes, skin, hair, hands were all as substanceless as thought; but is not thought the source of all creation? We made love. In the darkling water, under the smog-streaked twilight. First she was Rachel-Roseanne, my daughter, a virgin, her mother's lipstick smudging her soft cheeks; slowly the woman in her awakened, and she was the Jennifer of my deepest dream, like the time we made love on the inflatable raft in the Olympic-sized pool in a Bangkok hotel at midnight; it seemed as though the water itself had become my wife, and I, a man-sized dildo, lanced the lubricious lake with the strength of a god; I hated her, I loved her, I killed her, I brought her back to life; and then, at last, she became Bridget, the source of all the waters, the great mother, the dragon, the world; and thus it was, at the heart of a kingdom of illusion that was itself the heart of a kingdom of illusion that was itself the heart of a kingdom of illusion, that the sword grown flaccid seven years before was given back to me at last; I found my lost manhood.

Would I have to awaken now? Must every human being be roused from shadowland? Were there only a few seconds of blissful madness left to me? Did it matter? I was loving the triple goddess, daughter, wife, mother; I was piercing the moon with my silver sword. The ocean was love itself. My seed burst forth not only from my penis but from my palms, my feet, and my wounded side. With the coming of manhood, fear returned to me at last. I trembled. I shuddered. I exulted in the feeling of this fear: the pounding heartbeat and the racing blood, the last, most vibrant colors of this transient world.

Any moment now would come the *snap* of final wakefulness. Perhaps the last seven years of my life had been but a series of rêveries, that when the *snap* came I would still be in that living room in Beverly Hills, about to twist free from my bonds and lunge toward the murderer of my wife. Perhaps I would find that it was *I* who killed her, and that the brother, son, and daughter were merely different personalities trapped inside my head. Perhaps I would find that even Jennifer was one such personality, and that the person I was stabbing to death was, after all, myself.

Perhaps even that would prove to be a dream. If so, then all that a man can ever learn is that the one true journey ends in *Oscuridad,* and that darkness is another word for love.

Dr. Rumpole

When all this started, it was during the Darlov regime, and I was working in the mailroom at Stupendous Entertainment, which is this monstrous medieval-looking faux castle in the hills, overlooking the Hollywood Freeway. I had ambitions, but I kept them to myself. I had an agent, Bobby Detweiler, but he was about as much an agent as I was a writer; he was an archnerd, worked in the computer room at Sullivan-Lechner, and moonlighted as a production assistant.

That Bobby Detweiler, Elena Darlov, and I would end up in the same stuck freight elevator in a soundstage in Valencia was the kind of coincidence you might find in a Victorian novel. The aftermath of that meeting, on the other hand, was the fabric of fairy tale.

The movie was *Encino Exorcist*. Bobby was going upstairs to try to sober up the star. I had dropped in to see Bobby, and volunteered to carry the mug of espresso on the off-chance I could wangle Brad's autograph. We took the freight elevator because I didn't want to spill the coffee running up the stairs. One floor to go, and the door slides open to reveal Elena Darlov.

"Fuck this script," she said, waving a jelly-stained sheaf of papers in my face. "It's the worst piece of shit I've ever seen in my life. If I can't get a page one rewrite by tomorrow, Brad's gonna walk."

Opportunity knocks but once, and Bobby sprang into action.

"Elena," he said, "Bobby Detweiler with Sullivan-Lechner. Ran into you at Cannes, Jeff's party, remember? Boy, you sure have lucked out. We have just signed the hottest new writer. Name's Adam Villacin. Wild imagination. Scintillating dialogue. Give the man twenty-four hours, and he could turn your pile of shit into a mountain of gold."

Elena looked pained. "I wasn't at Jeff's party," she said. "You shouldn't believe everything you read in *Variety.*"

An awkward silence was averted when the elevator sort of wheezed to a stop between floors. I picked up the red phone and called for help. Bobby went on talking up a storm. He raved about my spec script, which had just bounced back from Dreamworks unopened. About scripts I hadn't even written. About an idea I'd once almost pitched to Roger the time I found myself in the next urinal at a horror convention.

Elena was looking more and more pained by the minute, and presently she seized the espresso earmarked for Brad and downed it in one gulp. She scrutinized me. "I know you," she said at last. "Villacin, eh!"

"But Ms. Darlov, I mean Elena ... you've never seen me before in your life."

"I'm a very hands-on studio head," she said. "I personally okay every personnel file ... every errand boy, every secretary ... even every mailroom flunky."

Bobby—of all people—actually shut up. I smiled wryly. "You caught me," I said. "Gotta hand it to you."

She cackled. "Well, since you're already on my payroll, and since your scrawny little ass is mine to do with as I please—"

I gulped. Her appetites were legendary.

"I see my reputation precedes me."

I gulped harder.

"All right," she said at last. "What the hell." She thrust the dog-eared screenplay on my coffee tray. "Fix Bill's script by morning, and I'll give you ten grand. If it sucks, you get sacked."

"I—" I said.

"Union rules don't allow that kind of a deal structure—" Bobby began.

"This rube's not union," Elena said. "But I *will* throw in a couple of perks. You can have my permanent suite at the Beverly Plaza for the duration. It should be a little better writing environment than whatever miserable garret you're in. No hookers, though. Actually, I'll have you locked in. Unlimited room service, of course. Cable turned off, though. Nah, leave it on, there may be something worth stealing. All right then. I'll see the rewrite over breakfast." She began barking orders into a cell phone.

The elevator suddenly jerked up the final three feet, and Elena stalked off in the direction of Brad's private lounge. We never made it there; two of Elena's goons materialized from behind a stack of packing crates and escorted us off the premises.

•

The suite at the Beverly Plaza! You've seen it in movies, but actually setting foot in it was—different. I unpacked my laptop, found the dedicated data line, plugged everything in at a mahogany desk next to the French doors that opened out to the private Jacuzzi in its polarized-glass gazebo on its own little marble balcony. My agent left, the porters left, the room service waiter left after depositing a monstrous tray of beluga on toast points and a magnum of Moët, and there I was with the my computer and a pile of the worst shit the world's most highly paid screenwriter had ever produced.

It was unsalvageable. I don't know how much cocaine it takes to get this incoherent, but it smelled like old Bill had blown his entire fee on his nose. From the opening scene, where a dysfunctional white trash family gets raped by aliens, to the first plot point, when a psychic channels the spirit of JFK into an Egyptian mummy, through the chase scene where Mount Rushmore turns out to be a dormant volcano and a swarm of killer bees attacks Washington—

It was a mess. It wasn't even psychedelic. It was just bad.

Bobby Detweiler had destroyed my life.

I had downed over half of the magnum. I had scarfed all the caviar, and sent down for the assorted sushi platter, and washed that down with a fifth of Absolut. I had gotten all the way to FADE IN. I had to face it. I couldn't save this script.

I wheeled the food trolley to the door and was about to rap for the waiting attendant to come and get it—they were watching the door in case I tried to escape. But just then, this weird little man rolls out from under the thick white tablecloth. "Need a script doctor, do you?" he squawked. "Dr. Rumpole, at your service."

"I've had too much to drink," I said.

"Indeed you have." This guy couldn't have been more than four-eleven, and he had little pointy ears, but he was dressed to the gills in Hollywood executive chic. I didn't know Armani came in his size. "So how much is Darlov paying you, about twenty grand?"

"Ten," I said ruefully. "And I'll be fired if I don't come through. She doesn't really mean that, does she?" I must be drunk! I thought. I'm confiding in a fucking leprechaun.

"Okay," he said. "So I'll make you a deal. You write me out a check for ten grand. Postdate it forty-eight hours. I'll spin this shit into gold, and if it doesn't work out, you can stop payment tomorrow."

I didn't have much choice, so I let this guy sit down at the desk. I went back to drinking. You know, it is perfectly possible to do a screenplay in a night. Eight pages an hour, that'll run you maybe eleven, twelve hours. Even I've done that, though admittedly it was only for Roger.

Well, this guy didn't type any eight pages an hour. He typed so fast you couldn't see his fingers. The screen itself scrolled by in a blur, so I couldn't follow along. Not that I could read by then. I don't think I could have read my own name. In fact, I passed out, and when I woke up Dr. Rumpole was gone.

It wasn't even dawn, and there were 120 flawlessly typed pages on the coffee table, and when I started to read I knew I had a winner. Rumpole had relegated all those outrageous fantasy elements to a single dream sequence. The dreamer was the young son of the dysfunctional trailer park family, the aliens profound metaphors for alienation ... and redemption. The sister's multiple personality stemmed logically from the family's searing trauma, and backdating the entire tale against the background of the Vietnam War provided a trenchant symbology for illuminating these drab characters' lives and giving meaning to their miserable existences ... I'm not ashamed to say that I was weeping my ass off, and in a year's time I got to weep on national television, too, because I got to share the Oscar with Bill, who didn't bother to tell the press that his final contribution consisted of little more than the names of the characters.

I didn't mind losing the ten grand. Elena put me on a hundred grand retainer to come up with one high concept a month. Thank god they never actually used any of them.

•

Bobby Detweiler was still my agent a year later, which was just as well because I had blown the hundred thou on Vegas and an alimony, and I was living in the same temp apartment I was in before it all started, only the carpet had gone from beige to brown, what with the coffee stains, the cigarette ash, and the occasional barf binge.

I was standing in line at social security, trying to talk them into giving me food stamps, when my flip phone went off. Bad thing to happen when you're claiming to be destitute.

It was Bobby. It seemed that Elena Darlov had gotten greedy again. Two hundred grand, a two-day turnaround, or I'd never work in this town again. It wasn't Bill this time. It was Joe, who'd run off to Monte Carlo with his three mil, leaving behind only a tattered treatment to which Dustin, Bette, and Arnold were inseparably attached. Each star had received a ten million dollar retainer just to sit around, and with overhead that made forty-nine megabucks already in the hole without a single frame having been shot.

Elena was late, so Bobby and I had a couple of drinks at Musso and Frank's while we waited for her to show up. "There's a confession I've got to make," I said.

"Don't tell me," he said. "The little man with pointy ears?"

"You knew?"

"Dr. Rumpole's a kind of legend around this town," he said. "At least, among certain top agents." He grinned smugly. He was now a top agent, you see ... all because of that frantic night two years before. In fact, he was doing a whole lot better than me.

"Who is he?"

"Some say an incredibly eccentric studio executive who's on the payroll of all the top studios. Some say he's a sort of screenwriting idiot savant, such a klutz at the Hollywood shuffle that he's reduced to ghosting other people's scrips. Someone told me he's channeling D.W. Griffith. They say he has the Oscar committee in his pocket."

"Great. So my whole career now hangs on the whim of some bozo who's possessed by dead directors."

"Well," he said, "if Dr. Rumpole has come into your life, then you shouldn't have any trouble doctoring Elena's latest project."

"Yeah, but what if Dr. Rumpole doesn't show up?"

"I have my own theory about that," I said. "I think that Dr. Rumpole is an archetypal construct, brought to life by the frenzied collective agony of Hollywood screenwriters. You know, when reality fails you, fairy tale kind of takes over. We make our own magic here. This is Hollywood."

"I see. So if he ever gives me any shit, I just pull the Rumpelstiltskin gambit, I suppose."

"Hey, it could be worse, Adam. At least he's not demanding your soul."

"You are so fucking glib," I said. "You were a lot more palatable when you were Sullivan-Lechner's official computer nerd."

"Oh, I still am a nerd," he said. "Only I have much more expensive toys now. You should see my custom web search engine. It can sift through a trillion megs in a nanosecond. Why, with this new algorithm, I could rule the universe." I started to glaze over.

Elena showed up then, and we had the usual hour-long Hollywood lunch, studiously avoiding any mention of business until the last five minutes, when Elena produced the keys to the Beverly Plaza suite from her purse and announced that my limo was waiting. "Forty-eight hours," she said. "Because on Monday, our option runs out on the original property, which means that we kiss the whole forty-nine million goodbye. A lot is riding on this, Adam. You may even get a promotion."

She rolled her eyes. The truth is, I was still drawing my salary as a mailroom clerk, though I hadn't set foot in that hellhole for a year. That's how Stupendous is. People's job titles have absolutely nothing to do with who's really minding the store. For example, Elena was still only vice-president of development. Rumor had it her theoretical boss had set up permanent residence in a Thai brothel.

•

Two days and a postdated check for two hundred thousand dollars later, I was once again on the road to the Oscars. This time I had to share credit with Joe *and* Paul, who tinkered with the dialogue on the set, and the two of them got to appear on Larry King ... but what the hell? I had a contract for half a million a year, and I only had to come up with a new high concept every two months. Not that they ever used any of them.

But I was getting nervous. These things tend to come in threes, and you know that the third time's the killer. And the stakes were higher. Elena had begun to indulge her legendary appetites. She was particularly fond of the Oscars. I always had to clean them off with soap and water every time she came to my condo. Did I say condo? Soon I was moving into the Stupendous complex itself, that medieval castle athwart the Hollywood Hills, the legendary labyrinth of a thousand rooms. Like some primordial tree, the complex burrowed deep into the hills themselves. There were forgotten passageways and monastic cells without windows. There were also fairy penthouses perched on crenelated parapets. And security within security, once you were part of the inner elite. The Pentagon had nothing on Stupendous.

But the little old man was giving me nightmares. I remembered him hammering away at that second script. *The Lover,* it was called. A chillingly sadomasochistic love story about a concentration camp commandant and a Ukrainian prisoner—Bette lost sixty pounds to play the role, Dustin gained fifty—Joe's entire treatment tossed into the trash, the setting changed from Fire Island to Auschwitz—one little shift in perspective, and God, the characters went from yuppie stereotypes to mythic archetypes, the games from petty suburban bickerings to huge vistas of love, death, and eternity.

Thing about it all—and you don't see it in a lot of screenplays—the dialogue, the settings, they all seemed absolutely real. The illusion was astounding. Whole characters were painted with just a few deft details, a few telling words. The screenplay made you ache. The actors, the director had all their work done for them; they might as well have been puppets.

Dr. Rumpole hadn't even bothered to talk to me. He'd been in the suite, waiting, on the bed, watching an Oprah rerun. He put out his hand for the check, tucked it in his pocket, and went straight to my laptop.

And I went straight to my Valium.

•

Valium had been the drug of choice for a while, but the nightmares still wouldn't go away. Usually I'd wake up in medieval tights—worse yet, a dress, though I'm totally not that way—spinning straw in a monstrous stone castle. And Dr. Rumpole would be leaping and cavorting and cackling and shrieking out, "My name! My name! My name!"

Since when does a fairy tale make you wake up screaming in the night? Wandering the Stupendous corridors at three in the morning was a gothic experience. The business towers were all locked, of course; Elena had her own wing, accessible only by punching in a seven-digit code; my own little area was as medieval as my nightmares, complete with suits of armor and *Beauty and the Beast* wall sconces shaped like human arms.

My living room overlooked the Hollywood Freeway and the Capitol Records building ... and all the lights and speeding cars below made me feel even more isolated somehow, even more imprisoned ... and Valium became an addiction, soon to be joined by those little blue and red pills from a little pharmacy on Melrose, the one that's disguised as a bondage boutique.

So, doing lunch at Le Dome with Bobby Detweiler, admiring his new Rolls, I blurted it out. "I've gotta know, Bobby. Who he is. *What* he is."

"Really?" said Bobby. "Look, Elena has a job for you. Well, this is bigger than Elena, actually. It's Steve and Jeff as well, they're buying Stupendous out, you know; and there's a script that's just *got* to be fixed."

"Don't tell me. By tomorrow."

"They've already committed a hundred million. You've got the rep now, the ultimate script doctor. They're willing to go two point five, points even."

"No," I said. "I'll just have to sign it over to the little man. And the leftover perks won't sustain any of my habits."

"Look, Adam, you're overdoing it ... I know a great place to dry out ... Cancún, secluded, nobody will know who you are...."

"Look," I said, "what else is Elena willing to give me?"

"She's desperate, Adam," said Bobby. "I think she's running out of bargaining chips with Steve. Oh, and there's even a rumor of a hostile takeover by Rupert. I think she'll go for the proverbial 'half my kingdom' deal—co-equal status with her. She'll even throw in her shopworn body, though I don't doubt you've already had your fill of that—who hasn't?"

"You mean actual stock participation? Part ownership of Stupendous?"

That was a exhilarating thought for someone who still, technically, was a mailroom clerk.

"I think I can get you that," Bobby said, and he smiled that devilish grin that only agents know how to do, straight of the Mephistopheles method school of agenting.

"All right," I said. "But I need some ammunition for little old Dr. Rumpole when he shows up. Like, for example, his true name. Surely not Rumpelstiltskin—that's too obvious. But a man like that, makes his entire living sneaking up on desperate screenwriters, accepts no credit, well ... he's gotta have some kind of dark secret."

"Well, why didn't you tell me?" said Bobby. "Underneath my Versace jacket, I'm still Mr. Nerd Hacker Supreme, you know. You got anything to go on?"

"Like what."

"Social security number? Old I.D. cards? Maybe even ... fingerprints? I've got a back door to the FBI's fingerprint archive...."

"Well," I said, as I cut off one more little bite of my $60 rack of lamb, "he did use my laptop."

"Then," my agent said, reprising his grin, "I can deliver him to you. Dr. Rumpole has no secrets. If I can't dig up dirt on the man, my name's not Robert Ilan Detweiler, III."

"By tomorrow?"

"I might need time," he said. "Hacking's not as easy as it used to be."

I took my laptop from my Dior attaché case and handed it over, half expecting Bobby to pull out the old print dusting kit from his utility belt right then and there, over the soufflé and espresso. But he merely put it away and we sat for a moment, pretending to be normal, waiting for a very harried Elena Darlov to come dashing into to join us for a quick cognac before her next meeting.

•

These days, I merited an entire floor of the Beverly Plaza, but I was still locked in. It was all part of the myth, you see, like Houdini. And I still had the threat of execution hanging over me, in the shape of a signed confession from my dealer. The stakes got higher each time, but this time I was determined to quiz the old elf.

He ripped aside the shower curtain this time, reenacting *Psycho,* wielding a pen instead of a kitchen knife. I didn't scream. I was expecting some kind of apocalyptic entrance. "Two point five and half the kingdom," said Dr. Rumpole, "or ten years for possession and conspiracy. Not much of a choice this time."

"You might have let me get cleaned up in peace."

"You can clean your body," he said, "but you'll never get all the lint off your soul."

"Has the champagne come? Wait for me in the living room. I'll sign it when you're done."

"I'll have coffee," he said.

I took a really long shower. Make him wait, I thought, make him sweat. Though of course, I was the one sweating.

When I emerged, I presented him with the latest misbegotten masterpiece—which had cost the studio five million dollars, and was perhaps the worst screenplay of all time—and I said, "How do you do it?"

"What, you want my trade secrets?" said Dr. Rumpole.

"Well, yes. I mean look at the last one you did. The pathos, the palpability of that concentration camp experience. It was as though you were telling your own life story."

Dr. Rumpole smiled. A wan smile, and only for a moment. Then he said, "Well, come on, we haven't got all night. A new computer, I see! Well, I'm glad your excesses have left you a little something for a few toys. Well, I'll just start now. You go sit over there in the corner and get yourself royally smashed."

"Not this time, Dr. Rumpole," I said. "I'm going to go in the other room and work on one of my own projects."

The little man cackled. "So the hackmeister has one of those Great American Novels hidden in a drawer, eh! Or a slender volume of earth-shattering poetry? Or perhaps even a real script!"

I did go in the other room, but not to work on my novel. It was to set up my other other computer, hook up the modem, and get a frantic message to Bobby Detweiler. Who messaged me right back. I fixed myself some strong black coffee. I was going to have to move heaven and earth tonight. Which was a lot easier than you might think, with the resources of Stupendous at my beck and call. I made some calls. Now and then I went to the door and peered at the old man, who was wordprocessing up a storm. If anything he was wilder than before. You could almost see the smoke twirling up from the keyboard. His eyes burned red in the monitor screen. The text was scrolling up in a blur. He was in his own universe. He was inspired. He had the touch, the creative spark, the thing that mediocrities like me can only dream about. Oh, but I hated him. I needed to hate him. Otherwise....

I drank more espresso. Went to the bathroom to flush a packet of pills, in case I got too tempted. Sat on the bed watching *I Love Lucy* reruns, waiting for dawn.

•

Over a croissant, I paged through the screenplay as the polluted sunrise streamed into the suite. It was a work of unmitigated genius. A story which could otherwise have been the most maudlin, cliché-ridden, barf-inducing pile of turds had been transformed into the most refined, the most trenchant, the most soul-stirring paradigm of the human condition.

It was a simple enough situation. A kid dying of AIDS becoming the vehicle for the reuniting of his dysfunctional family. I mean, come on, there's a movie of the week like that every week. But Dr. Rumpole made the old tropes sing. A hideous plot device—the kid having visions in which he experiences his past lives—became a Jacob's ladder to enlightenment. There was hope in the ultimate horror of his life. There was vision. There was redemption. God, but I wept.

"It's all right, then?" Dr. Rumpole said, and handed me the pen so I could sign over the entire profits of my perfidy.

I ripped up the deal memo. "Not so fast," I said, "Mr. Rumpelstiltskin—or should I say *Herr Professor Doktor Rumpelstilzchen?* This time I've got something on you."

And then I told him what Bobby Detweiler had found out.

The fingerprint search at the FBI website had led to a photograph. A signature had led to a Swiss bank account by way of a CIA back door. An account number had led to the website of the Wiesenthal people. This harmless little dwarf, seer into men's hearts, explicator of the human condition, was also a Nazi war criminal on the lam.

"Ah well," said Dr. Rumpole, "it was bound to happen sooner or later. But no publicity, if you can avoid it. One way or another, one pays for everything, but I do have grandchildren, who know nothing ... have you already called the authorities?"

"Yes," I said.

And soon, all too soon, they came to the door and carted him away.

•

These days, I don't have to pay for rewrites anymore. Dr. Rumpole sits in a very gothic-looking cell, without windows and without companionship. He helps me out just to have someone to talk to; and I bring him cookies sometimes. He hardly even speaks to the guards; his mind has turned inward. All he ever does now is remember. He hardly needs the prison walls; he has made his own hell.

Last week, he wrote a stunning miniseries about Buchenwald. It's odd, because the villain he depicts, the horrifying commandant who rapes, maims and kills without compunction, seems curiously sympathetic. It's almost as though he gets into the monster's mind. And toward the end, when he recapitulates the monster's childhood dreams....

At least four Emmys in the bag with this one.

"Elena works for me now," I told him. "Fancy that. She even has to visit the mailroom from time to time. That's what I call a fairy tale ending."

Dr. Rumpole smiled sadly. "Next time," he said, "bring the oat nut ones. I'm tired of chocolate chip."

"We're working on your appeal," I told him. "Soon, you may even be able to fly back to America."

"It's good of you to visit," he said, "but please, no more chocolate chips."

I waved for the guard. The heavy doors clanged shut. There is a filthy wormhole of a corridor that ends in an elevator; I punched a secret code and went straight up to my penthouse.

Stupendous is a big place. Lot of hidden corridors. There's no limit to the art of illusion. With money, with special effects, sets, actors, you can create anything. Trips to the Hague, World Court tribunals, guards, windowless prisons, all can be conjured up by the magic of Hollywood. Why have the man put away? Why kill the goose, when it's good for at least another decade's worth of golden eggs?

I glanced at the nubile creature draped on the couch, and paused to admire my wall-sized Hockney. Wasn't I myself the ultimate triumph of Hollywood sleight of hand? I was a phony screenwriter who had won three Oscars, I was a bogus producer, I had a hairpiece, and I was a fake studio head just marking time until the real honcho crawled out of that brothel in Bangkok. So many illusions ... and yet ... how real I felt, how alive!

I stepped out of my medieval castle onto the balcony, and breathed in a heady lungful of the smog-filled air. It's a wonderful life, I told myself, and tried to forget the old man in the cellar.

The Sleeping Ice Princess

Nobody liked to pull sleeping duty at the cryo-warehouse. It was a lottery deal—your number would come up at the front office, you'd see your name on the roster a day or three in advance, which sometimes gave you enough time to dig up an excuse—doctor's note, whatever—or find someone to take your place.

Usually you could get one of the new guys—Forever Corp has a *fast* turnover—tempt him with the 200% overtime—don't mention the nightmares. Failing that, you could talk to one of the perverts—who tended to be the only old-timers on the staff.

Or you could get Barker.

Barker *lived* for sleeping duty.

It was, in a way, true love. He had a girlfriend on the inside. Now wait a moment, you say! Forever Corp is a cryogenic facility for rich people who get themselves frozen in the hope of waking up one day with perfect toned bodies and fat bank accounts … so what, this Barker was some kind of sicko, a necrophile?

Not exactly. You see, most people think that Forever Corp's clientele are all dead.

That's not exactly true.

•

I am the resident shrink or exorcist, depending on which side of the science versus magic debate you want to take; as a card-carrying Jungian, my training is in straddling the fence. I get to interview most of the recruits.

That's how I met Barker. Interesting guy. Little guy, no more than five-four, five-five, intense eyes, blue I think, scruffy. Really young-looking. At first I thought he was applying for the office boy internship.

I have a faceless office without windows, in the Hollywood showroom—the actual warehouse is off-premises, in Sun Valley, lot of warehouses there—we don't publicize that part of the operation. Barker was the only job applicant, but I wanted to make it look good.

"No, no," he said, gulping his Pepsi, "the other want ad. Technician. I can fix about anything. Program, too. Got my bachelor's, 'puter science. You want to see?" He pulled a dog-eared diploma from the sleeve he'd just wiped his mouth with.

"I'll be damned," I said. "Know anything about cryogenics?"

"Only the stuff in your journal, I mean, I, I have a subscription. Read it cover to cover."

"Well," I said, "if anything, you're overqualified. The 'technician' job description's there to make it sound more attractive; it's little more than sitting in a booth, pushing a button now and then ... and occasionally there's sleeping duty. A lot of the guys don't like that, I'll be honest, but someone has to mind the cryo-warehouse at night, keep the clients company, switch on the backup power in an emergency, that kind of thing."

"That's where they keep them? The, ah, clients? You call them clients? The corpses."

"Mike," I said, "can I call you Mike? If we're going to be working together and all that. Mike, one thing we have to get straight is, these people are not corpses. They are what pays our salaries. And they're not dead, per se. To make this process work, we have to decapitate the clients seconds *before* brain death would have occurred. And to correct another misconception—these heads are *not* frozen. Water expands when it freezes, and our bodies are mostly water ... expansion would rupture the cell walls, and I don't think *any* future technology could reverse that. So, just make sure you understand. They're not frozen, and they're not dead."

"They're a fraction of a degree above freezing, and a fraction of a second before death." Barker looked puzzled for a moment, and then he smiled broadly. "Cool," he said. "I mean, cool, totally cool. I'm going to love it here."

"I suppose that's why you need to be aware that a lot of our technicians have experienced unpleasant psychological effects from sleeping duty ... aural hallucinations, a feeling that our clients are somehow still—"

"Oh my god! Talking heads!" He was cackling now. Then, abruptly, he stopped. I pegged him for a potential pervert, but we don't mind those at Forever Corp—a decapitated head is unlikely to sue for sexual harassment.

"Actually, the reaction is generally known as the Khandelwal Syndrome."

"Whoah, doc! You are sly! Named it after yourself, huh." I had to like this strange little guy, especially when he went on to say, "Really, doc, I read your article about it in *Scientific American*. You were, I mean, gotta say it, you were, are, like, brilliant."

I poured myself a cup of tea. "Do call me Jon," I said. He had disarmed me.

"So you got a lot of famous people here, huh," said Barker.

"Sure do. Elvis, Marilyn Monroe, Eva Peron, Tupac Shakur; had JFK for a while, but sold him to the Smithsonian—" My standard answer. We assure total privacy. You'd be amazed who we actually *do* have.

"You're gonna say, but of course our client list is classified. But tell me ... you really do have Alyssa Derwood. I read it in *Weekly World News.*"

"Well, okay. With such an impeccable source, I don't dare deny it."

"So are her eyes still emerald green?"

"Last time I looked."

"And that hair of hers, still long and so black it's almost blue?"

"I daresay."

"And her lips? You still use that wet-look deep-purple lipstick on her, the color of a Thai eggplant salad?"

An alarm bell went off in my head, naturally; chalk up another one for obsessive-compulsive disorder. Not really a strike against prospective staff; you almost *have* to have OCD to want to work here. "So," I said. "You're really into Alyssa Derwood. How many times did you see *The Beast that Decapitated Nuns?* Did you watch the horror spectacular she co-hosted with Forrest J. Ackerman? Did you masturbate over her centerfold in *Hustler?"*

"More than that, Doc. I killed her."

•

OCDs tend to lie a lot. Just to be sure, I checked, of course; Alyssa Derwood died in some kind of freak car crash, and now and then the tabloids would connect her death with aliens or the CIA; no mention, however, of any Michael Barker.

On the other hand, Barker talked a lot—to me, at any rate—and, in bits and pieces, I managed to extract a sort of story. Parts of it do jibe with the forensic information I was able to glean.

His claim to have killed Alyssa Derwood did seem to have a kernel of truth to it, after a fashion. It's certainly true that he stalked her. I realized that she'd told me so herself during client counseling ... oh yes, I wear a lot of hats.

She was a fussy, nervous woman. I had been settling in for a long-term counseling situation, because at her age she was likely to be around for quite a while, and it's company policy to nurture the clients—make sure they don't pull out, since they pay only a token retainer during life, with a large balloon payment due twenty-four hours *post mortem.*

"There's a funny little man who watches me from across the street," she told. "It's weird, but I think about him a lot. He gives me the creeps, but sometimes I almost want to invite him in."

"He's a polite stalker then—waits to be invited—the vampire type."

"Yes," she said, and she did that famous, somehow very sexual blinking thing that her fans all love to imitate.

That funny little man, it would see, was our friend.

As an initiate in the secret science of the mind, I'll try to reconstruct his point of view.

•

Imagine this then: He's standing across the street from her gate. She's not Bel Air, not Mt. Olympus—a scream queen doesn't make that kind of dough—but a comfortable place in Studio City. He watches her go in, come out. Day after day.

He does have a day job, mind you. He's a clerk in a video store ... for which he is somewhat overqualified since he does in fact have that 'puter science degree. Alone in the store a lot, he runs all of Alyssa's tapes back to back ... from the Madonna video where she is glimpsed in a street corner in one shot all the way through her Roger Corman work and her culminating performances in *The Were-Woman* and *Were-Woman II—The Emergence.*

In *Were-woman II,* there's a scene where Alyssa lies on a morgue table naked. Dr. Thanatos, a demented scientist in a wheelchair, is about to plunge in a scalpel when he is overcome by her beauty. There's a lingering closeup of Alyssa's face. Just when you think she's totally dead, comes that seductive blink. This is the last scene on Michael Barker's shift; it always plays just after he has locked up, when he's adding the receipts and tallying the till.

"I know you're still alive," Michael murmurs from behind the counter. Just as he always murmurs.

But this time, she whispers back.

"What did you say?"

"You keep me alive," she says. "You're so devoted."

She's about to say more, but Dr. Thanatos moves into the shot and the scene continues—Michael has it memorized—with his attempts to desecrate the body and her dramatic transformation into the were-creature of his nightmares.

So that night, when he drives by her house, and he sees her, sitting silhouetted in her bedroom window, staring out at whatever she stares out at every night, Michael makes a point of stopping to thank her. She doesn't, of course, acknowledge him—why should she? She knows he knows she knows he's there, there always, always hers.

In the morning, when he stands for an hour to catch her as she walks from her front door to her silver Lexus, she smiles at him. A dangerous moment. She shouldn't have acknowledged him. They'll get her for speaking to him, you know. This raises the stakes.

That night at closing he asks her if she loves him. She says, "You know we can't talk of such things." Then Dr. Thanatos moves into the shot and the scene just carries on. It's so frustrating, only having those few stolen moments together. She stares down from the monitors that encircle him. But she won't meet his gaze no matter which monitor she looks at. What's she afraid of? To acknowledge the reality of their relationship ... wasn't that already more than he could ever hope for?

When he drives by her house that night, she is just coming home. A man is leading her to the door. The silver Lexus is in the driveway.

In the porch light, the stranger kisses her. But she rebuffs him. He is more insistent. She looks from side to side, wondering, perhaps, whether she should scream; if only she knew that her secret lover were right there, across the street, ready to rush in and rescue her at any minute ... but she does know, doesn't she? That's why she's sending the other man away.

Barker is touched by Alyssa's loyalty.

After midnight, unable to sleep, he puts on his special videotape, which shows the scene in the morgue table over and over and over, and he puts the television right by his head, and he strokes himself into uneasy sleep.

•

"This funny little man," I asked Alyssa. "You ever talk to him?"

"No ... well, once. I told him the time."

•

She is sitting on the doorstep. She is weeping. It's a few days after the incident with the stranger. This time she has come home in the Lexus, slamming on the brakes. She has stormed toward the door but now she won't go in. She sits there in a diaphanous green dress, which matches her eyes. The porchlight is harsh and unforgiving, and even from across the street, Michael knows that her makeup is running a little.

Surely if she only knew I was here, Michael thinks, if she only knew that the man she talks to nightly in the video store, the man she visits in dreams and visions, was standing within a few yards of her! Well of course, he reflected, she does know, really. We have a bond. If only I dared to speak to her....

Too late to worry now. He has already crossed the street. How could I forget myself like this? he thinks. We have a pact, don't we, an unspoken agreement? No one must know, no one....

"Don't you know what time it is?" she says. She doesn't look at her.

"Haven't checked," he says.

"One or two in the morning," she says. "Don't you ever sleep?"

That's it then! He knows for sure now that she knows. She has watched him too ... knows of his desolate nights. He clutches this new knowledge to himself. It's hard and shiny and frightening.

And in the nights to come, the videotape of *Were-woman II* begins to reveal more nuggets of information. That man who made her cry isn't a lover; he's a wicked, demented scientist who's been stalking her, trying to get her to consent to medical experiments.

Michael doesn't know *how* she manages to make that scene convey so many different messages. Probably she slips into the store during the day shift and switches tapes, or beams her commands into the video box via satellite. She's so cunning, that woman, and so into all this *Mission Impossible* kind of thing; it's amazing how she does it. And all of it without a bead of sweat, without one giveaway smile. How she must love me, he thinks. How she must dream and plot and connive and obsess. And to think, I'm just some nerdy little guy to most people. She's the only one who sees the great figure of tragedy within, the monumental thing that's trapped inside my slim slight body.

•

"I killed her," Barker had told me, and that got me to thinking. He had come to Forever to be with her. Well, that might seem morbid to some, but there's a fine line between death and near-death. Not even a line, really, just a blurry, shifting boundary, and our salesmen straddle that boundary every day when it comes to the fine print.

"You're saying I won't be dead when you cut off my head." Alyssa said, the day she signed the deal. I wear many hats, as I've said; I'm also a notary public, and I also have the right to call the whole thing off if the client appears psychologically unprepared ... our insurance requires a statement from a shrink.

"Not *quite* dead," I said. "Hence the release."

"So technically," Alyssa said, "you'll be murdering me."

"That's true, Ms. Derwood," I explained, "but that's really only a technicality. The courts are trying to find just the right language to satisfy the constitutional lawyers ... and anyway, what is death? If you are successfully revived, that will only prove that you never were dead, you see. So how could you have been murdered?"

Alyssa did that little half-laugh thing that she is known for, and then she went ahead and signed, although of course no one realized that she had less than a week to live.

•

Naturally, Michael knows that she's been going to Forever Corp—the showroom, on Hollywood, not far from the Egyptian Theater. He's been in the showroom too, slipping in just as she leaves, browsing the literature, which shows smiling faces and the sun over suburbia.

He knows she has signed up. He's seen me shaking hands with her, seen her stuff some papers into a shopworn Louis Vuitton handbag, seen her hurry, eyes downcast, cracking her knuckles, toward the parked Lexus against which that man leans.

He's already slipped a job application into his pocket, and now he saunters down Hollywood, skipping over Cary Grant, stomping on Hitchcock, spitting on Michael Jackson.

That evening in the store, he stares at the monitor, mechanically checking the rental tapes with the scanner, manning the till with a vacuous robotic smile. Alyssa's words seem to come from everywhere. The speakers blaze with her sighs, her whispered invitations. Dead on the undertaker's table, she speaks to him with motionless lips—how does she do it? some strange variety of ventriloquism?—and his name echoes in the clank of surgical instruments on metal trolleys, in the squeak of wheels on linoleum, *Michael Michael Michael—*

And all night long he plays that tape, the endlessly looped morgue scene, waiting to catch each word that slips out, enthralled by those trademark fluttering eyelashes; and by morning she has finally said it to him: *I love you, I love you, I love you.*

And then she is dead.

Of course, there is an intimate linkage between love and death.

•

I wear many hats, as I have said. One of my many duties is to guard the guards. So, figuring that his obsessive-compulsive disorder might come laced with a jigger of necrophilia, I decided to keep a close watch on Barker. Not that he would intentionally harm the clients, of course, but what if he, for example, violate the strict sterility rules of the warehouse in a moment of ardor? I told myself that my interest in the matter was strictly one of clinical observation—as the discoverer of the Khandelwal Syndrome, I had a duty to study all its manifestations.

Duty, however, has a way of overdoing itself....

A few weeks after he had been hired, Barker pulled several stints of sleeping duty in a row. It was on the third night that I decided I would check up on him.

There is a secret room in the Sun Valley warehouse, where all the feeds from all the monitors in the building end up, and you sit there ringed with television sets, stacked up six high. Staring down from those screens are our clientele. The heads are cooled, and shrouded in condensation, and each one rests in a pool of nutrient fluid, though none has ever been seen to absorb nutrition.

There they are, all staring into the swivel armchair in the center of the room. Each head, and its attendant apparatus, lies inside a sterile plexiglass womb, accessible only by a master key. Oh yes—another hat I have—the key hangs on a ring in my office—and though most people know what it is for, it is rarely used. Using it requires a form, two signatures, and a rubber stamp from the head office. That stamp, alas, is not one of my hats.

Enough scene setting. Suffice it to say that that night I spied our friend Barker leaning against the plexiglass wall, whispering sweet nothings to his beloved. The camera lingered on him—it automatically lingers when in senses motion—and I heard him murmur, "Oh Alyssa, I'm sorry, baby, I'm so fucking sorry," and then I looked away, and when I glanced back, our friend was hunched over and appeared to be celebrating the rites of Onan.

A common enough sight, and really nothing to worry about ... yet. Even I've been known to talk to the heads. But when they start talking back ... well, you see, that is the Khandelwal syndrome. To which I was immune, and always would be, with any luck.

•

Of course, when I started piecing his story together, I realized he was a prize Khandelwal case even before getting this job ... had a predisposition, as it were. His perception of things was a little different; he had what some of my colleagues refer to as a rich fantasy life.

Thus:

From the moment Michael saw her walking out of my office, fiddling with those papers, he knew that Alyssa wanted to die. Not *die* exactly, just die within the the Forever Corp's

limited definition. Not so much an ending as a transformation.

The man who had tried to kiss her on her doorstep ... he
made her very unhappy. Perhaps he had an inkling of her
other relationship, the dark secret encoded in the thin black
Mylar of a B-movie video. That's why she wanted so much to
become something new, to evolve to her next level of being.

But like all women she might need a little prodding.

Michael's mother had always needed prodding, too. Dad
had prodded her right into the grave, and he was serving
time somewhere for that; once, as a child, he'd spoken to
Daddy, with that thick glass between the two of them, and
Daddy had spoken without moving his lips. *Get me outa here,*
he said.

And looked down at him, a five-year-old or so, with the
eyes of a man already dead. Which wasn't surprising; Uncle
Jerry had already warned him about that. "He's as good as
dead," he said. "You best forget he ever lived, Mikey-boy; or
he'll haunt you from beyond the grave. That's a dead man
looking at you, remember that. Thing about that electric
chair, Mikey—it starts to change you even before you sit in
it—the waiting changes you. The chair only finishes you off."

"You mean he's kinda like Frankenstein," Mikey said.
He liked that movie a lot. It was the only good video in the
trailer. The others were like preacher crap.

"Yeah. Already dead, but zapped into something new by
a bolt of electricity."

And Uncle Jerry made that Halloween face, which always made Mikey laugh, only this time he didn't.

I wonder why I'm thinking about that now, thinks
Michael. And then he sees the connection. Alyssa. The morgue
table. Dr. Thanatos. Death and transfiguration. That's what
she's telling me, he thinks as he watches the Lexus thread
through the traffic on Hollywood Boulevard. She's not stopping at Musso and Frank's for a burger this time. The job
application's burning a hole in his pocket. Where does he
start?

Perhaps a .45. You can get those anywhere along the
Boulevard, and it's a lot cleaner than a knife ... or a bolt of
lightning. And then there's other magics too. Cloaks of in-

visibility you can draw up over yourself. Shapeshifting mantras. It's love, you see. Love can put you anyplace, transform you into anything.

Love is the one true magic.

•

He materializes in the middle of the street and points his gun. She swerves and crashes into her house.

No one has seen him. No one has connected him. *It's our little secret.* Now, on to Forever.

•

I watched him communing with his beloved, squatting for hours before the plexiglass, occasionally rising to caress the clear plastic or to unburden his passion with a quick jackoff. The things he murmured proved clearly that for him Alyssa was fully alive, responsive, and in love; he was in the advanced stages of the Khandelwal syndrome.

"You're not saying much tonight ... it's okay, no one can hear us when we do this ... yes, yes, I'll put myself in there with you one day, we can wait for the future together, we can awaken to the light, you and me, hand in hand...."

Not that he had enough, on *his* paycheck, to purchase our services, although we do have a layaway plan. But there he was, on one side of the barrier, and there *she* was, a head on a silver platter with fine hair of deepest midnight blue, with purple lips lightly parted as though about to kiss, and those strange grassy eyes. ... oh, but he loved her.

And I know what he hears her say. She's saying oh yes, yes, yes, oh yes, Michael, one day when I get out of here I'll be with you always ... like your Daddy ... the things you love the most are always under glass ... because they're precious ... because they can break. But oh, how I want you...."

"Take me," say the unmoving lips.

"Oh, baby, baby," he cried out, "are you living? Are you dead?"

And he hears her whisper: "Michael, I'm in the border-land ... come here ... come to me ... come and wait with me ... because I'm so terribly alone."

And he embraces her and knows she has forgiven him for trapping her here. "I wanted to keep you safe." he whispers, "safe for all eternity."

"Why can't you come a little closer? Why can't we kiss?"

"But we *do* kiss...." Through inch-thick plexiglass they kiss. The scent of her, a subtle melange of musk and medicines, filters through the barricade and invades his nostrils, a fragrance no one else can sense ... oh, but he does love her, and she him. And they are making love, because it is she who controls the motions of his hands, she who blows over his tender skin the painful breath of life and death, she who causes him to convulse with the spasms of desire.

I did nothing. No. I am lying. There in my womblike throne room, surrounded by the heads of the undead, I watched this scene unfold and found myself racked by the pangs of a discomfiting, voyeuristic arousal. Why not? What, after all, is a washed-up shrink to do, now that he can no longer afford malpractice insurance?

I did nothing every time. In fact, I connived in their passion; I was their unknown Friar Laurence, tinkering with the 'puter so Barker could pull more sleeping duty, encouraging him to unburden himself to me, and always, when it happened, watching, watching.

Then came the night he went too far....

•

I knew he was going too far when I saw him get out the blowtorch. There it was in the monitor. And him murmuring, moaning, "Alyssa ... be with you now ... be with you ... yes baby yes...."

I knew he was going to try to get in there. Who knows what else? Was he going to reprogram the computers, recharge the nutrient bath, hook her up to a lightning rod to restore her to a simulacrum of life? I knew it was time to put on my final hat.

I unlocked the safe behind monitor number one, and I pulled out the company's official .357 Magnum.

I, who never walked among the clients as such, who was always content to observe them on those little TV screens, found myself punching in the combination to the cryo-unit, found the door swinging open, found myself in the arena of the undead.

Nothing like as tidy as we made it out to be—that's why the showroom is in Hollywood and the warehouse in Sun Valley. The plexiglass walls all seemed so neat from the control room, but in fact the head-boxes were piled up every which way, and the tubes that led to the central vats of liquid nitrogen and other fluids were bunched up overhead, loosely velcroed to the ceiling and tied up with string. The video cameras hung from battered poles like clumps of coconuts. The floor was a mess of writhing wires, wrapping papers, and old beer cans. After all, what did the corridors matter as long as the atmosphere inside the plexiglass wombs was pure and uncontaminated?

You might think that there'd be warning lights, moving walls that sealed off sectors, disinfectant sprinklers, and the light, but there was really only one primitive system for preventing germs from getting into the head-boxes ... me.

I worked my way through the labyrinth. It was easy enough to know where to go. Barker's whine was the only sound above the thrum of machines and the drip-drip-drip of condensation from the cooling units.

"Yes, my darling," he was saying, "I've had enough waiting too ... I'm going to kiss you back to life ... I'm going to bring you back from the borderland...."

And I could hear the hiss of acetylene. And there was the acrid stench of burning plastic.

I came right behind him. Watched him for a moment. He had hung his clothes up on one of the camera poles. He had the blowtorch in one hand, and he was doing a strange sort of dance. He rubbed himself against the plexiglass, made circular motion with his palms, wriggled from side to side, perhaps in an effort to stir the cold plastic to arousal; then, once in a while, he would turn on the flame with a piercing yell of—pain? erotic passion? I could not tell—only that I had to stop him.

A sterile environment at all times is the only guarantee we make in our contract with the clients. And that environment was in jeopardy. He had almost broken through. One pinhole and there'd be hell to pay.

"Mike," I said softly—you can't be blunt with these people, especially once they've become unmoored from the real world—"Mike, let's get going now."

The tears were running down his cheeks. "Yes, yes," he said, "let's get going ... I see the way, the way is clear, clear the way, the clear clear way—"

"It isn't time," I said.

"I know, my love," he said, "that's why I'm going to wait here with you—"

"No, no," I said, "We're going home now, Michael."

"Home," he said, "yes, home, together, through the clear way, gotta let you breathe now, gotta let my breath touch your breath, that's the only way—"

It didn't matter what I said. He was going to twist it to his own reality. He was going to bust through to wake his sleeping beauty and consummate his passion. He turned on the torch. Pointed it at me. Sparks flew. I dodged. He trained the flame on the weak spot in the plexiglass, and I fired.

•

It is very important that there be not one hint of scandal at Forever Corp. I had not killed Michael Barker; it was not a lethal wound, though he would surely be paralyzed from the neck down.

What we do at Forever Corp is not murder. Our clientele do not die. They are put, as it were, on hold in the seconds before death would have occurred, and they are preserved, as it were, in that borderland between life and death; the facilities being always available on the premises, and authority to initiate the procedure having been signed over to me by our beneficent—but quite uninterested—board of directors, it was simple for Michael Barker to become Forever Corp's first non-paying client. A sort of *pro bono* case. As it were. And there's no murder, and no personal injury lawsuit.

It seemed only fair to let them share a double cubicle....

Lately, I have spending a lot more time at the cryo-warehouse. I sit in the little room there, and I glance from head to head, and I consider the possibilities ... how it would be if they really *could* talk.

And then there are those moments when they actually *do* seem to....

"But you *killed* me, Dr. Khandelwal ... there wasn't any call to *kill* me. I just wanted to be with her...."

And then I find myself wanting to answer: "How can you say I killed you? There is no death in the cryo-warehouse. There is only the simulacrum of death...."

I stop myself ... because I realize I have actually spoken aloud. I guess giving your name to a syndrome doesn't make one immune from it. What should I take? Idly, I pull out the pad and write out a prescription for Xanax.

"Why don't you find out for yourself, Dr. Khandelwal? Why don't you come down here and join us? Maybe there's something down here you don't know about with all your scientific instruments and high-end drugs. Maybe when all that's left of us is a head, it frees us, and our minds can range through all of time and space, and touch everything, and make love in a thousand places all at once ... you've never thought of trying?"

One evening, I realize that I've become a shell of man, and they are more alive than I. I envy them.

The night that Alyssa seems to blow a kiss at me, I decide it's time to depart the womb, leave the television screens behind, enter the labyrinth, see for myself. Nothing like empirical observation. What would it be like to feel ... how did Barker put it ... the painful breath of life and death? To feel a spectral tongue on mine, to smell the perfume of putrefaction and desire?

After all, there's no danger for me. I don't need a blowtorch. I'm a doctor. I know to scrub, to disinfect, to sterilize.

And I have all the keys.

Though I Walk through the Valley

Uncle Will never meant no harm. Dude, he was *down*. Last Christmas he gave me a Super Nintendo and a dirt bike. Once a month or so we'd like get drunk and stoned and shit. When my brother was gunned down in a drive-by, he took me down to Hollywood after the funeral and bought me a big old chocolate sundae, and he told me I could come and live with him if I wanted to. And I'm all, "Thanks, but like I don't want to hurt Mom's feelings even if she don't got no feelings since she became a junkie."

He's all, "I hear you, but don't be such a stranger anymore. I only live two floors down. I like you, Oz. You really have your head screwed on straight for a kid who's had so much shit happen to him in his life. So maybe you can do me a favor, talk some sense into Little Ferdie; he's so fucking stubborn."

That's how I come to see a lot more of my cousin Ferdie, and how I found out that Uncle Will was a child abuser.

Cousin Ferdie was twelve like me but he was totally skinny with big bulging eyes like a hunger poster. When I started hanging out at Uncle Will's apartment after school, or when I would ditch, I didn't see much of him. His door'd be closed and there wasn't no reason for me to go in and see him and maybe he wasn't even home, maybe he was like out cruising with his own friends somewheres. I didn't like Ferdie. He was so quiet he made you nervous, and when he would say something it would be like sudden, out of nowhere, something that had nothing to do with anything ... like when my grandmother would do her speaking-in-tongues thing in church.

I didn't go to Uncle Will's to see Ferdie anyways. I was there to see Will. He was always there because he'd been laid off for three months. His girlfriend, a directory assistance lady, was paying all the bills, except his liquor bill which he would get the money for by standing at the entrance to the Sacramento Freeway with a big old sign that said he was homeless. By lunchtime he would always have enough for a couple of forty-ouncers.

He often had his homies over. There was Bill and Ted, forty-year-old surfers, from the apartment next door, and Armando, who was dying of AIDS, and Lupe the hooker, and Jungle George the loan shark, but most of all there was Mr. Death, an old black dude with long white hair. His real name was Daniel Moreau. Mr. Death was his professional name. He was a *houngan*—a voodoo witch doctor. Retired that is. Used to hang out with Baby Doc in Haiti. Told wild stories: political prisoners getting burning tires hung around their necks, magic potions, and zombies, naturally, except, the way he told it, there wasn't nothing supernatural about them. He was my favorite of Uncle Will's friends, but his stories about Haiti made the East Valley sound like buttfuck Egypt, I mean *nothing* happens here except like, drive-bys and drug busts and shit.

My cousin Ferdie was usually nowhere to be found. That was fine with me. Then, one too-hot day in April, I totally saved his life.

It was kind of an accident. I was at the 7-11 trying to buy a pack of cigarettes. Usually the dude just sells them to me but this time I think it was a different person even though it's like hard to tell them apart. He stood there, six-feet-six in his turban, and he's all, "You cannot be purchasing cigarettes here, young man."

I'm all, "Why not?" and he's all, "Because you are being too young," so I'm all, "You motherfucking camel jockey," and slamming the hardpack on the counter and jamming out of the store. But because I'm in such a hurry, everything

I've jacked starts tumbling out of my pocket: two Twix bars, a packet of condoms, a bag of peanuts, and a Bic lighter.

"Shoplifter!" he screamed, and started loping out from behind the counter.

But I'm all, "So what are you gonna do about it, fag?" because I knew I could outrun anybody, and I started running, but he pushed some kind of alarm button and I didn't make it out of the parking lot before a cop car pulled in and two big dudes jumped out with big old PR-24s. They started chasing me but they didn't know the alleys like I did. I lost them but then I heard the sirens and I knew they were going to try and head me off somewheres. I hopped a chain-link fence and dove through a hole in a churchyard shrubbery and I came out behind our apartment building. I was in an alley that was too narrow for the squad car to squeeze through but I seen it through the gap and the lights flashing and I knew that they'd be running after me again and I didn't feel like getting beat up. Them plastic ties they put around your wrists can really cut you.

I shimmied up the wall where a orange tree grew, swung over the branch, and found myself on the balcony outside my cousin's room. I could tell they hadn't seen me because I heard them running all the way past the complex shouting, "Stop you little cholo shit stop or I'll shoot your fucking face off," and I knew I'd gotten clean away. They'd never even gotten a good look at me since they thought I was a cholo; I may dress like one but I don't look like one.

So I slide open the door into Ferdie's room and there he is, standing on a chair with a belt around his neck, tightening the buckle and getting ready to kick. His eyes were all empty and he had wet his boxers.

I didn't waste no time, I just grabbed a hold of him and yanked the belt out of the buckle. There was like a red bruise all around his neck where the leather had cut it. I lifted him up real easy (he was a head shorter than me) and carried him to the lower bunk and I'm all, "What do you think you're doing, dude?" and pulling off his boxers and drying him off with a Ren and Stimpy towel.

"Jesus, Ferdie," I said, "you could at least have pissed in the bathroom."

"Not allowed in the bathroom."

"What do you mean?"

"Not allowed to leave my room for two weeks on account of I'm stubborn."

"Not even to go to the bathroom?"

"Sometimes there ain't no one out there to let me out in time."

I tried Ferdie's door. It was locked from the outside. Then I heard my Uncle Will's voice: "Don't you try the door, it's no use, I'll double your time if I even hear you breathe."

I held my breath. This was another Uncle Will than the down dude I could get stoned with. I'd never heard Uncle Will scream like that before. Never even heard him raise his voice.

Ferdie was all shivering even though it was probably 106 outside and the swamp cooler wasn't working too well because of the humidity. I looked around the room for some clean underwear, but when I found it he wouldn't let me take away his towel. I had to trick him and whisk it away and that's when I saw all the bruises because he stepped out from the shadow of the bunk, into the harsh summer light. There were some thin red stripes, like maybe an electric cord, and some wide purple ones with punctures, like the buckle end of a belt, and a couple of cigarette burns. I was too shocked to say anything at first, and then all I could say was "Why?" because something this bad had to have a reason, it couldn't just happen.

And he's all, "I dunno." And he shrugged. "I guess it's because I'm stubborn, that's all, stubborn."

"How stubborn?"

"I forget. I think I wouldn't eat my cereal." He gave a sharp giggle, like a girl. "I don't like Captain Crunch."

There had to be more to it than that. I figured maybe he wasn't thinking straight seeing how he'd just been this close to history. Uncle Will wasn't like one of them dudes on *Geraldo,* you know, one show they had with like kids who had been locked up in cages, used in satanic sacrifices, shit like that. Was he? I've known Uncle Will since the fourth grade, when we moved down to the Valley from the trailer park in Lancaster. Maybe Uncle Will had gotten weird from being laid off so long.

"You still shouldn't of tried to kill yourself," I said. "It's a sin."

"I know, Oz," Ferdie said, "but hell can't be no worse than this."

Then he looks at me with big sad sunken eyes and picks at a scab on the back of his hand. The way he looks at me is all, *I'm in hell now, Oz, and you gotta help me, cuz I'm sinking fast.* But I still couldn't believe that Uncle Will would have done that to him. I didn't like Ferdie, you understand, on account of he could stare anyone down and he made you nervous just being around him. And he read books, too, and he could toss of a string of facts that would make you feel totally stupid and want to punch his head in. But he was my cousin and you know, family is all you have, and less and less of it because they keep getting gunned down in your back yard.

"You don't got to help me any," Ferdie said, "next week they're gonna put me on Ritalin and maybe I won't be so stubborn no more."

I'm all, "Shit, Ferdie, of course I'll help you." I gave him a piece of bubble gum that I'd jacked along with the other stuff, that hadn't fallen out of my pocket. He swallowed the whole thing. "Me and Uncle Will are homies. Maybe I can find out what's making him act this way." Because I still thought that it was just some kind of temporary craziness and I could get Will to come to his senses, and I knew we couldn't turn him in, because that would tear the family apart forever.

•

So I waited for a couple of hours and I snuck back over the balcony and around to the front of the apartment building. Mr. Death and Uncle Will were sitting in the living room chugging their forty-ouncers. They were talking in whispers and they didn't see me come in. So I sat down on the bean bag behind Will's armchair and pretended like I wasn't there.

Uncle Will's all, "I don't know what to do, I try so hard, he's so stubborn."

"I would say you was probably stubborn too," Mr. Death said. "Stubborn runs in families." His voice was deep and it rolled like a tubular wave. The way he talked wasn't like the black people in my school exactly, I mean it had like a foreign lilt to it, French or something.

"Yeah," Uncle Will said, "I reckon I was. Stubborn I mean. My Dad used to whip the shit out of me. But Ferdinand's a different kind of stubborn. He's stubborn like a block of granite that you want to carve into a statue and it won't give. Drugs don't help him, whipping don't make it any better."

It's weird. *Stubborn* ain't a word you hear people use much about kids, well, just old people, and they're more'n likely talking about a mule or a dog when they say it. When I heard Uncle Will talking this way it was, you know, like when I heard his voice booming through Ferdie's locked door—it didn't sound like the Will I knew, my bud. Suddenly I realized that it sounded like Grandpa.

And like I'm all cold suddenly, cold and clammy, even though the air from the electric fan is as burning hot as the smoggy air outside. Because I seen my grandfather dead, at the wake. They made me kiss the corpse on the cheek. The makeup rubbed off on my lips and I sucked in a cold and bitter-tasting wind. Even though that had been a totally hot day too, a heat wave, and me six years old and standing on a crate and sweating like a motherfucker.

Uncle Will said, "I wish there was another way." And popped the cap off the second forty-ouncer. "Jesus I try so hard but him and me, it's like I'm butting my head against the biggest-ass wall in the world."

And Mr. Death said, "Well, Will, there *be* other ways. There is things in the world you can only see if you choose to open your eyes. There is doors you can unlock but only if you know they there."

I could tell that like, Mr. Death was about to totally launch into one of them stories of his. Maybe if Uncle Will got all involved in the story I could slip out from behind the armchair and act like I just arrived. But Will cut him off and he just said, "Daniel, I got no patience for your bullshit today. I'm scared, man, scared for me and my son. What if I accidentally kill him one of these days? I ain't a bad man, I ain't a murderer, but the kid just plain makes me go berserk."

"Well, back at home there is a little trick I do," Mr. Death said. "And after I do this little trick, my patients they all calm, they do what they told, they never ever complain no more."

"What is it, some kind of voodoo therapy?"

"Maybe you call it that."

"Is it expensive?"

"Not for you. You can't afford not to have it done. You drinking yourself into the grave because how much it trouble you. You want to feel that love God say you got to feel for the child of your own loins."

"I'd give anything."

"And you will. Not just anything. Everything."

"But what will you give Ferdie in return?"

"I will give him a new life," Mr. Death said. "A kind of being born again, starting with a clean slate."

That's when I really got scared, because before you can kind of be born again you have to kind of die. And I knew Mr. Death was talking about turning Ferdie into a zombie.

•

I didn't come out from behind that armchair until long after Daniel Moreau had gone home and Uncle Will dozed off after his second forty-ouncer. I crept up the stairs to my mom's apartment. She was lying on the living room floor, past noticing anything.

I dreamed about my brother. I never saw him dead because they couldn't fix his face and so they had a closed coffin funeral. Then I dreamed Ferdie was dangling from the end of a noose, swinging like a busted naked light bulb. Then I dreamed about Grandpa. Bending down to kiss the body. His eyes popping open. Staring straight at me. Fixed. Like the lens of a camcorder. Staring. Videotaping me, my lips still freeze-dried from brushing his cheek, too scared to scream.

Then I dreamed it was me in that coffin, and I'm all rigid but not from death only from terror because the three of them are standing around me and all of them are dead and all of them with their fixed-focus eyes …

I woke up and I thought: Uncle Will didn't come to the funeral. I didn't meet him for another three years. I wondered why he didn't come. I'm all, I think I'll ask him tomorrow. I looked over at the VCR and the timer said 3:30 in the morning. I tried to go back to sleep.

But like, every time I closed my eyes I would see all three of them again. *Night of the Living Dead* style, with their arms hanging limp and shambling around my grave. And their heads swiveling like the security cameras at the K-Mart. And that's how it goes on, all night long, so I can't get to sleep, so when I finally do it's almost dawn and I know I'm going to have to sleep through first period or totally ditch.

•

I got up around twelve. I couldn't leave the house because there's always a cop prowling around somewheres and they can't wait to truss your wrists with them plastic ties and haul you off to school. So I decided to go down to Uncle Will's apartment.

Actually I went down the fire escape first, slipped Ferdie a couple of cookies and a wine cooler—he just sat staring into a broken television set—then worked my way back around to the front, let myself in.

Uncle Will gave me a big old hug and I told him I had nightmares all night long and he's all, "It's okay, son, I'm here for you, calm down now."

And I'm all, "Dude, I dreamed everyone was dead."

"You've had it rough, kid." He steered me toward the sofa and gave me a couple of Valium. "You want to hang out here for a while? Your mom don't give a shit."

I sat on the sofa juggling the Valium from hand to hand. "Uncle Will? Why didn't you go to Grandpa's funeral? Like, he was your dad, wasn't he?"

"Don't got no father," said Uncle Will.

"Well but … Uncle Will? Why do you beat up on Ferdie so much?"

"Because he's a stubborn little motherfucker."

"Yeah, but … over not eating his cereal? I mean like, cigarette burns and shit?"

"How d'you find out?"

"I saw him yesterday."

"Saw him? I told him to stay in his room!"

"I know, I went in through the balcony."

"I told him not to—" I could see that Uncle Will was getting real pissed. Frothing at the mouth almost. He strode down the corridor to Ferdie's room and started trying to kick it in.

I'm all, "Don't you have a key?" and he like calms down, but only a little bit, and fumbles in his jeans and pulls them out and unlocks the door. There's Ferdie, sitting on the bunk in just a pair of *Terminator 2* boxer shorts and crisscrossed with cuts, and I see what Uncle Will means when he says *stubborn* because there ain't one shred of fear or self-pity in Ferdie's eyes, he just glares at Will and there's more anger coiled up in them eyes than you can imagine. Will just throws himself on Ferdie and he's all punching him and Ferdie just sits there, taking it, but no matter how hard he's hit he never gives up one little bit of that fury that's in his eyes. After a while I couldn't stand it no more and I'm all trying to pull Will off of him and I'm all, "You're crazy, dude, you're not yourself, you're fucking possessed or something."

And then it all suddenly snaps to. Ferdie, rigid, Uncle Will stepping back, looking away from those blazing eyes. "It's them eyes," he said, "it's all because of them eyes. Devil eyes. They just keep daring me and daring me. They taunt me and they haunt me."

He grabbed my shoulders and pushed me out of Ferdie's room and then he slammed the door shut behind us and locked it again. "I got to do something," he said. "Or else I'm going to murder him, I really am."

Once Ferdie was out of sight he started changing back into the Will I knew. "Let's go cruising," he said. "I can't stay cooped up here. I'll keep thinking about *him.*"

So we took off down the San Fernando Road toward Sun Valley, past Foothill Division, with speed metal all blaring on the stereo. I had to shout and he did too. And he's got his arm around me the whole time, and he's all, "Ozzie, I wish you were my kid. We have such good times together."

"Don't you love Ferdinand, Uncle Will?"

"I love him with all my heart." But there's no tenderness in his voice when he says it, only fear. "I don't know why I want to kill him so bad. He's got some devil in him."

"Maybe it's in *you,* Uncle Will. You know"—we turned a sharp corner, bounced across the railroad tracks somewhere around Tuxford, nothing but big old gray warehouses covered with taggers' writings, and the smog totally hiding the San Gabriel Mountains from sight—"when you were all screaming and shit, you sounded like another person. You sounded almost like Grandpa."

"Your grandfather was a good man. He never laid a hand on me. Do you hear that? Don't you ever forget that."

The tape was getting chewed up, so I had to stop the stereo and pull out the cassette and wind the little ribbon back with the end of a Pilot marker. So we caught the end of some news thing and it was that the cops were all found not guilty up there in Simi Valley, and then Uncle Will switched the radio off. "Motherfuckers," he said softly.

"Uncle Will, where are we?"

We were threading down a narrow winding road, half paved, half dirt, and weeds waist-high on either side of us, and like, it was suddenly getting dark. Then, poking out of them weeds, there's a big old sign that reads *Daniel Moreau, Doctor of Divinity.* I get that chilly feeling inside me again because of what I heard them talking about last night, which I've been trying to forget all day.

"I'll be damned," Uncle Will said. "It's Mr. Death's place."

After we parked we had to walk through a path winding through trees and weeds and here and there little piles of rocks, pyramids kind of, decorated with bunches of wildflowers. Like the place was a kind of homemade graveyard. The house wasn't much more than a shack, and it was set way in back of the lot. It looked abandoned, but when we got closer we could see the TV flickering behind closed blinds, and Uncle Will knocked on the door. There wasn't no answer but we went in anyways.

Mr. Death was in a lazyboy rocking back and forth and looking at the television. "Gone be riots," he said softly. "I just know it."

Uncle Will's all, "Gosh, Daniel, I don't know what happened. We were just cruising is all, and the road twisted and turned and we somehow ended up here."

"I been expecting you." Mr. Death's voice was all booming and hollow. On TV, the sun was setting and the streets were totally filling with angry black dudes and they were shouting and breaking store windows and beating up Koreans and shit. "You come for that service we done talked about."

"No, Mr. Death," Uncle Will said, "I swear, we were just passing by."

"You at your wits' end, Will. And Mr. Death, he at the end of every road."

Now I was getting totally scared because the way Mr. Death was talking, it was like this house, this whole encounter, was supernatural somehow. And I was staring at TV, it was Fox 11, and I could see fire running down the streets of South Central, and once in a while they cut to the videotape of the Rodney King thing, I remembered us driving past Foothill Division, I thought of my dream and my grandfather's shambling toward me with camcorder eyes.

"Don't be ashamed you come to me," said Daniel Moreau. "You done tried everything you can. You a good man, Will, but you have one streak of darkness in you, and maybe this gone lighten your darkness, maybe not."

"I just ... want to be able to love my son ... you know. They way I love Ozzie, my nephew."

And the way he said it, it made me feel like me and Ferdie were more alike than I'd of ever thought; like Ferdie was my own self's shadow, locked up in a dark room, sucking the hatred out of Uncle Will so that all that was left for me was his love. We were different like night and day, but the sickness in Uncle Will's mind had made us Siamese twins, joined at the heart.

"Give me a few minutes," said Mr. Death, "and I'll get all my tools."

"How much is this going to cost me?"

"It against the law for me to charge for this kind of thing. But you make a voluntary donation, that's fine."

"How much?" said Uncle Will, who always counted every dime, even when he was panhandling for change next to the freeway.

"You will know what the price will be," Mr. Death says, "and it will be the right price."

We followed him into the kitchen which was totally filthy. On the counter there was a bell jar with a big old frog inside, and hanging from the ceiling where a light bulb should be there was a a bunch of dried puffer fishes. At first I thought the frog was dead but he was only sleeping, and Mr. Death lifted the jar and made me hold him in both my hands, and then he jabbed it in the head with a needle, so it was dead and undead at the same time, and then he cut down one of the puffer fishes and got a whole mess of other shit off the shelves and then he throws everything, including the dead twitching frog, into like this big old blender, and he like turns it on.

While it's whirring all I can think of are frog-in-a-blender jokes.

Okay so then he pours this gooey mass out of the blender and then he does something with it in the microwave and finally he's all pounding it in a mortar and he's all mumbling in some kind of foreign language. After a while the chemicals and the dead animals were reduced to about a handful of dark powder and Mr. Death used a flour scoop to fill a Ziploc bag with it. A black-and-white TV on top of the microwave was on the whole time and the riots were getting uglier every minute, but so far they hadn't mentioned San Fernando, it was all like mostly downtown.

"You know," Mr. Death said, "if we cruise up to Mulholland drive, we'd see, the whole city, she a sea of fire."

He closed his eyes like he was remembering that sea of fire. But I knew that Mr. Death had been here the whole time. Maybe he had an inner eye for seeing things like that. Or he could send his spirit out hovering over the city. Maybe that was how we been led to his house ... shit all I know is he scared me, and I couldn't take my eyes off the things he was doing, and maybe it was the words he mumbled and maybe it was the two Valium, but my mind was all fuzzed up and I couldn't see straight.

Mr. Death put the powder in a black tote bag and took a human skull out of the refrigerator and he stuck that in the bag too. Then we drove back to the apartment and what was weird was it only took a minute or two to get back and I never seen the road we took before. In front of the complex there wasn't nobody cruising, only a patrol car with its lights flashing at the corner of Aztec and Hubbard. We went indoors and the TV was on and it showed a helicopter view of the city and like Mr. Death said, it was a ocean of flames and the people were streaming down the streets like termites.

We went to Ferdie's room and we found him exactly where he was sitting before, on the bunk bed facing the television.

Mr. Death is all, "We must introduce the *coup poudre* through a cut in the skin; it has to get into the bloodstream before it start to work."

"Come here, Ferdinand," said Uncle Will.

Ferdie comes toward us. He's thin as a shadow and there's his eyes, clear blue and deep sunken and full of rage, and some of his welts are bleeding a little bit where he's been picking scabs.

"And now," says Mr. Death, "please remember, my homies, there is no magic, no superstition. This a ancient and venerable science that come all the way from BaKongo times. The *coup poudre* gone send the boy into the sleep of no dreaming, and then, when he come back, he don't be stubborn no more."

I'm all, "You're gonna kill him, dude!"

Mr. Death said, "Death is transformation."

Ferdie comes up to Uncle Will. He only comes up to his chest. His sandy hair is all matted. I'm all, "What the fuck do you think you're doing, Uncle Will?" but he pushes me away real rough like, I never seen him be this rough to me before, he sends me reeling across the carpet and I hit my head against the bunk post. I'm all, "Why are you hurting me, Uncle Will," but then I look across the room and I see a strange thing in the cold light of the street lamp through the orange tree that leans against the balcony: I see Uncle Will take Ferdie into his arms with all the tenderness that he shows me, sometimes, when I knows I'm going through a lot of pain, and he hugs him, and he's all, "Ferdie, I'm only doing this because I want us to be a real family, I'm doing this for you as much as for me," and while he's hugging him his fingernail is searching out a long thick scab that goes diagonally all the way across Ferdie's back like a burned-on shoulder strap, and he's all digging his fingernail into it, flicking off the dry blood and exposing the quick, slick flesh. And the weird thing is there is a kind of love between them, or anyways a kind of dependency, because they are like each other's liquid sky, they are each other's addiction. Uncle Will still has Ferdie in his arms and he turns his back to me so I can see right into Ferdie's eyes and them eyes are all shiny, like the contact lenses a monster wears in a cheesy horror movie. But Ferdie's smiling too, like he's telling me, *This is what I've been waiting for. Yeah, maybe you like saved my life yesterday, but you couldn't snatch me away from Mr. Death forever.* And I'm all like standing with pain pounding in my skull from hitting the post and breaking out in a cold sweat because now Mr. Death has crept up behind Ferdie, with his cupped hands full of the powder, and even bending down he's a head taller than them and standing against the balcony door he's all black and shadowy and big and terrifying, and then I guess when there's enough raw flesh showing he like blows the powder all over Ferdie's back and he begins to chant and the powder goes everywhere, it wraps itself around the three of them like a cloud for a moment and then it all gets totally swallowed up in the dust and darkness of the room.

That's when Ferdie starts to scream.

Uncle Will's all, "God damn it, bitch, stop whining or I'll whip your motherfucking ass to kingdom come," but Mr. Death puts his hand on Will's shoulder and says, "It too late, my friend, you already have."

•

We left him screaming and went into the living room and Uncle Will broke out a brand-new bottle of Jack Daniels. We drank the whole thing in less than fifteen minutes and then we got totally fucked up on weed and downers. We had to. Because that screaming went on and on and it made me feel cold all the way into my guts. I don't know how long it went on but when I finally woke up it was because Uncle Will was prodding me with an empty bottle, and he's all, "Help me load him into the car, dude."

"Where's Mr. Death?"

"Gone already. But he's left us a note."

The note read:

> Bring him to my house
> Bury him in my yard
> Wait

And that's what we did. We found an open wooden box lying out under the trees, all ready to receive the body, and we dug a hole and buried Ferdie and we set up a pile of stones like we seen other places in Mr. Death's yard. We hung around all day. It got to late afternoon and Uncle Will kept going up to the house and knocking but the whole place was locked up. When the sun got near to setting Will was all pacing up and down and he's all, "We can't stay after sunset, there's a fucking curfew on and we'll have to spend the fucking night if we don't leave now."

"But we can't just leave Ferdie behind."

Just when Will was about ready to explode, this beat-up old Packard comes screaming into the driveway and there's Mr. Death. He's all dressed in black and he has a bottle of pills in his hand and he throws it to me and the bottle says on it, *Datura*. "Sorry I'm so late," he said, "I had to see my pharmaceutical contacts. It difficult to track anybody down with all them riots going on."

"What's that stuff for?" said Uncle Will.

"Insurance," said Mr. Death. "Now let's dig up your new son."

Digging him up took a lot longer than burying him because every now and then Mr. Death stopped to chant and then, when the moon came out, he went into like a trance and his eyes totally rolled up into their sockets he danced around us, hollering and shrieking.

But we finally pulled the coffin back out of the ground and we opened the lid and there was Ferdie, his eyes wide open, trying to breathe and his knuckles and knees were all bloody from clawing and kicking at the coffin lid. Mr. Death forced a pill down his throat and he calmed down, and Mr. Death's all, "Ferdinand, you a zombie now. You one of the living dead. You understand what that mean?"

Ferdie nods, slowly, and yeah, I can tell that he's changed. It ain't that he looks much different. There ain't no smell of dead things on him, just the usual toilet smell because he didn't have nowhere he could go in that box we buried him in. His eyes have that look though. The look I remember from my grandpa. The camcorder look. The eyes suck in, but they give nothing out.

"Now," Mr. Death says, "embrace your father, and don't you be stubborn again, cuz next time you dead for good."

"I won't be stubborn," Ferdie says, and he sounds more like a toddler than a twelve-year-old, "I love my father."

We went back to the house and camped out on the living room floor because the curfew. Ferdie lay on the floor and slept with his eyes open and didn't move a muscle. Maybe Mr. Death was right when he said this was all science, not magic, and maybe it was true that Ferdie wasn't really dead but had only been called back from a coma caused my the nerve poison in the puffer fish, but I knew that Ferdie didn't think so. Ferdie had watched zombie movies before. He knew that he didn't have his soul no more. He knew he was just a animated corpse.

•

I didn't ditch too much that week because of the riots and there was so much to talk about with my homies. A lot of them taken the bus down to South Central and did their own looting and they were all telling me about their new watches, Sega Genesises, boomboxes, shoes they jacked. I couldn't tell them I had spend the last two days raising the dead so I pretended I didn't care. In fact, whenever they tell me about all the shit they stoled, I'm all, "Who cares? It ain't no challenge looting a big old Circuit City with five hundred other people and the cops too scared to come in. Me, I can jack a CD player right from under the security guard's eyes. I'm down and you ain't."

So anyways I didn't see too much of Uncle Will that week. But whenever I would go there, the apartment was totally different. It was all clean and vacuumed and all the forty-ouncer bottles were all neatly lined up against the wall ready to be recycled. The blinds were all up and the living room was flooded in sunlight. At first I thought Uncle Will must have a new girlfriend but actually she had dumped him and it was just him and Ferdie living there now. And it was Ferdie cleaning the house. One time I caught him at it. He was all dusting the blinds and he was dressed different, too, in freshly laundered Bugle Boys and a white tee shirt.

"Yo, Ferdie," I said.

And he's all, "Hello, Ozzie, can I get you something to drink?" like he's a fucking waitress at Denny's or something. I was amazed and I just let him fetch me a wine cooler from the refrigerator. Then he went back into the kitchen and I followed him. He didn't walk like a zombie. He wasn't all shambling. He held his shoulders back and stood straight and didn't slouch around like a wuss. And he was all smiling. I mean, all the time. Only his eyes didn't smile. His eyes took everything in, gave out nothing.

I'm all, "What the fuck's happened to you?"

"I think I'm enjoying being dead."

"Ferdie, you ain't dead. Mr. Death explained the whole process to us. The datura makes your mind all fuzzy but you ain't *dead*."

He's all, "Of course I am. It's what I been praying for all my life. I'm happy now and so is my dad. You should try it, Oz. I look at you and I see, you're so unhappy."

"I seen dead people before," I said. I thought of Grandpa. I thought of my brother, which I never saw dead but they all told me about his brains being splattered on the pavement and his eyeball impaled by the hood ornament of a parked Impala. "You ain't one of them." But his eyes, his eyes … "And I don't want to be one neither."

"Suit yourself," he said, and scrubbed the counter with a sponge, scrubbed it to death even though it was already shiny except the spots where his scrubbing had wore off the laminate.

Uncle Will came home.

Ferdie's all "Daddy!" and he runs over to embrace him. Uncle Will kisses him on the cheek. He takes a pill out of his pocket and feeds it to Ferdie. They hug each other again. It's kind of sickening actually, like *The Waltons.*

"Shit," he says, "last one. I'll have to ask Mr. Death for more." Then he sees me and he's all, "Oh, it's you."

I'm all, "I stopped by to see what's up."

Uncle Will looks me over and then he's all, "Look at you, Ozzie, jeeze you're a disgrace. Look at them jeans. What are you doing wearing them jeans, they look like they're about ten sizes too big."

"It's the style, Uncle Will."

"Fucking cholo style. You want people to think we're nothing but white trash?"

I backed away in real hurry. I looked at Ferdie but he didn't seem to think anything was wrong, he was hanging on every word Uncle Will spoke, like a ten-year-old girl at a NKOTB concert.

"And what are you doing drinking that wine cooler anyways?"

"You always let me drink wine coolers, Uncle Will."

He knocked the bottle out of my hand and Ferdie dove after it, caught it one handed, got on his hands and knees to sponge the mess off of the carpet. While I was all standing there stunned, Uncle Will slaps me hard right across the mouth a couple of times. I can't believe this is happening to me even when I start to taste blood.

And Ferdie's all smiling.

"Uncle Will," I said softly, "you never done this to me before."

"I'm seeing you with new eyes, you good-for-nothing juvenile delinquent scumbag."

"Come on, Uncle Will, you said yourself every kid has to steal a few cars and jack a few stereos once in a while, and get drunk. You said it was just a phase, that I'd get over it, that it was like harmless."

"Don't sass me."

But it's hard to get out of the habit of answering back because it's always been this close between me and Uncle Will and I can't understand why he's turned against me until I realize that it's the Siamese twin thing, that Will can't love his zombie son without hating me. So I'm all backing out of there real fast because I think any minute now he's going to starting laying into me with his belt or his fists or a cigarette, I get out of there as fast as I can and I go sprinting up the stairs three steps at a time to my mom's apartment, the place where I most hate to be.

•

Mom was sitting at the counter and what was weird was she was actually making dinner when I arrived and the whole living room smelled of enchiladas. She was all dressed up, too. I realized she had been out looking for a job, and she didn't look wasted. She was all shredding lettuce and watching television, which was showing the riots, naturally.

"How's the job market, Mom?"

She's all, "I actually *got* a job today, Oz, they're going to train me to be a checkout lady at Alpha Beta."

"Coolness."

"I get a discount on food, too. We're not gonna be hungry no more."

"We wouldn't be hungry, Mom, if you would have spent them disability checks on food instead of—"

"I know, I know. Let's not argue about it no more. I want to start again. I done a lot of things I regretted in my life. And Jesus, I don't know how to tell you this, but ... there was this lady from the rehab program, she got my name off some mailing list, she was over here to talk about shared needles and ... Jesus, Oz, do you think I have it?"

"Don't say that, Mom."

"I'm scared to take the test, son. I'm scared to stick another needle in me and I'm scared not to because if I don't then I know I'm going to be scared by everything around me, the whole world."

She's all crying and the oven timer goes *dingdingding* so I took the enchiladas out and then I put my arm around

Mom's waist and let her cry for the longest time, and dinner was totally cold when we finally got around to it, but it's the thought that counts and it was like the first dinner she'd made in six months.

After we ate I asked her what Grandpa was like. "Was he ever mean to you?" I said. "Did he like hit you and stuff?"

"No. I got everything I ever asked for. It was Will he hated. He always said Will was stubborn. He'd lock him up in the tool shed for days at a time. Me, though, he loved me. He loved me to death. His love was a scary thing. It engulfed me. It ate me up. I guess that's why I became a junkie."

And then I understood everything. Uncle Will's sickness didn't just come from nowhere. It had been handed down through the generations and maybe, one day, it would even come down to me. Grownups are always all, what a big deal it is to grow up, to become mature, to set aside childish things as my grandma says, quoting the Bible ... I ain't grown up yet but I already know that growing up is a big old joke ... you don't grow up. You just live through your childhood again and again and again until the day you die. Your childhood is who you are.

"I'm going back down to Uncle Will's place," I said. "There's something I just got to tell him."

"All right," she said. "But don't go outside. The curfew hasn't been lifted yet and you don't know what the cops will do, they're in such a state over these damn riots."

Yeah. We could hear sirens in the distance. Mom switched channels and an anchorman was talking about the fires again ... behind him, the city was burning ... in a little window on the screen, they were replaying the video of the Rodney King beating for the millionth time. They had preempted the fucking *Simpsons*. They showed a clip of Pat Buchanan visiting South Central. He might just as well have been an alien from *Close Encounters*.

I went down to Uncle Will's to tell him my big new insight. I figure if he would have known that he was just slow-motion-replaying a scene from his childhood over and over, he could maybe step back from it, get it in perspectve, and then maybe we could pull Ferdie back from his so-called death and Will out of his madness. But when I got to Will's I could tell that things had gone wrong, more wrong than they ever were before.

Will and Ferdie were standing on opposite sides of the living room. Between them, on the big TV, was the bird's-eye-view of the ocean of fire. Will was shouting into his portable phone. "God damn it," he was saying, "I need the fucking pills *now,* he's getting stubborn again, I'm gonna fucking lose control!"

He had run out of datura. But what difference did it make? Ferdie was standing there and he was all submissive, all smiling, didn't seem like he was doing nothing wrong.

I heard Mr. Death's voice, "You know I can't come out there now. The curfew. And my supplier he way out in South Pas."

And Uncle Will's all, "Fuck, fuck, fuck, I'm fucking desperate!"

He slammed the portable phone against the wall. Then he turned and saw me. "Kid's being stubborn again," he shouted. "He won't mind, he just stands there, won't do what he's told." Then he turned to Ferdie and screamed, "I want you to whine, you hear! I want you to wipe that grin off your face! I'm sick of watching that smile day in, day out!"

Ferdie tried to frown but the smile was soldered on his face. He said, "But I can't be unhappy, Dad. I have the kindest father in the world. I have a great life."

"You don't even *have* a life, you're just an animated corpse, and I want you to obey me!"

Ferdie's all, "Okay, Dad. I'm as sad as you want me to be." And he goes on smiling. And Uncle Will's going berserk, I mean like, more berserk than he's ever been before, he's like frothing at the mouth and shit. And Ferdie just goes on smiling. And Will's all, "I'm gonna hurt you, Ferdie," but Ferdie's all, "I don't hurt anymore, Dad. There ain't no hurting where I am, the dead country." And he goes on smiling.

Uncle Will picks up the first thing he sees which is one of the empty bottles lined up against the wall and he strides over to Ferdie and he starts swinging it and it cracks against the wall and he cuts Ferdie's face a couple of times and Ferdie goes on smiling. Will socks him in the jaw and a bloody tooth flies on to the carpet and Ferdie smiles a gap-toothed smile, wider than ever. Will's weeping with rage and he just goes on punching and punching and for a long while I'm all standing there and staring because I can't believe it's happening, it's worse than I've ever seen before. I forget all about the big old revelation I was going to make. I think maybe even though it's true, that we're all together in this generational cycle of violence, that just saying it isn't going to make it stop because we're stuck in it, we're part of it, we're the spokes of the wheel and when the wheel turns we can't just turn the other way. I'm so full of despair I want to go hang myself like Ferdie was trying to. I want to be dead.

While I'm all standing there with these terrible emotions raging through me, Uncle Will's never stopped trying to whip that smile off Ferdie's face. And now he's all, "You ain't dead, you ain't dead, it's just your stubbornness speaking, and I'm going to *shock* you back to the way you are, you can't escape from me by playing possum cuz I know you're inside there and you're laughing at me, laughing at me ..." and he sounds just like Grandpa used to sound sometimes. I stand there and watch while he ties Ferdie to a chair with an extension cord and now he's all getting more cords out of a drawer and I realize that when Uncle Will says *shock* that's exactly what he means, he's going to fry Ferdie's brains and this time he'll *really* be dead. And finally this shocks *me* out of my despair and I do what I should have done the first day I saw my cousin cut and bruised and caged ... I crawl over to where the phone's lying on the carpet and I pull up the antenna and I dial 911.

It takes forever to get through because of the riots I guess. And the whole time Uncle Will's all storming through the house and throwing things around and there's blood all over Ferdie's white shirt but Ferdie's all smiling, smiling, smiling, and even I can feel a piece of Uncle Will's madness in me, the smile that goes on and on and driving you all crazy and shit. Then there's a lull in the shouting, Uncle Will's out of breath or something maybe, and that's when I get through to the police and I give them our address and tell them there's a child-beating going on right now and please come, please Jesus come fast or I think my cousin's going to get fucking killed.

I put down the phone and I see the two of them, face to face, frozen in a moment of concentrated rage. Uncle Will turns to me and says, real soft like, "Traitor."

I'm all, "I'm sorry, Uncle Will." And I'm thinking of the times Uncle Will's been good to me, put his arm around me, wiped my tears with his sleeve, and all the time there's been a mirror image of this love between us, locked up like a dirty secret. And I'm all crying. We can hear sirens in the distance. They're already coming.

"I've gotta get out of here," says Will. "Can't let them catch me. There's a warrant on me, parking tickets and shit, car registration, I don't know."

"You got nowheres to go, Uncle Will. There's a curfew."

Someone is knocking on the door.

Uncle Will bolts past both of us toward Ferdie's room. I let the officer in and she takes one look at Ferdie, tied to the chair and covered in blood, and she's all pulling out her gun and running toward the back of the house.

I untie Ferdie and then me and him follow. We hear the rustle of the orange tree and we know he's going down into the alley. The sirens are wailing from every side now. The police officer's all, "Stay right here, kids. I'm going down to radio for help."

So there's me and there's Ferdie standing on the balcony looking down through the branches the orange tree into the alley below. And there's Uncle Will. Staggering. Confused. Two police officers come in from Aztec and two from Astoria and they have their PR24's out. They don't read him no rights, they don't call out to him to surrender. They just surround him and they start beating the shit out of him with their power blows. The whistling of the nightsticks and the crunching of bones blend in with the other sounds of the night, the swaying of the orange branches, the rattling of garbage cans, the thrum of helicopters, the wail of sirens and stray cats. The night air totally smells of citrus and smog and garbage and gunsmoke. Though this is all happening for real and not on television there's something about it that's less real than televsion: it's because we're standing in the warm wind of night and seeing the San Gabriel Mountains through the veil of smog and we feel small and we feel powerless, not like

TV where you're bigger than the people on the screen and you can turn them on and off with a flick of a remote. I look down and I don't see a man I used to love, I only see flesh and bone and blood, and I try to feel but I don't feel nothing, *nothing*.

And like, now I understand why Ferdie prefers being dead.

The beating goes on and on and afterwards Uncle Will isn't moving no more and I'm sure that he's not gonna see the morning.

And I'm all, "Ferdie, come back from the dead now. You don't have to be dead no more. We've killed him."

But Ferdie doesn't come back from the dead. I look into his eyes and they have the lifeless look of a camcorder lens. There won't be no videotape of Uncle Will to play on national television. No, there'll just be the videotape that's burned into me and Ferdie's brains, with the erase tab popped forever.

Ferdie smiles. And smiles.

And smiles.

•

Me and my mom and Ferdie are in family counseling now. We were on a waiting list for a foster home for a while, but nobody wanted us. Mr. Death has disappeared, and we've never been able to find his house again.

Our counselor says it's true what Mr. Death said: that there's no magic to what happened, that Ferdie never was dead or came back from the dead. He says that Uncle Will wove a tapestry of illusion around us, that we were trapped inside his warped reality. He says that coming to terms with this will help us to change, to heal.

Well like, *I've* changed. I hardly drink no more and I never shoplift. I try to read books sometimes, like Ferdie used to. Ferdie don't read books. I don't think he's even growing any. He's all frozen in time.

But Ferdie hasn't stopped smiling. He smiles through everything: happy times, sad times. A defense mechanism, the counselor calls it. My mom says, "Give him time and one day he'll feel again."

Sometimes I ask him if he's ever going to come back. And always he's all, "Nu-*uh.*"

"Why not, Ferdie?" I'll ask him. Because like, there's no reason for him to play dead no more. Mom's in rehab and we're getting taken care of, and he don't have to feel pain all the time like he used to.

But he'll just look at me with them dead eyes, and he'll say, "I like it better here."

Mr. Death's Blue-Eyed Boy

Darrell Sachsenhauser loved money and hated children. Children had always frightened him, even when he was a child himself.

He did not know why, although by middle age he had paid a great deal of money to therapists, analysts, and occultists to find out. There were those who wanted to probe his dreams; they elicited little but recurring images of wild, fanged creatures with slitty eyes. They tried to regress him to that singular trauma of childhood that always seemed to motivate their clientele; but this client did not seem to have had much of a childhood at all; he had sprung into being sometime around puberty; they could find no mismanaged potty training, no virulent rape, no devastating primal scene. It seemed to the Freudians that the trauma must be so deeply lodged that only a larger infusion of cash could draw it out; and so Darrell Sachsenhauser, who loved money more than he loved himself, went to the Jungians instead.

The Jungians tried to get him to confront his Shadow and communicate with his Anima, only to discover that he seemed to have neither. A variety of New Age therapists had a go, but they ended up telling him that he simply didn't want to change. And then there was a shamaness who told him that some enemy had worked a spell on him, and that he should bury a thousand dollars in a certain graveyard by the light of the full moon; Darrell Sachsenhauser balked at that and so received no succor from the spirit world. The last straw had been Marilyn Firth, whom he'd run into at the Long Beach coin fair: beautiful in a shopworn kind of way, a former Jungian, now some kind of vaguely Joseph Campbellian counselor; she had tried to help him communicate with his inner child, only to discover that there was no inner child within him—a shell without an oyster, she'd called him in a fit of pique.

At least she had been good in bed. Surfers always were. They bucked and heaved in time to an imagined tide.

After he weathered his midlife crisis, it occurred to him that the attempt to fathom his phobia had become increasingly subject to the law of dimishing returns; he gave up trying to find out why. He merely avoided them whenever possible; and when, as often in the course of his daily business, he could not do so, he kept his distance as best he could.

It was not necessarily as discomfiting a phobia as it might appear. Darrell Sachsenhauser lived in an all-adult condominium, and he took a circuitous route to the coin store in order to avoid passing the playground and the elementary school. However, there were times when they did cross his path. After all, the coin store was a public place. There *was* a sign in the window that read NO CHILDREN ALLOWED, but it was not, of course, enforceable.

One particular Sunday he had planned to close the shop early. The last customer was a snotty-looking child who was clearly not about to buy anything; and Darrell wanted to count his money without having to experience the unreasoning terror he suffered in their proximity. He retreated to the farthest corner of the store, switched off a few lights, and began emptying the display cabinets so he could put the coins back in the safe. But the child seemed to sense where he was. When Darrell looked up, he was right there, sniffing the dusty air like a rat.

"Scram," Darrell Sachsenhauser said. "Show's over."

The child had a skateboard under one arm and a teeshirt with neon pink skeletons dancing against black. "Wow!" he said. "Is that, like, really a *billion* on that banknote? How much is it worth?"

In his thirty years as proprietor of a second-rate coin store in the northeast side of the San Fernando Valley, Darrell had gotten pretty fucking tired of that question. Nevertheless, having to concentrate on the stock answer distracted him from the terror. He rattled off: "It's *Notgeld,* emergency scrip put out by local governments during the great inflation that hit Germany after World War I ... a billion marks could buy you maybe a dozen eggs ... that's how Hitler came to power, by taking advantage of the economic—" He paused. The unease was creeping back up on him.

The kid just stood there. Feral. Ready to pounce. Beady-eyed, slavering. No teary-eyed moppet, but a monster, a vampire. Darrell mopped the sweat from his forehead. Damn you, disappear! he thought. *Retro me, Satanas!*

"You okay, dude?"

... and something clammy slithering down his spine. "Take it," he said. "You can take the goddamn thing for a buck if you'll get out of the fucking store so I can close up!"

"Fresh," said the child, "gimme two of 'em, dude."

Darrell selected a worn City of Bamberg "eine Milliarde Mark" note and a crisp Heidelberg "zwei Millionen," hurriedly inserted them into mylar envelopes and handed them to the boy. He tried to make himself relax with the thought that, even at the discount, he was still clearing a 400% profit. You could buy German *Notgeld* by the carton. It was worthless. A novelty item at best. His pulse raced. Any minute now he'd be gasping for oxygen—

The door clanged shut. Darrell was safe.

He put away more coins. He turned off the neon sign. Smog-filtered sunset streamed in through the window bars. He coughed. It had been a narrow escape. Another minute or two and he might have fainted dead away, like the time his neighbour's nieces came over to use the swimming pool.

Darrell packed up the last of the gold, a handful of 2x2's containing liberty half-eagles in shitty condition, slammed the safe shut, and lugged it into the toilet, where he had a secret panel behind the medicine cabinet. That's where he kept the real treasures: an Athenian dekadrachm of the archaic period, a roll of CC Morgans, a mint state Caligula denarius with an unrecorded reverse ... coins that could one day put him in a mansion on Mulholland. Coins he had killed for.

He held up the dekadrachm, feeling its weight and the weight of its past. The face of Athena was in profile, but the eye was askew; it glared straight up at him. Time hadn't touched the coin since some Ionian merchant hoarded it away in a wine jug and buried it against catastrophe. Darrell had snatched it right under the nose of that Turkish dealer in a Paris hotel. Then the dealer had died, somehow. Heart attack. Poison. Darrell couldn't recall.

Darrell held the Turk's death between his fingers, a chunk of metal with the face of a goddess.

There was a tap at the window.

Quickly Darrell put away his guilty pleasures. He locked the medicine chest and came out of the bathroom. There was a shadow in the doorway. He mouthed "We're closed. Go away."

The shadow didn't leave. It was a slender figure in a leather coat, silhouetted in sunset and the flicker of sushi bar neon signs. It was banging hard now. Any minute it would set off the alarm. Insufferable. But it least it wasn't another kid.

It was a sharp-featured young woman with a page-boy haircut. She pummeled the door with operatic desperation.

"Closed! Come back tomorrow."

A high-heeled patent leather boot jammed the doorway. *"Bitte. Entschuldigung, Herr Sachsenhauser. Sie müssen mir ja helfen."*

"I don't do any of this old country talk, lady. Just English." Darrell could understand German perfectly, but he had no memory of ever having learned it.

"Mr. Sachsenhauser?" A limousine was waiting by the curb.

Darrell looked her in the eye. Could she possibly know about the trail of blood that led to the medicine cabinet in the lavatory of his coin store? Was she Interpol, maybe? But why so distraught? Why the heaving sex appeal? Surely anyone with a dossier would have known that his interest in women was confined to his regular Saturday night outing to Mrs. Chernikov's—quick, impersonal, and modestly priced.

"I have been searching for you for months, Herr Sachsenhauser." She handed him her business card.

It read:

Eva Rotwang
Office of the Municipality of Hameln,
Westfalien, Germany

"You've come a long way, lady," he said.

"It was necessary." Maybe she *was* with Interpol after all. But Darrell had never killed anyone in Germany. Or robbed a collection. No. He'd always kept my hands off Germany. The Fatherland, he supposed, although he had no memories of it. He started to fidget. "There isn't much time, Mr. Sachsenhauser. Your passport is in order, I hope? But of course it is; you travel a great deal."

"Am I going somewhere?" he said. Sensing my unease, she tugged at his sleeve and pulled him out of my store so that they stood, face to face, on the sidewalk. She no longer seemed distraught. She gripped his wrists. Her mid-calf overcoat and leather gloves were overpoweringly Aryan. She seemed strong ... so different from the wishy-washy Marilyn. She allowed him a moment to lock up and set the alarm system. Then the chauffeur ushered him into the back seat.

He protested that he had his own car, but no one listened. The Rotwang woman followed. "Are you kidnapping me?" he said.

"No, of course not," said Eva Rotwang. In a few moments they were on the Ventura Freeway. She picked up the car phone and dialed, said, "*Ja, ja,*" a few times, hung up.

"*Nach dem Flughafen,*" she said to the driver.

"Bullshit," Darrell said. "I'm not going to the airport. Do you have a warrant?"

Eva Rotwang pulled something out of her purse. "Do you recognize this man?" she said.

It was a polaroid shot: a pretty nondescript man, actually, long, scraggly blond hair, not too thoroughly shaven—

the caveman type. His cheeks were hollow and his his face gaunt ... it was an Auschwitz sort of a face ... a skull.

Mr. Death, Darrell thought. But he had no idea who he was, and said so. "Whatever you're looking for," he said, "you obviously have the wrong man."

"I don't think so."

Darrell peered at the photograph again as the freeway crossed the Santa Monica Mountains. They were speeding; these people were used to the autobahn.

The man in the picture was wearing some kind of mediaeval costume, he realized, one side red and the other side yellow; maybe he was an actor. But still, it wasn't someone he had robbed or cheated. No, Darrell told himself firmly, I don't know him. And yet....

Eyes on a cavern wall, dancing in candlelight....

"The man insists on seeing you, asking for you by name. And he's very persuasive."

"How so?"

"Enough to cause the city of Hameln to send me here to get you ... by hook or by crook."

"I don't even know where the fuck Hameln is."

"In Westphalia. Germany. But you know of it, *natürlich* ... the rats ... the Pied Piper ... the thirty guilders...."

"Oh, you mean Hame-*lin.*"

"Ja, ja, Hameln. Hamelin is the anglicized version."

"Well, listen, Eva, or whatever your name is, this doesn't seem to have much to do with me, so if you're not arresting me, you might as well let me off at the next exit. I'll take a cab home."

"You don't understand ... we'll pay you."

"Usually, in a kidnapping, it's the kidnappee who pays." They were really flying down the San Diego Freeway now. He reckoned they'd reach the airport in about ten minutes. Perhaps he'd be able to lose her there.

The Rotwang woman said, "If not for the sake of a reward, then at least do it for the children!"

"Now you've really said the wrong thing." She scrambled in her purse and produced several more polaroids. They were all kids. Cute little blond things. Children in sailor suits. Children waving Nintendo Game Boys and Barbie dolls. Each image filled him with revulsion. They're only pictures, he told himself, but he found himself sliding toward the window. "Children make me nervous. It's a phobia of mine." He gazed at the billboards as they reeled by, strident in the purple-streaked smog of sunset. The polaroids were all over the seat and he caught the reflection of one of them in the window ... eyes superimposed over the cityscape ... floating in the void. Animal eyes. Hungry. Glowing in the dark. Devil eyes.

"I *hate* children," he said softly.

"In that case," said Eva Rotwang, "you won't mind coming to Hameln. There are no children there at all, you see. They've all vanished. And you're the only one *he'll* talk to."

•

It was an old familiar dream ... the cave ... the cold. And the hunger. Seeping into his bones. And the darkness. The only sound a steady drip ... drip ... drip ... echoing. Echoing. Drip. Echoing. Then slowly, out of the cold and dark, a faint light. Flickering. Ebbing now, sucked back into the limestone void. Ice-floes that hugged the interior of the mountain. Dark. Dark.

Candlelight....

Flash! The glint of a razor-sharp incisor. A hint of drool. A deathsmile forming out of the dimness ... eyes that burn crimson ... eyes. Eyes. And then the laughter: squeaky, metallic, punctuated by the drip-drip-drip ... and the cold. The cold. Eyes. More eyes. Eyes. Screeching.

The laughter of feral children.

Darrell screamed.

•

He felt a cold compress against his brow. "There, there." a familiar voice ... one he had never thought to hear again. "My, my, our inner child's sure going through a shitload of anxiety today."

"Marilyn Firth?" said Darrell. "Get out of here, go back to Santa Monica, find some new yuppies to torment."

She stood there, resplendent in sari and—this was new—dreadlocks. The Indo-Jamaican look. Underneath it, still the middle-aged surfer woman from Santa Monica. "Now you listen to me, Darrell. You're not paying for my services, so don't have a cow. Me all taken care of, mon."

"Talk about an identity crisis," Darrell said. "You with your bleached hair and your Santa Monica sun-weathered face and your"—he noted that she had now become a dothead—"third eye."

"Hey, I found myself, okay? In Jamaica, on the rebound from you, I might add. More than can be said of you, you old miser."

Eva Rotwang was coming through the partition into the first class section now. "What a commotion," she said. "Do you want me to ask for you some sleeping pills? We have a doctor on board, at your disposal." Darrell seemed to be the only passenger in first. "I see the doctor has found you."

"Yes. Give me a Valium or something. And get this witch doctor off the plane."

"Got a parachute?" said Marilyn, shrugging. "Relax! Money's no object to these people; they *desperate*."

He looked at Eva. "What possessed you people to bring *her* along? Don't you know she's a total charlatan? Her psychic powers come and go, just like her quaint and colorful West Indian accent."

"Oh, you've no imagination, Darrie ... we're all spokes in the great cosmic wheel. Karma, mon. Hey, we could have sex. Old times' sake."

"I'm sorry," Eva said. "Our records indicated that ... you're not the most stable of individuals ... and this woman was listed as your most recent therapist."

"And you didn't want me to flake out on you while I negotiate with the Pied Piper."

There was a long silence as the women looked at each other, each waiting for the other to do something. At last Darrell said, "Okay, give me the damn tranquilizer."

But the nightmare came back as soon as he closed his eyes. It was more vivid than ever. And this time he could not wake himself up, because he had taken one Valium too many. The children laughed all the way from Los Angeles to

Hamburg ... all the way through customs ... all the way along the autobahn ... all the way to the office of the mayor of Hamelin.

•

Sculpted wood paneling; frayed carpeting; on the ceiling, a baroque fresco of cupids, nymphs, shepherds, and the like.

They were sitting at a round table. Each wore a business suit of the identical shade of gray, and each wore a dark blue tie. They were the city council: all male, all old, all tired. Darrell had not had time for even a coffee break; the two women ushered him in, standing on either side of him, as though he were their prisoner.

"Herr Sachsenhauser," one of them, bearded, perhaps a nonagenarian, began. *"Wie glücklich, daß Sie schon angekommen sind."*

"He won't speak German, Dr. Krumm," said Eva Rotwang. "Darrell Sachsenhauser: the distinguished members of our city council. Unfortunately, the mayor will be unable to attend this meeting."

"He is in hiding," said the old codger, and introduced the others quickly by name; Darrell soon forgot who they were. Confusion was kicking in. They weren't Interpol. They had dragged him halfway across the world because they thought he could save their children. He, the one person in the world who could not be in the same room as a child without experiencing an mindless, uncontrollable panic.

A man in a butler's uniform can into the room. He was carrying a television set on. He set it down in the middle of the round table, and Dr. Krumm finally remembered to invite Darrell to sit down. The seats were dark green leather, the central heating oppressive. The butler turned on the television, and one of the councillors activated a speakerphone.

"There he is," said Dr. Krumm.

It was the straggly-haired blond in the medieval costume. *"Er ist im Gefängnis,"* said one of the other councillors.

"You jailed him?" said Darrell.

"Of course we did!" said Krumm. "He could be serial killer or something like that. A madman preying on ancient legend."

The man on the screen looked up at them; a prison guard handed him a telephone. He seemed unsure of its purpose, but after an brief explanation from the guard, he lifted the receiver.

"I want to speak to Sachsenhauser," he said in a strangely accented German. Even through the speakerphone's distortion, there was something compelling about his voice. His eyes, too, were hypnotic, so sunken that they were encircled with shadow.

"Herr Sachsenhauser is here now," said Dr. Krumm. "Enunciate clearly, though; he hasn't spoken the *muttersprache* for a long time."

Darrell said, "Good morning, Mr. Death," in German, surprising himself by how easily it leapt to his tongue.

"Why do you call me that?"

"I ... I don't know."

"It is not I who kill the children."

"What are you accusing me of?"

The stranger said, "Five hundred years ago, your many-times-great-grandfather made a pact with me. I have come to collect the money. With, of course, the accumulated interest."

Dr. Krumm said, "Which comes to, Herr Sachsenhauser, four quadrillion, seven hundred and twenty-two trillion, sixteen billion, four hundred and twelve million, six hundred thousand and seventeen marks and thirteen pfennigs!" And he handed Darrell a piece of computer printout on which were row upon row of figures ... and that ominous final figure, 4,722,016,412,600,017.13, underlined and circled.

"These folks mad as hatters," said Marilyn Firth. "Just my kind of people."

Dr. Krumm went on, "We have a document that has been in the city archives for some centuries. It is an ... ah ... a sort of trust deed. It certifies that ..." He put on a pair of hornrimmed spectacled and rummaged in a drawer. Then he looked up in frustration. The butler came in, sideways, bearing a silver casket; Dr. Krumm took out a xerox of a handwritten document. "I'll translate it for you: 'in consideration of services rendered to the municipality of Hameln, the sum of thirty guilders, plus interest, to be awarded, to be collected no sooner than one hundred years from this date, with the children of the town, their bodies and souls, to be pledged as mortgage collateral ... that this agreement be binding upon myself and my heirs until such time as the obligations therein be fully discharged, as witness of which I herewith commit my living soul and the souls of my heirs living or as yet unborn ... signed this day by me, having been granted such authority by the citizens of the municipality of Hameln, Antonius Sachsenhauser, mayor.'" Krumm removed his glasses and looked expectantly at Darrell.

"What the hell is this supposed to mean?" Darrell said. "Anyway, everyone knows what *really* happened ... oh, I don't mean *really,* I mean in the fucking fairy tale ... the piper *did* get paid ... with those children ... good fucking riddance ... and ..."

"Apparently not," said Dr. Krumm. "Apparently there was some kind of compromise ... the piper agreed to ... ah, carry paper, as you might say in the mortgage business ... and the balloon payment has come due."

An even more geriatric fellow, jabbing his finger in the director of Darrell's face, said, "You are the only traceable living descendant of Antonius Sachsenhauser, author of this document."

"Awesome," said Marilyn. "I mean, it's like, a visitation from the collective unconscious. I think I'm in love!"

"Bullshit," said Darrell Sachsenhauser.

"Oh, but it's beautiful, mon," Marilyn said. "It's not just that Berlin Wall she come a-tumbling down; it's the wall between reality and illusion ... the wall between mythic time and modern time. This is so cool I could piss myself."

"I'm not descended from any mayor of Hamelin," Darrell said. How could they possibly know such a thing when even he himself had no memories of childhood, of being *anybody's* heir? And how could a fairy tale come true? Was it all something to do with the childhood Darrell could not remember, the childhood that seemed to have been walled up within the same mountain walls that had hidden the children of

Hamelin? It was too ridiculous for words. Yet here were all these decrepit old krauts, sitting around a table in a plush old office building, waiting for him to be their messiah. "It's beyond belief."

"And yet ..." said Marilyn, causing all eyes to turn to her, even the eyes of the madman in the prison cell ... "and yet he does have this irrational fear of children."

... the cave ... the cold ... the laughter ...

The old men all looked at each other, nodded, muttered, murmured, as if Marilyn's revelation proved everything.

"You will negotiate with the piper," said Dr. Krumm. "You'll be well paid."

"Your city doesn't have a good track record in paying for pest control," Darrell said. It was easy to fall into the reality of the fairy tale because all of *them* believed it.

"You'll like what we have to offer." The butler, suaver than ever, came in with another casket, this time gold. Inside, on a blue velvet lining, lay a coin. A dekadrachm. It was a twin of the one in Darrell's bathroom safe. Except that *this* one was perfect. The last such dekadrachm to be auctioned had sold for $600,000, but it had only been in EF.

Darrell reached out to grab the box, but the butler snatched it away. "You certainly know what I like," Darrell said, "but somehow—"

"There is, of course, also the leaden casket," said Eva Rotwang. The butler whipped it out, opened it, and Darrell saw what was inside: a photograph of a dead Turkish coin dealer in a Paris hotel. There was another photograph of a glass case full of ancient coins, with one conspicuously missing. There was a third photograph—a closeup of the glass case—a fingerprint.

"I'll be damned," said Darrell. "You *are* from Interpol." Eva smiled a little, then clammed up.

"This is *so* fucking mythic!" squealed Marilyn.

"You have twenty-four hours, give or take a few," said Dr. Krumm. "That's the deadline *he* gave us."

"What if he has nothing to do with the disappearance of your children? What if he's just some lunatic taking the credit and trying to blackmail the city?"

"That is possible. But walk our streets ... look out over the town square from your hotel window ... go to the playgrounds ... you will see that there are no children in Hameln. *None!*"

And all the old men began to weep.

•

Darrell did walk the streets. There were indeed no children in Hameln. If, as their records seemed to indicate, Darrell Sachsenhauser had actually been born in Hamelin, and had emigrated to America with his parents and aging grandfather sometime after the war, it was strange that he felt no twinges of recognition.

Darrell walked down cobblestoned alleys, past rococo churches, past squat apartment complexes and medieval storefronts. Toy shops were boarded up. In a pastry shop, old women in black dresses sipped hot chocolate and glared at each other. In Los Angeles, there would be times when Darrell was just walking down the boulevard to buy a magazine ... feeling quite safe, quite at peace with himself ... and then there'd be a shrill cry in the air ... a child whizzing by on a skateboard, brushing against him, and his nostrils would get a sudden blast of that smell they had, an odd amalgum of ketchup and chocolate and sweat and *Teenage Mutant Ninja Turtles* bubble bath. The contact would last for a split second and yet by the time he'd reached the newsstand he'd have become a nervous wreck, unable to remember what he had come for. Or sometimes, just the dread that such an encounter might occur would be enough to reduce him to a gibbering idiot.

After an hour of walking, he had yet to feel that dread. There was no turning a corner and suddenly running into one of the creatures, sprinting toward school. There was no metal-tinged laughter.

There really were no children here. Darrell could breathe deeply without fear of sucking in their breath, their odor. After another hour or so, strolling along the left bank of the Weser, it occurred to him that this was the first time he had ever felt free from oppression. He walked with his head held high, unafraid. All cities should be like this city. He waved at passersby, but no one waved back. It was autumn, and moist rotting leaves fluttered along the narrow streets, and people walked with their eyes downcast. One storefront was plastered with dozens of polaroids of children, with a banner that read, *"Wo sind die Kinder?"* and Darrell was tempted to shout back, "Who cares where they are?"

At length he found himself beside souvenir stand that sold plastic Hong Kong rats and wooden flutes. There was no vendor. It stood beside a stone gate, an obvious tourist spot, though there were no tourists; a Latin inscription noted that this gate was dedicated, two hundred and seventy-two years later, to the hundred and thirty children abducted from the town and immurred within Mt. Poppen. Sitting down on a bench, feeding the pigeons with a bag of birdseed pilfered from another abandoned souvenir stand, Darrell could see the celebrated mountain itself, rearing up behind the town's skyline, an unharmonious blend of the sixteenth and twentieth centuries. He helped himself to a Pilsner. It occurred to him that they must be following him, and sure enough he could see the leathery outline of Eva Rotwang in the shadow of the gate; but he didn't care. It was wonderful to know such freedom from anxiety. The therapists hadn't been able to do it. Maybe there never had been anything wrong with him … just with the rest of the world.

"Pretty grim, huh." It was Marilyn, sitting down on the bench beside him, opening an apple juice.

"On the contrary," said Darrell, "I've never felt better in my life."

"Oh, you old solipsist! I didn't mean you, I meant this town."

"I don't miss them."

"Oh, don't be silly. How would the human race replicate itself without children? Your ancestor did the right thing, in a way … life expectancy was much shorter in the middle ages … you eliminate one generation, you kill the whole town." She wasn't putting on some accent now, which meant she was dead serious.

"You're buying this malarkey?"

"You take their money, you take their shit," she said. "Besides ... when old Krumm there was telling you how the children were all gone ... and you were just staring into the piper's eyes, on the monitor ... there was something in your expression ... it didn't look like doubt to me. It looked like *recognition.*"

"Maybe," Darrell said. Two women, dressed in black, walked past, not looking at them. A man walked toward them wheeling a baby carriage, but Darrell felt no frisson at all ... as the man went past them, Darrell realized that the carriage contained only a Cabbage Patch Kid ... and the man was weeping.

"I can totally tell what you're thinking, mon," Marilyn said. "You've been inside that cave with the laughing children and you're all shuddering inside—and now for the first time you feel the walls crumbling."

"Maybe," Darrell said again. But as he breathed the clean pure childless air, he thought: I don't need healing.

"Me think maybe time for you to try to touch your inner child one more time."

"I thought it had been scientifically determined that I *have* no inner child."

"Ain't no living being don't not have no inner child," she said.

"Speak English!" said Darrell, cringing at the quintuple negative.

"Tubular!" she said, and rubbed the red dot on her forehead. "But Darrell Sachsenhauser, I am a shapeshifter in my own way, you see; I dart from mythos to mythos; yet the heart is always the same. But, it seems, not your heart; perhaps you aren't human after all. What were those photographs they were blackmailing you with ?"

"Nothing. I killed someone once. I think."

"Eww! Let us explore."

And then, right there in the empty plaza, Marilyn Firth began to dance. At first it was only with her eyes; they darted back and forth to a music Darrell could not hear; yet after a while, as by hypnotic suggestion, he thought he could hear a kind of rhythm in the cooing of pigeons, in the flapping of old newspapers in the wind, in the footsteps of the passersby, heads bowed, who were too absorbed in the community's grief to be interested in the strange woman dancing. Marilyn danced and Darrell watched her eyes ... fluttering ... glittering ... strobing ... suddenly she began to whirl. Her sari began to unravel ... and unravel ... and unravel ... veils of sheer silk jetted out in all directions ... she unwound and unwound and unwound herself and still the silk seemed infinite ... like a magician's string of handkerchiefs ... billowing upward, twisting, weaving into mandala-like patterns against the gray sky.

I must be dreaming, Darrell thought. But the colors were more garish than any dream ... crimsons and ceruleans and vermillions and apple greens and cadmium yellows ... dancing ... dancing.

"You never used to do this sort of thing," he said.

She didn't answer him but he could hear her voice pounding in his head like the wind in a tubular wave ... *I've learned a lot of new tricks, Darrie. And you've helped me. You've heard the cracking of the cavern walls, not me ... you told me you were ready ... now take me. Take me into your dream. We will go together so you need not be afraid. We will go together and this time you will be awake, conscious, understanding.*

Darrell still could not believe that this phantasmagoric display could lead to a therapeutic epiphany, but he could not help be mesmerized by the streams of color as their patterns shifted and undulated. After a time it seemed that the silk was darkening, taking on the shades of the overcast sky. He could smell the wet limestone and the dust that had hung for centuries in the sunless air. And the cooing of the pigeons ... wasn't it transforming itself into the mocking laughter of children ... children with predatory eyes?

And Marilyn danced, and the cave walls coalesced out of the lowering sky. The veils rained down around him and hardened and turned to stone. And it became dark. And he could hear the drip-drip-drip of water. And he felt the fear for the first time that day. Until Marilyn's voice echoed in the chamber: *Speak to me from your dream. Tell me what you see.*

"There's a cave."

Yes.

"There's voices. Laughing. Cruel voices. The children."

This is a dream, Darrell, but it's a waking dream. And it's a journey. There are caves within caves, and the darkest cave is the one inside your own soul. Tell me what you see.

"I see eyes."

But wait a minute! There were more than eyes. There were names attached to those eyes. There was a *real* cave. Wasn't there? Darrell stood up, grew accustomed to the darkness that was shot through with streaks of phosphorescence. He turned a corner and saw—

The dead Turkish coin dealer, mummified, sitting up in his coffin, holding out the glistening silver dekadrachm and—

Deeper. Deeper into labyrinth. He steadied himself against clammy walls. There were cave paintings here. He could hear the pattering of rodent feet. Movement in the shadows. A pair of eyes. Nothing now. The laughter came closer. The hairs on the nape of his neck prickled.

Go on, said the voice of Marilyn Firth.

He didn't know at what point the cave became, not the metaphorical caverns of his recurring nightmares, but a real cave. He had stepped through the wall behind which he had sealed his childhood. Images of it were hurtling through his mind in a surreal montage—

The belt buckle lacerating his buttocks, the rhythmic refrain of *Pay the Piper! Pay the Piper!* and—

Mt. Poppen ... the town square with the medieval gate, the tourists, the plastic rats, balloons, the mousetraps in the attic, weathered faces of dead parents, sneaking over the bridge and pissing into the Weser....

Grampa showing him his most treasured possession. It's a hammered silver coin, thirteenth century, some German principality ... "I was disappointed because it was all tarnished. I wanted precious coins to be shiny." He laughed ruefully.

Saxenpooper! Saxenpooper! Childish voices ringing out in the clear summer air.

... another country. A cave. Children. He hadn't always been afraid of children, he realized ... and this discovery filled him with awe. "There's a cave," he told Marilyn. "A real cave this time. It's in America. It's summer, a hot wild place, Montana maybe. In the summer I stay with grampa. Or maybe my parents are already dead. Yes. I just remembered the funeral. A car crash."

Tell me what's happening.

... "I'm a child. It's an unfamiliar feeling because I've never been able to remember it before ... how big things seems ... how slender my hands and feet ... I'm with my friends, Stevie Dunn and Mikey Austin and Johnny I-can't-remember-his-last-name. We're dissecting a rat. It's neat. It was stuck on a glueboard in Mikey's mom's sewing room. It's still alive but barely. I just stuck a pin through its head, one of those shiny pins that come stuck in brand-new shirts, the kind you wear to church. Okay the rat's sort of twitching now. Its guts are neat. I didn't know there was so many of them. It's fun. Johnny says, 'Pretend like we're Mr. Death.' That's the name of a child-murderer in this part of the state ... there's been a manhunt for some months now.

"Mikey says, 'Mr. Death slices off their heads. He eats their brains.' Johnny says, 'Bull. It's their livers.' Mikey says, 'Nu-*uh.*' And I just watch the rat twitching, twitching, twitching, but finally I put it out of its misery by squishing its head with a rock. The odd thing is that I'm not scared of these children at all. I'm more scared of the rat, even though it's a helpless thing, and now it's not even moving any more."

Go on.

Images came flooding now. "Stevie comes running. 'C'mon, Saxenpooper! There's something you gotta see.' It's deeper in the cave. Deeper. We follow him. We're in a tunnel. We have to go in single file. There's a little bit of light because the walls are glowing. Mikey remembers his flashlight and he turns it on and then it gets weird because of the beam of light that darts back and forth. There's graffiti scrawled on the walls. Skeletal figures. A medieval dance of death.

"The cave widens. There's candlelight or something. Flickering. First thing we see, crouching behind a low ridge of limestone, is a face. Larger than life. Painted on the wall. Its eyes are a clear deep blue and it's holding a flute to its lips. It's a face that shows no emotion at all but to me it's scary. It's a thin, pinched face, like a skull. I look a little lower and see that he's wearing a medieval costume, one side red and the other side yellow. And I can almost hear the music.

"'Jeepers,' Mikey whispers. 'What is it?'

"'It's a shrine or something. Or a human sacrifice place. Yeah.'

"Around the image of the piper, are children. They're not realistically painted, but drawn the way a kid might draw them ... a circle for a face, a wavy line for the lips, a sketched-in skirt or overalls ... only the eyes seem real. You can't help looking into those eyes. They're the eyes of creatures who were human once, but now they've gone dead. But the candlelight lends them a kind of life.

"'Jeepers Creepers,' Mikey whispers urgently. 'There's a bum in here.'

"We look at where he's pointing. There is an old man huddled against the far wall, and there's a candle on either side of him and that's where the flickering light is coming from. And he's wearing a tattered piper's costume ... and he has a flute in his hand ... and he's trying to blow a tune. So I haven't imagined the music after all. 'It's Mr. Death!' Stevie says suddenly. 'This must be his secret hideout or something.'

"The old man is my grandfather. But I don't dare say anything. I'm starting to feel the fear now, for the first time.

"'Let's *get* him,' says Mikey. 'C'mon, there's four of us and only one of him.'

"'I bet this is where they're all buried,' says Johnny, the littlest.

"Mikey takes a rock and heaves it at my grandpa. It hits him in the forehead and he gets up and I can see a spot of blood between the eyebrows ... it doesn't seem to hurt him."

Oh! Cosmic! Mythic! The wounding of the Fisher King! The opening up of the third eye!

But Darrell had no time for the intrusive voice of Marilyn Firth. In all the time he had lived without a memory, without a past, the world had been populated with phantoms, two-dimensional figures. Oh, God, this was different. He could taste, touch, smell this memory.

Darrell? Darrell?

"My grandfather stands fully erect. He's holding up the flute like a talisman. Mikey and Johnny and Stevie are throwing stones like crazy now. They're screaming, 'Take that, you baby-killer ... take that.' And my grandfather just stands there, tottering a little, there's a big gouge in his left cheek and his arms are pitted and bloody. And Mikey says, 'He ain't much. Let's kill the fucker. Let's carve him to bits.' He takes a Swiss army knife from his shorts. 'Yeah,' Stevie says, 'let's do him.' And I'm watching all this, not participating, and I see the three kids converge on my grandfather and surround him, and they're pummeling him with their fists and bashing him with rocks and biting and scratching, and he's just standing there. Finally I can't take it any more and I scream, 'Grandpa,' and he looks up at me. The boys are surprised for only a minute and then they go on beating up on him, I guess they're too much into it now to stop ... there's all this rage in them ... their eyes are glowing. They're laughing as they kick him and punch him in the stomach. Finally I run down there and I'm trying to pull them off him ... and he just stands there, taking it ... his eyes darting back and forth ... as though there were hundreds of kids, all over the cave, kids with glistening fangs and slitty eyes ... and I wrest the flute out of Grandpa's hand and then I bring it smashing down on Mikey's head and I hear bone cracking ... I see blood trickling down his face ... I see a whitish goo squishing out of the fractured cranium and ... Stevie and Johnny step back. And I say, 'Grandpa, Grandpa,' and my two friends are chanting, 'Mr. Death, Mr. Death, Mr. Death.' And Grandpa says to me, 'Now we have to go all the way.' Suddenly he's strong. He's like a demon. He grabs the two boys. He slits the throat of one of them, then the other. I help him, I hold them down. We pile the bodies up in front of the icon of the Pied Piper. We're soaked with blood. I taste the blood. The blood's all gooey and crusting on my skin and hair. And I'm crying and saying, 'What's going on, what are you doing here, why did we kill them, are you Mr. Death?'

"Grandpa's weak again. He looks at me and I see hopelessness in his eyes as he says, 'Damn kids. They're out to destroy you, body and soul, because of who you are. The know about the past. They haunt you wherever you go. They lurk in the shadows. They leap out at you from the darkness. Their eyes glow and their teeth glisten. It's always been this way.' I say, 'Why, grandpa, why?' and he says, 'When the Piper comes, you pay him. You hear? *Pay him!* Then all this will end.'

"The dead boys are stacked in a heap. We don't suck out their livers or anything like that. We just light candles around them and leave them as an offering to Piper. The pictures of the children on the walls seem to draw life from the dead boys because now their eyes are animated. I can hear them laughing. My grandpa puts his bloody arms around me and says, 'Forget, my blue-eyed boy, forget.' And I forget.

"Except for the nightmares...."

Darrell followed Marilyn's voice, out of the cavern within the cavern, back to the square beside the memorial gate. She sat down beside him, securely cocooned in her sari now. There was no evidence around them of any supernatural happenings. There were only autumn leaves skimming the cobbled pavement ... and pigeons ... and the sun setting ... and the lengthening shadow of Mt. Poppen.

"What was that all about?" cried Darrell. "Was that true? Did all that really happen?"

"When was the last time you wept, Darrie?" said Marilyn, her arm around his shoulder, her other hand swabbing at his cheek with a fold of her sari.

Darrell said, "I don't know. Back then, I guess."

Marilyn said, "So maybe I am a kind of sorceress after all, and not the crank you think I am. Reality has warped itself around you so that you'll get to replay this ancient myth. You can be a fatalist, and you can say, myths are eternal, the outcome can't be changed ... or maybe you can face up to this Mr. Death ... and find the peace that's eluded you all your life. Good?"

And Darrell Sachsenhauser returned to his hotel and slept all night without dreaming. When we awoke, he had a plan.

•

Darrell asked Dr. Krumm's office to buy up all the *Notgeld* they could find. "You can even print more, if you have to," he said. "Just make sure it adds up to the four quadrillion or whatever it is."

"But it is worthless," said Dr. Krumm.

"That," Darrell said, "is in the eye of the beholder."

To Eva Rotwang, he said, "When you threw him in jail, did you confiscate any items?"

"Yes."

"Any flutes? Pipes? Shawms? Woodwind instruments of any kind?"

"A wooden flute."

"I'll take that with me too."

They piled up the sacks of money in the Piper's cell. Then they left the two of them alone together. Darrell faced the nemesis he had not known he had until the previous day; he looked him square in the face; and he cheated him of his quadrillions.

Mr. Death examined the sacks of useless money with interest. "It's only paper," he said. "Astonishing."

"But paper with promises written on it," Darrell said. "And that makes it more than paper; that lends it a kind of magic."

"I suppose you're right," said Mr. Death. "I'm glad you understand that a bargain is a bargain."

The Pied Piper was a little man after all, despite the monstrous icon on the cavern wall. In real life, locked in the cell, with his two-day stubble and his unwashed joker's costume, there was nothing to him.

Darrell handed over the flute.

The Piper broke the flute across his knee. Then, with his sacks of money, he vanished.

As Darrell left the prison, his new dekadrachm in a velvet pouch in his pocket, he heard children's laughter. It didn't bother him anymore.

•

Darrell had dinner with Marilyn in one of those riverside coffee shops: schnitzel, one of those desserts drowning in whipped cream, a lot of beer to wash it down. He told her, "You were right. I shouldn't be fatalistic about it. Guilt's not genetic. I didn't do anything wrong."

Although he thought to himself: I *have* killed people.

But what did it matter now? The flute was broken. The phobia was no more. Soon he would be back in Los Angeles. He would think of the trip to Hameln as one of those weekend therapy retreats he'd tried so frequently in the past ... only this time it worked.

"You really *are* a sorceress after all, Marilyn." A wind rose from the river and blew out their candles. A girl ran past, her pigtails flying. Darrell laughed.

"I'm not a sorceress," said Marilyn. "Whatever it was you did, *you* did. And if there's any price to pay, *you'll* pay it."

"What price?" He couldn't resist taking the dekadrachm out of his pocket, sliding it out of the pouch, as the waiter relit the candles. "What's to pay? I got away with it. The way I always do."

Marilyn smiled and scratched the dot on her forehead. It wasn't a real dot at all; just a stickon thing. She peeled it off and stuck it in her purse. Sensing his surprise, she said, "Hey, all the girls do it this way now."

That night, she showed him that the sari, which had seemed endless, could in fact be completely unwound. They made love; he remembered how well she used to thrash about; tonight though, it was he who thrashed with newly-learned abandon, and she who, eyes closed, rode him, serenely, as though he were a surfboard and their bed the infinite sea. And then, as he drifted into sleep, she left him.

•

Later that night, Mikey Austin stood by his bedside. He was still eleven years old, and his brain was still oozing from the crack in his head.

"Long time no see, Darrell Saxenpooper." he said. And laughed that high-pitched, metallic laugh that had haunted Darrell all those years.

But Darrell wasn't afraid. "Oh," he said, "a ghost."

"Come on," said Mikey. And his eyes glowed. And he gripped Darrell's hand in his death-cold fingers. "Time for you to go now."

"Where to?" said Darrell. "Is this a fucking dream?"

"No more dreams, Darrie." The cold of Mikey's touch was burrowing into his flesh and creeping up his bones. "You know where we're going."

He tugged and Darrell found himself getting out of bed. Mikey walked quickly. They penetrated the wall of the hotel room and sank through the floor ... they reached the town square. It was deserted, and there was a full moon, and the dead leaves glistened like tarnished silver.

"Come on! Quick! You don't have much time left," Mikey said. And laughed again. And this time Darrell did feel a ghost of the old terror. But the cold had seeped deep into him, and he was too numb to shiver.

They reached the café beside the Weser. The tables and chairs were overrun with rats. Rats darted back and forth over the flagstones. Rats swam to and fro in the brackish water. The only sound, save the sighing of the wind, was the pattering of rodent feet; for he and Mikey made no noise as they trod the cobblestones of the city.

They flitted through the memorial gate. They skirted the autobahn for a moment. There were no cars. Then they turned uphill, toward Mt. Poppen. There was a winding path that narrowed, narrowed, narrowed, narrowed, narrowed, and the mountain loomed higher and higher until there was no sky, and still the pathway narrowed until it was a man-wide cleft cut into the face of the rock ... and finally there was no pathway at all ... there was only the mountain ...

... and the darkness. The cold. And the hunger. Seeping into his bones. And the darkness. The only sound a steady drip ... drip ... drip ... echoing. Echoing. Drip. Echoing. Then slowly, out of the cold and dark, a faint light. Flickering. Ebbing now, sucked back into the limestone void. Ice-floes that hugged the interior of the mountain. Dark. Dark.

"Hey, there, Saxenpooper! Been a while!"

Flash! The glint of a razor-sharp incisor. A hint of drool. A deathsmile forming out of the dimness ... eyes that burn crimson ... eyes. A shock of blond hair and a slit throat. And the blood, drip-drip-dripping.

"Stevie?" Darrell said.

"You should've paid the Piper with real money, Saxenpooper."

"Johnny?"

"There's a lot of us here, Saxenpooper. And there's only one of you," Johnny said. His voice buzzed in his severed windpipe.

"But I didn't put you here! *He* did. It wasn't me who made that bargain."

"There's only one bargain, and you all made it," said Stevie. You and every Sachsenhauser and every man who can't come to terms with Mr. Death."

"You can cheat the Piper, but you can't cheat yourself," said Mikey.

"You're our new Mr. Death, now," said Stevie. "Neato."

Darrell looked around. The panic gripped him. He couldn't breathe. His pulse pounded. Darkness ... and the eyes. Glimmering, Glowering, Angry. Then the laughter: squeaky, metallic, punctuated by the drip-drip-drip of children's blood ... and the cold. The cold. Eyes. More eyes. Eyes. He could smell their breath ... and the sweat and the junk food and the baby shampoo ... as they surrounded him, touching him, sucking the warmth from his body with their icy fingers ... and laughing. Laughing. Laughing.

This time it would never end.

A Hummingbird among Angels

*H*uitzilopotchtli.

It was the will of the god named Hummingbird that our people should cease to be a wandering people, a desert people, an impoverished and simpleminded people. That we should journey down into the rich green valley at the world's heart and claim its lakes and forests for our own, and rule over all the nations of the earth. We were a people with a grand and glorious destiny; we had been called to a special covenant with our god; and if there were things that our god commanded us to do which, to those who did not share our special relationsip with him, appeared brutal, cruel, uncompassionate, it was only that we alone could see the higher purpose; that we alone were charged with the guardianship of the knowledge of the secret workings of the universe.

It was the will of the god named Hummingbird that I should be the one to hear his voice and bear his message to my people; that I should lead them from the wasteland into the place where they would build the greatest of all cities, set in the center of the world as a turquoise in a circlet of gold. And it came to pass that I spoke, and the people obeyed, and we sealed our covenant with our own blood and the blood of the countless conquered. This was as it should be. Our people had been chosen.

Later I would come to understand that there were others, people no less proud than our people, no less confident of their moral rectitude, no less certain that the salvation of the entire universe lay in the application of secret knowledge that only their tribe possessed; there was even, across the great ocean to the east, a people whose god had called them to cross a great desert and seal a covenant and conquer and build a great temple. We Mexica were not, after all, unique; we were merely a repeating pattern in the wheel of history; and our history was not even the only wheel that was in motion at the time.

We didn't even have wheels then, anyway. After a dozen centuries I suppose one might be forgiven a few anachronistic metaphors. I learned about wheels a long time after the covenant was broken, in a place called Los Angeles.

I learned about the other chosen people from Julia Epstein.

•

There is a gap of about five hundred years in my existence. One moment, the fire was raging in the streets of Tenochtitlán, and I was watching the stars fall from the sky, and cursing the silver-clad man-beasts called Spaniards who had blundered into shattering the equilibrium of the universe. Then, in a blink's breadth, it seemed, I was lying in a glass case, an exhibit in the Los Angeles Museum, being pointed at by a petulant youth.

That I might have slept for a time—a century or two even—would not have been surprising. I had done that before, though only of my own volition. I had slept all the way through the conquest of the people of Tlatztelhuatec; I knew it would be dull; they were little better than cattle. But there were no signs that I had been in suspended animation. No cognitive disjunction. No sensation of falling, falling, falling into the bottomless abyss.

The room was gloomy; it had been designed to simulate the rocky chamber in which I had been found. There was no daylight. Torches flickered, yet they did not burn; the fire in them was cold and artificial.

Even lying under the glass, unable as yet to move more than the twitch of an eyelash, fighting the inertia of the dreamless sleep, I was aware that the world had become far stranger than I could have imagined. The youth who stared down at me was a mongrel; he had the flat nose and dark skin of the Mexica, but there was also something about him that resembled the man-beasts from across the sea. He had no hair save for a crest that stood unnaturally tall and was dyed the color of quetzal feathers. His robes were of animal hide, but black and polished to an almost reflective smoothness. He was not utterly inhuman—his ears were pierced at least—but from them hung, upside-down, a pair of those silver crucifixes that symbolize the man-beasts' god, whom they call Hesuskristos, who is in reality Xipe Totec, the flayed god, as Hummingbird once revealed to me in a dream.

He called out to a companion; this one's tufted hair was the color of fresh blood, and he wore a silver thorn through his left cheek. The language, at least, I knew, though the accent was strange and there were unfamiliar words; I had taken the trouble to learn the language of the man-beasts. There are two dialects; one, spoken by the black robes, is called Español; the other is the language of their enemies, known as English. It was the second of these I heard, in a boyish voice muffled by glass.

"Dude! It says he's been dead for five hundred years."

"Pulled him out of the foundation of a fifty-story office building after that big Mexico City quake. Yeah, perfectly preserved and shit. A hollow in the rock, a natural vacuum."

"Yeah, I saw it on *20/20.*"

"Did you see that? He moved, dude!"

"Yeah. Right."

Five hundred years. But that was impossible! Hummingbird himself had told me that in a few short years the world would end in an apocalypse of blood and fire. How could five hundred years have gone by? Unless, of course, the world had already ended.

That would explain the surpassing alienness of my surroundings. Even the air smelled strange. Even the blood of the two boys, which sang to me as it pumped through their arteries, exuded an unaccustomed odor, as though infused with the pulped essences of the hemp and coca plants.

The one with the crimson hair said, "No, dude, I ain't joking. Look at him, man, I swear his eyelids are like, flickering."

"You shouldn't have dropped acid at the Cure concert last night. You're still blazing, dude."

I turned my head to get a better view.

"Jesus Christ!" they screamed.

So the world had ended after all. The time of Huitzilopotchtli was over. There had been a fiery apocalypse—my memories had not deceived me—and we were now well into the World of the Fifth Sun, foretold to me by the god, and a new god was in power, the hanged god whose name those boys evoked, Hesuskristos.

I was full of despair. I did not belong here. Why had I been suffered to remain alive? Surely I should have been destroyed, along with the city of Tenochtitlán, along with the great pyramids and temples and palaces of my people. Could the gods not have been more thorough? But then that was just like them; come up with the grand concepts, leave their execution to imperfect mortals. I raged. My heart gave a little flutter, trying to bestir itself from its age-old immobility. My fury fueled me. I could feel my blood begin, sluggishly, to liquefy, to funnel upward through my veins like the magma through the twisty tunnels of Popocatapetl.

Soon I would erupt.

I lashed out. I heard shattering glass. The smells of the strange new world burst upon my senses. Then came the hunger, swooping down on me as an owl on a mouse in the dead of night. No longer muffled, the rushing of young blood roared in my ears. The odor was sour and pungent. I seized the first creature by the arm, the one with the quetzal-feathered hair; the second, screaming, ran; I transfixed the prey with my eyes and filled him with the certainty of his own death; then, drawing him down to me, I fed.

I do not know how long we lay together, locked in that predatory embrace. His blood was youthful; it spurted; it permeated my pores; I drank it and I breathed it into my lungs; for a fleeting moment it brought back to mind those nights of furtive, unfulfilled encounters in the chill desert night; the burning curve of a young girl's thigh, the aroma of her liquidescing pubes. Those were the times before the god called me, when I was mortal and barely man.

At length I realized that I had completely drained him. I let go and he thudded on the polished floor like a terracotta doll. It was then that I became aware of a noisome clanging sound, a whirling, flashing red light, and men in strange blue clothing who brandished muskets of a sleekly futuristic design as they surrounded the plinth on which I lay. The boy who had fled stood beneath an archway, babbling and shivering and pointing at me and at his friend's desiccated corpse.

Perhaps, I decided, it would be more prudent to play dead for a little while longer.

•

I awakened in another chamber. It was lined with leatherbound codices of the kind the black robes favored. The room was lit by candlelight, and I sitting on a wooden chair. I tried to move, but I had been bound with ropes—metal ropes, artfully strung, and padlocked, the way the Spaniards keep their gold. Across an immense desk, cluttered with the artifacts of my people, jeweled skulls and jade statuettes and blood-cups, sat a woman.

She was of man-beast extraction, but not unattractive. I had never seen a woman of their kind before; they had brought none with them from their country, which was perhaps why they had become so ferocious. She was sharp-nosed, and had long brown hair. When she spoke to me, it was, to my amazement, in Nahuatl, the language of the Mexica people.

"I'm Julia Epstein," she said. "I'm the curator of our Latin American collection. Would you care for a little blood?"

"I'm quite full, thank you," I said.

"In that case, you might want to start telling me what the hell is going on. It's not every day that a museum exhibit gets up and starts attacking the public. Who are you?"

"It's not proper for me to give my name to you. A man-beast."

She laughed. "Man-beast! I know. You Aztecs used to think that the Spaniards and their horses were some kind of hybrid monster. But times have changed. We drive automobiles now. I think it's safe for you to tell me your name. I'm not going to acquire any mystical power over you. Besides, you're just going to have to trust me; I'm the one who talked the cops into believing that that punk's story was just some kind of acid-trip fantasy; they have him under wraps now, the poor child, deciding whether to get him on murder one."

"Very well," I said, "I am Nezahualcóyotl."

"And I'm Santa Claus," said Julia Epstein, frowning. "So you say you're the Nezahualcóyotl, who claimed descent from the great gods of Teotihuacán, the greatest poet, musician and prophet of the Aztecs, their first great ruler, a man who was an ancient memory when Moctezuma was king and the Conquistadores swept over Mexico?"

"You are well informed," I said.

"Well, why not? It's no harder to believe that than to believe that an exceptionally well-preserved mummy, just dug up from the newly discovered catacombs in Mexico City, and my museum's prize exhibit, would get up, walk around, attack a few punks, and drink their blood. And to think that I dug you up with my own hands."

"So it is to you that owe my continued. Existence."

"If you want to call it living."

"What else would you call it?"

"You're a vampire."

"I'm unfamiliar with that word."

"Oh, don't give me that bullshit, Nezzy. I know everything about you guys. I can't get anyone to believe me, but I've gathered a shitload of information. Yeah, I'm an archaeologist, sure, but vampires are kind of a hobby with me, know what I mean? And this city's crawling with them. I know. I've got tons of evidence. Clippings, photographs, police files. Tried to sell this shit to the Enquirer, and you know what? They rejected it. Said it wasn't, ah, convincing. Convincing! From the people who did the 'Alien Endorses Clinton' story and the piece about the four-headed baby! Let me tell you what really happened. They found out about it. They're everywhere. Big cities mainly, but even the smallest town has

one or two. They're running everything. Your worst nightmare about the Mafia, the CIA, the Illuminati, all rolled into
one. They read my submission and they squelched it! Sounds
pretty damn paranoid, doesn't it? Welcome to the quackpot
world of academia."

"But what is a vampire?" I said. I was beginning to feel
the hunger again; just a prickle in my veins. Normally the
blood of a whole young male would have kept me going for
days, but it had been so long. I glanced down at myself. Saw
my papery skin. Knew it would take a few more feedings to
restore me to the semblance of life.

"A vampire?" said Julia. "Why, you're a vampire. You
drink blood. You live for a long, long time. You are a child of
the shadows, a creature of the night."

"True, but—are you saying that there are others?"

"Are you saying that there aren't others?"

"There was one other." It pained me to think of my young
protégé. The one who had betrayed King Moctezuma to the
man-beasts, the one whom the black robes called Hortator,
which signifies, in their language, the man who beats the
drum to drive the galley-slaves who row in the Spaniards'
men-o'-war. Because of the drum he stole from me, made
from the flayed skin of the god Xipe Totec himself. The one I
thought would succeed me, but who instead had destroyed
my whole world. "There was the god at first. He called me to
his service. I had thought to hand on the power to another,
but ..."

"That's where you're wrong, my friend," said Julia.
"There's a whole network of you people. You have your ten-
tacles in everything. You run this whole planet. You're in
Congress. In the U.N. In the damn White House, for all I
know. And all top secret. Don't worry. I won't give you away.
They have a certificate on file that says I'm a paranoid schizophrenic; so who'd believe me anyway?"

"Even among the white men, people such as I?" It was
hard to grasp.

"The New World was a universe unto itself in 1453. Maybe
you were the only one here. Maybe your god came over the
Bering Strait, nurtured his secret alone for twenty thousand
years. Perhaps he forgot, even, that there was a race of crea-

tures like himself. Perhaps, after milennia, he became lonely; who knows? Or he needed another cowherd. He made you. You, Nezahualcóyotl, coming of age with an entire continent for your domain, completely ignorant of the customs, traditions, laws, identities of your kindred. A law unto yourself. They're not going to like you."

"I think I'll have that drink now."

Julia Epstein rose and went to a white rectangular cabinet. She opened it. A searing cold emanated from it, as though winter had been trapped within its confines. She drew out a skin of chilled blood; not a natural skin, surely, for it was clear as water. "It's my own," she said. "I have a rare blood type, so I keep some around in case something happens to me and I need a quick transfusion. Yeah, more evidence of paranoia."

She tossed the skin to me. I sank my teeth into the artificial skin. The blood was sweet, a little cloying, and freezing cold; then I remembered, from my childhood, how much I had enjoyed the snow cones flavored with berry juice that the vendors used to bring down from the mountains; I savored the nostalgia. Twice today I'd had a remembrance of the distant past, before my changing. It is strange how one's childhood haunts one.

Julia herself drank coffee, which she poured from a metal pot and blended with bleached sugar. She shook back her hair. I was taken aback at the immodest way she stared at me; truly my god had no more power in this world, or she would have been trembling with awe. There was a faint odor of attraction about her; this woman desired me. And that was strange, for no Aztec woman would have dared think sexual thoughts about one who spoke directly to the gods.

"You need me," she said. "You'll be flung into a cutthroat society. Dozens of your kind, with bizarre hierarchies, internecine politics, games of control and domination. You been asleep for five hundred years, and since then there's been a mass emigration. They like it better in the New World; fewer preconceptions, the American dream and all that. And the prey are a lot less careful than back in old Wallachia. Where everyone believes in vampires, it's hard for one to catch a decent meal."

"What? They do not give their blood willingly?" For that was the hardest new concept to grasp. Was it not the duty of humans to give freely of their flesh and blood that their gods might live? Was blood not the life force that kept the sun and the stars in their courses?

"Willingly!" said Julia. "You do have a lot to learn."

"You'll help me."

She smiled. "Of course. But only if you help me."

"How?"

"By telling me all about yourself."

She unchained me, and I told her about the coming of the white men, and about Hortator's betrayal. And she in turn told me of her own people, who had once been nomads, who had crossed a tremendous desert to find a land flowing with milk and honey; who had made a covenant with a great and terrible deity who spoke in the voices of wind and fire; and I came to know of the vastness of the earth, and of how my people had been but one of many; how nations had risen and fallen, how even mankind itself had not always been the pinnacle of creation; how the great globe had formed out of the cold dust of the cosmos, and would one day return to dust.

In time, I came to love her; and that in itself was a strange thing, for our kind do not feel love as mortals feel it.

•

The man who came to be called Hortator belonged to me. I had captured him in the Flower Wars, which we hold each year when there are not enough captives from normal wars to feed the altars of the gods.

This year the war was held in a plain not far from the city. Moctezuma himself had come to watch; on a knoll overlooking the battlefield, he and the enemy king, Cozcatl, picnicked on tortillas stuffed with ground iguana, braised in a sauce of pulped cocoa beans, which the man-beasts call chocolate. I, as the mouthpiece of the god, sat above Moctezuma on a ledge lined with jaguar skin and feathers. It was a pleasant afternoon; the courtiers were wolfing down their packed lunch while I sipped, from a sacred onyx cup, the blood of a

young Mayan girl who had been sacrificed only that morning; yes, the blood had been cooled with snow from the slopes
of the volcano.

"It's not going well," said the king. "Look—the jaguar
team has only snared about a hundred, and the quetzal team
less than half that."

Once touched by the sacred flower wand which was the
only weapon used in these artificial wars, a soldier was sent
to the sacrificial pen. It was a great honor, of course, to be
sacrificed, and a thing of beauty to behold those hordes of
young men, oiled and gleaming, rushing across the grass to
embrace their several destinies. "They seem more reluctant
than usual, Your Majesty," I said.

"Yes," said the king darkly. "I wonder why."

"I think," I said, trying to put it to him delicately, "it has
something to do with the man-beasts from the sea."

"You'd think they'd be all the more anxious to get sacrificed, what with the present danger to the empire."

"Yes. But. They've been spreading sedition, Your Majesty. I've just come from the prison; they've been interrogat-
ing that black robe they captured—a high priest of sorts. He
says that our sacrifices are ignorant superstition; that the
sun will rise each morning with our without them; and he's
been babbling about Hesuskristos, their god, who seems to
be a garbled version of Xipe Totec."

"You shouldn't say bad things about the man-beasts. Last
night I dreamed that the Plumed Serpent was returning to
claim his kingdom." He was speaking of Quetzalcoatl, the
god-king who left our shores five hundred years before, vow-
ing to come back.

"Quetzalcoatl will not come back, Your Majesty."

"How do you know? Am I not the king? Don't my dreams
have the force of prophecy?"

"You may have dreamt of him, Your Majesty; I, on the
other hand, was his friend." It was because he lost the land
in a wager that he had been forced to cross the ocean to look
for a new kingdom, though that part of the story never made
it into our mythology.

"So you say, Nezahualcóyotl. You say that you're a thousand years old, and that you personally led our people out of

the wilderness. That sort of thing is all very well for the peasants, Nezahualcóyotl. But I'm a modern king, and I know that you often use the language of metaphor in order to enhance the grandeur of the gods. No, no, I'm not blaming you; I'm a mean hand at propaganda myself. It's just that, well, you shouldn't believe your own—"

It would not do to argue. I finished my blood in silence.

"Anyhow, I think we should have a bit of propaganda right now, Nezahualcóyotl. Why don't you go down there and lead the jaguar team personally? Give them a bit of that old-time religion. Stir up their juices."

"Sire, at my age—"

"Nonsense. Guard, give him one of those flower wands."

I sighed, took the wand, and went down the hill.

The war was being conducted in an orderly fashion. Seeing me, members of the jaguar team made a space for me. I gave a brief and cliché-ridden harangue about the cycles of the cosmos; then it was time to charge. Boys banged on human-skin drums; musicians began a noisy caterwauling of flutes, cymbals, and shrilling voices that sang of the coming of Huitzilopochtli to the Mexica. The armies ran toward each other, chanting their war songs, each soldier seeking out a good quarry. I too ran; not with supernatural swiftness, but like a man, my bare feet pounding the ground. Above us, the whistle of the atl-atl and the whine of flower-tipped arrows. The armies met. I searched for a suitable captive that would honor the god. I saw a man in the farthest rank of the enemy. more child than man, his limbs perfectly formed, his eyes darting fearfully from side to side. There was someone who saw no honor in dying for the god! I elbowed aside three pairs of combatants and came upon him suddenly, looming above him as he ducked behind a tree.

"I am your death," I said. "Give yourself up; give honor to the gods."

I touched him with the flower wand. He glanced at it, took it, stared me defiantly in the eye.

"I won't do it," he said.

I knew then that he had been polluted by the preachings of the man-beasts. A fury erupted in me. I said, "Why have you been listening to them? Don't you know that they're only human beings? That they bleed and die like ordinary men?"

But he began to run. I was surprised by his speed. He leaped over a bush, sprinted away from the mass of warriors toward a field of maize that bordered the battleground. My first impulse was to let him go—for there was no honor in sacrificing so abject a creature to Hummingbird—but my anger grew and grew as I watched him shrinking into the distance. I could stand it no longer. I called upon the strength of the jaguar and the swiftness of the rabbit; I funneled into the very wind; soon I was upon him again. He turned, saw me running beside him, matching him pace for pace. I could smell his terror; terror was only natural; what I could not smell was the joy, equally natural, that a man should feel when he is about to embrace the source of all joy, to die that the sun might live. He was less than a man. Only an animal could feel this terror of dying without also feeling the exhilaration. I decided to kill him as he ran. I reached out. He struggled, but I drew on my inner strength; I pinned him to the ground. The corn encircled us. Only the gods heard what we said to one another.

"I won't go," he said again. "Kill me now, but I won't die to feed a god that doesn't even exist."

"Doesn't exist!" My anger rose up, naked and terrible. I startled to throttle him. The odor of his fear filled my nostrils. It was intoxicating. I wanted to feed on him right then and there. I could feel his jugular throbbing against my fingers. I knew that his blood was clean and unpolluted with alcohol or coca leaf. His blood was pure as the waters of the mountain; but I could not kill him. "How long were you among the man-beasts?"

"Three years."

I had to let him live. He knew about the foreigners. Their languages, their savage ways. I could not kill him until he had divulged all he knew. With a fingernail I scratched his arm, sucked out a few droplets to assuage my hunger. I had to bind him to me. He could become a secret weapon; perhaps I could stave off the end of the world after all.

If only I had listened to the voice of Hummingbird! But I wanted to halt the wheel of time, and though I was a thousand years old I was still too young to understand that there is no stopping time.

"Who are you?" I said.

"I don't know. I don't have a name anymore; I've forgotten it. The Spanish called me Hortator. It pleased them to let me beat the drum on one of their galley ships. I've even been to Spain. That part of Spain that they call Cuba."

"Why aren't you still with them?"

"Pirates, Lord High Priest. I escaped; the others. Dead, every one of them."

"And the man-beast who is called Cortéz, who the king thinks is the god Quetzalcoatl, returned to reclaim his inheritance?"

"I don't know of him. The man-beasts are many—dozens of nations and languages. And all of them are coming here. They want gold."

I laughed; what was so valuable about gold, that would make these creatures come across the ocean in their islands made of wood? Was gold then their god?

"No, my Lord. They worship Xipe Totec; their name for him is Hesuskristos."

When I escorted my prisoner back to the pen, it was getting late. Moctezuma was bored and listless; Cozcatl was annoyed at having lost the war, though it would hardly have been good manners for him to be victorious over his sovereign lord. The two kings applauded as I approached them, and bade me eat with them; they had a fresh haunch roasting. "Excellent meat," said the king. "She was good in bed, too."

"You did her great honor, Sire, to inseminate her, sacrifice her, and eat her, all with your own hands."

"It was the Queen's idea, actually; she had been getting uppity. But what have we here?" He eyed my captive with interest. "A powerful-looking fellow; I didn't know you had it in you to bring in so fine a specimen."

He cast his eye about for his obsidian knife; when the king particularly favored someone, he was apt to sacrifice him on the spot. I had to think quickly to protect my source of information. "Your Majesty," I said, "the god has told me that this man is to be the next Unblemished Youth."

"Oh," said the king, disappointed, "we'll have to wait until the big ceremony, then." To Hortator he said, "You're a very lucky young man; you'll have the best in food, drink and women, including four holy brides; until you're sacrificed, a year from now, you'll be worshipped as a god. Even I will have to bow to you, though you mustn't get any grand ideas."

"Yes, Sire," said Hortator. I could tell he was grateful for his reprieve. Perhaps, in time, I would be able to wash away the silly notions the man-beasts had planted in his mind. A year was time enough, surely, to persuade him to look forward to being sacrificed properly.

•

"You were planning to deprogram him!" Julia said, having by then become somewhat drunk. I myself was on my second skin of blood; my appearance was far less corpselike than it had been in the exhibit hall.

"I'd better take you home with me," she went on. "At least until you figure out what you're going to do with yourself. I mean—no credit cards, no social security number, no car—you could be in for some culture shock."

I was not sure what she was talking about, but a few hours later I was numb from confusion. I had ridden in a cylindrical metal wagon that runs through tubes under the earth; I had been driven in a horseless chariot across a bridge that seemed to hang on wires above the ocean; I had seen buildings shaped like phalluses, strutting up into the sky; and the people! Tenochtitlán at its most crowded had not been like this. La Reina de Los Angeles—named, so Julia told me, after a celestial goddess of the Spaniards—was a hundred times as crowded. There were people of many colors, and their costumes beggared description. In my feathers, leggings, and pendulous jade earrings, I must have looked a little odd; yet no one stared at me. This was a people accustomed to strangeness.

At length we reached Julia's home, an apartment within one of those tall buildings, reached by means of a little chamber on pulleys which seemed much more efficient than stairs;

I could see that I was going to enjoy the many conveniences of this alien world.

Her home was an odd little place; she lived alone, without parents or children, without even any servants; and the apartment, though crammed with labor-saving devices, was little bigger than a peasant's hovel, and considerably more claustrophobic.

We had been there for only moments when she thrust herself at me. Her blood was racing, and scented with erotic secretions. She kissed me. I tasted blood on her chapped lips. I pulled away. "Be careful," I said. "I don't have the same desires as you. I don't feel lust. Not like that."

"Then teach me the other kind of lust."

"I'm afraid you would not like it."

"Yes, yes, I know. The desolation. The loneliness of eternity. I don't care! Don't you understand? I've always wanted to be a vampire. I've never been able to get this close to one before. Not for certain. I'm a historian. I want to get the long view. I want to see man's destiny unfold, bit by bit. I hate being a human being."

"It's not what you think it is." How could I tell her about those flashes from my childhood. Those faded images that still haunted me with their unattainable vividness? My world is a gray world; only the infusion of blood brings to it a fleeting color, and that only a simulacrum of color, awakened by long-lost memories; now, five hundred years beyond the end of the world, I had become even more of a tragicomic figure. How could this woman ever know. Unless I made her know? And then, poor thing, there would be no turning back.

I did not want to make her like me. I had tried that once. It had not eased my loneliness. And my creation had betrayed me. But the woman could be useful. For now I would pretend to hold out the possibility that she might one day become immortal.

"Make love to me," she said.

She smiled a half-smile and beckoned me into an inner room. There were mirrors everywhere. With great deliberation, she began to remove her clothing. There was a pleasing firmness to her, though she was not young. An Aztec woman of her years would have been worn out, her fists hardened from pounding laundry or tortillas. It would be necessary for me to go through the motions of lovemaking. In the end I did not mind. She had been menstruating.

Afterwards, I lay on the bed and watched her sitting at the mirror, painting her face. She opened a drawer and took out a gold pendant in the shape of a crucified man. Suddenly I understood why I had not perished along with the rest of the world. I had unfinished business.

"Where did you get that amulet from?"

"You recognize it, don't you?" She stood up, clad only in the pendant and her long dark hair. "I'm afraid you're not the first vampire I've dated. Actually I wasn't entirely sure he was one. Until now. They don't make a habit of telling. But you've just confirmed it."

"I have to find the person who gave it to you."

"I'll take you to him," she said.

•

Once more we crossed the bay in the steel chariot; once more my memories came flooding back.

They had seemed insane to me, those man-beasts; there were only a handful of them, yet they scoured the land as though they were an army of thousands. In only a short while they had conquered a city but a day's journey from Tenochtitlán. But in the palace of Moctezuma there was a strange calm. I did not know why. Each day, I sacrificed the requisite numbers of victims at the appropriate hours; I did nothing that dishonored the gods.

Except, of course, for the little lie I had told my king; it had not been Huitzilopochtli who had commanded that the man Hortator be consecrated as the Unblemished Youth. I had said so to ensure that the man would survive and remain useful to me. It was not the first time I had invoked the voice of the Hummingbird to bring about some personal decision. When one has been the mouthpiece of the god for centuries at a time, there are times when one's identity becomes blurred. Besides, what harm could it do? Hortator was the perfect choice, even if the god had not made it himself.

I visited him each evening in the compound sacred to Xipe Totec, where the four sacred handmaidens dressed him, bathed him, and tended to his sexual needs, for he was no longer free to walk about the city at will. He was, indeed, unblemished, a prime specimen of Aztec manhood, lean, tall, well-proportioned, and fine-featured. The god would be pleased when the day came for him to be flayed alive so that his skin could be worn by the priest of Xipe Totec in the annual ceremony that heals and renews the wounded earth and brings forth the rains of spring. There was only one thing wrong with it all; the Unblemished Youth did not seem particularly honored by the attention. It was all most unusual, a sign of the decadence of those times.

"I don't want to do it," he told me, "because I don't believe in it." For a nonbeliever he was certainly reaping its benefits—being massaged by one handmaiden, being fed by another, and the gods alone knew what was going on under the gold-edged table behind which he sat. "I mean that it's no use; the blood of human sacrifices isn't what makes the sun rise each morning; the god of the man-beasts is clearly more powerful than Huitzilopochtli even as Hummingbird was mightier than the gods who came before. I don't mind the pain so much as the fact that I'd be dying for no reason."

"You've been poisoning the king's mind, too, haven't you?" I said. For Moctezuma seemed to have lost all interest in the future of his empire.

"I am the Unblemished Youth," he pointed out. "It was your idea. And as you know, that means that my advice comes from the gods."

"You hear no voices from the sky!" I said. "It's all pretense with you."

"And what voice from the gods told you that I was to be kept alive to teach you the ways of the white men?"

He knew I had lied. Only one whose mind had already been tainted by the man-beasts' ideas would even have imagined such a thing. "But I do hear voices," I said.

"Then let me hear one too."

"All right."

I told him to follow me. We took a subterranean passageway—for he could not be seen to wander the streets of the city—that angled downward, deep under the great pyramid of Huitzilopochtli. The walls were damp and had a natural coolness from the waters that seeped underground from the great lake of Tenochtitlán. Hortator stopped to admire the bas-reliefs which depicted the history of the Mexica people in their long migration toward the promised land; there were sculptures in niches in the stone, some decorated with fresh human skulls or decaying flowers, some so weathered that they could no longer be identified, being the gods of unremembered peoples who had long since been conquered and assimilated by the Mexica; many parts of the tunnel were ill-kept; our torches burned but dimly here, far from the outside air.

At length we reached a chamber so sacred that even King Moctezuma had never set foot within it. It was guarded by the god of a civilization far older than ours—Um-Tzec, the Mayan god of death, whose skull-face was etched into the stone that blocked the entrance.

I whispered a word in the long-forgotten Olmec language, and the stone slid aside to reveal the chamber. Hortator gasped as he read in the flickering torchlight the calendar symbols and the glyphs that lined the walls.

"But—" he said, "this is the lost tomb of Nezahualcóyotl, your namesake, the first great king of the Aztecs!"

I smiled. I held up my torch so he could see all that the room contained—treasures of gold from ancient cities—magical objects and amulets—and a great sarcophagus, carved from solid obsidian.

"The tomb is empty!" he gasped.

"Yes," I said, "it is, and always will be, by the sacred grace and will of Huitzilopochtli, Hummingbird of the Left."

"The black robes told me of creatures like you. I've never seen you eat; you seem to subsist on blood. You're one of the undead. A creature of the devil. You sleep by day in your own coffin, and by night you prey on human blood."

I laughed. "What strange notions these man-beasts have! Though I admit that I have sometimes taken a nap inside the sarcophagus. It's roomy, and very conducive to meditation."

I showed him the treasures. Every one of them had an ancient tale attached to it, or some mystic power. The ring of concealment and the jewel for scrying the past. The great drum fashioned from Xipe Totec's skin, which, when beaten, confers the power of celerity. "Feel it, touch its tautness. That is your skin too. For you are Xipe Totec."

"There is only one Xipe Totec, who gave his life for the redemption of the world, who was killed and rose again on the third day."

"I'm glad the Spaniards haven't robbed you of that truth!"

"On the contrary," he said, "they taught it to me. And they say that theirs is the real Xipe Totec, and yours is an illusion, the work of the powers of darkness." He pulled out an amulet from a fold of his feather robe, and showed me the image of Hesuskristos; a suffering god indeed, nailed to a tree, his torso cruelly pierced, his scalp ripped by thorns. "It is an admirable god," I said, "but I see no reason why, accepting one, you must heap scorn on the other."

"Oh, they are not so different, the new gods and the old. The black robes have sacrifices too; they burn the victims alive in a public ceremony called auto-da-fés, after first subjecting them to fiendish tortures—"

"Wonderful," I said, "at least they have some of the rudiments of civilization."

"I did not say their god was better, Nezahualcóyotl; only that he is stronger. Now show me how your god speaks."

"I will need blood."

"Take mine," he said.

I took my favorite blood-cup, carved from a single, flawless piece of jade, and murmured a prayer over it. I did not want to scar the Unblemished Youth; I knelt before him and pricked him lightly in the groin with the fingernail of my left pinky, which I keep sharpened for that purpose; I drained a ounce or so into the bloodcup, then seared the wound shut with a dab of my saliva. The drawing of blood caused the man to close his eyes. He whimpered; I knew not if it was from pain or ecstacy. I called on Huitzilopochtli, drained the blood-cup, tossed it aside. The warmth shot through my ancient veins, pierced my unbeating heart; it was a bitter blood, a blood of destiny. I emptied out my soul. I waited for the god to speak.

And presently it came, a faint whisper in my left ear, like the fluttering of tiny wings. I could not see Huitzilopochtli—no one has ever seen him—but his still small voice lanced my very bones like the thunderous erupting of Popocatapetl itself. The world has turned in on itself, said the god, and the fire of the sun has turned to ashes.

"But—what have we done wrong? Didn't we slaughter hecatombs of warriors to your glory? Didn't we mortify our own flesh, build pyramids whose points grazed the very dwelling places of your kindred?"

The god laughed. The cosmos dances, he said. We are at peace.

In my trance state I saw Hortator standing before me, no longer in the consecrated raiment of Xipe Totec, but naked, nailed to a tree, the skin scourged from his back, the blood streaming from his side and down his face, and I cried out, "You abomination! You travesty of the true faith!" and I rushed toward him. When I was with the god I was more powerful than any human. I could rip him in pieces with my bare hands. I had him by the throat, was throttling the life from him—

You will not kill him, said the god. All at once, the strength left my hands. Instead, you will make him immortal.

"He doesn't deserve—"

Obey me! He too is a prophet, of a sort. Do you not understand that he who rises to godhead, who creates a world, a people, a destiny, plants inevitably within his creation the seeds of his own destruction? All life is so—and the gods, who are the pinnacle of life, are as subject to its laws as any other creatures.

It seemed to me that I no longer understood the god as clearly as I had once, when I came down from the high mountain to bring his message to a tribe of wanderers. His words were confused now, tainted. But he was the god, and my obeyed him without thought. I knelt once more before Hortator, and I began to feed, mindless now of damaging his flesh, for I knew that he would never have to suffer the rites of Xipe Totec. I fed and fed until there was no more blood at all, and then, slashing my lip with my razor fingernail, I moistened his lips with a few drops of my own millennial blood, blood that ran cold as the waters under the earth.

I cried out: "Do you see now the power of Huitzilopochtli? I have killed you and brought you back from the dead; I have awakened you to the world of eternal cold."

But Hortator only laughed, and he said to me, "I heard nothing. No hummingbird whispered in my left ear. The black robes were right; your gods do not exist."

"My gods have made you immortal!"

"I am already immortal; for the black robes have sprinkled me with their water of life."

I could not understand what had happened. Why had the god commanded me to make him my kindred, then allowed him to mock me? Why could Hortator not hear the voice of the deity when it reverberated in my very bones? The very fabric of the world was unraveling. For the first time in a thousand years, I was afraid. At first I could not even recognize the emotion, it was so alien; it was almost thrilling. I reached back farther and farther through the cobwebs of memory. I saw myself as a child. Scurrying beneath my mother's blanket. Fleeing the music of the night. With fear came a kind of melancholy, for I knew that I would never again truly feel what it was like to be alive.

Once, it seemed, I walked with my god; daily, hourly I heard his voice echo and reecho in my heart. Then came a time when he spoke to me but rarely, and usually only in the context of the blood-ritual. And now and then, I began to speak for him, inventing his words, for the people did not hear him unless I first heard him; it was I who was his prophet. Was it those little lies that had made my god abandon me now?

I cried out, "Oh, Huitzilopochtli, Huitzilopochtli, why hast thou forsaken me?" But the god did not see fit to respond.

•

We stopped at a bazaar to buy clothes more suitable to my surroundings. Julia picked out some black leggings which could be pulled over my loincloth, shoes made from animal skins, and an overshirt of some soft white material; she paid for the items with a rectangular plaque, which the vendor slid through a metal device, after which she made some mysterious marks on a square of parchment.

Then we drove on to another part of the city, one where the buildings were more ornate, not the monolithic towers of stone and glass I had seen before. We stopped in front of a low, unpretentious-looking building; Julia bade me follow her.

Inside, the surroundings were considerably more ostentatious. There were paintings, a floor covered with some kind of red-tinted fur, the pieces joined together so invisibly that one could not tell what animal it had come from. The place was full of all manner of people, jabbering away in many accents, though I did not hear anyone speak Nahuatl; perhaps my native tongue had gone the way of the language of the Olmecs.

We stood, a little uncomfortably—for though no one questioned our being there no one made us welcome—and I began to notice a pervasive sickliness in the air—the sweetness of putrefying flesh that has been doused in cloying perfume—I knew that it was the odor of the dead—I knew that I was in the presence of others of my kind—not one or two but dozens of them. What had happened in the past five hundred years? Had I been reborn into a world of vampires? Again fear flecked my feelings, the same fear I had felt when I doubted my gods for the first time.

"Your friend is sometimes to be found there," Julia said. She pointed to a door, half-hidden by shadows. "Go along. I'll stay here and have a glass of wine."

"You're not coming with me?"

"I can't," she said. "No human being has ever come out of that room alive. But if you're really what I say you are, you won't have any trouble. That room," she went on, her voice dropping to a whisper, "is the Vampire Club."

"Why are you whispering?"

"I'm not supposed to know." Her eyes sparkled. I could see that she loved to flirt with danger. That was why she was so obsessed with my kind.

I put aside my fear. I had to confront Hortator. Already I knew that he was close by. From the dozens of clamoring voices in the building, my attenuated senses were able to isolate him. I could even hear his blood as it oozed through his veins; for every creature's life force pulsates to a personal rhythm, unique as a fingerprint, if one has only the skill to pick it out.

I was becoming angry. I stalked to the door and flung it open. There came a blast of foul and icy wind. I stepped inside and slammed the door shut. There was no mistaking the odor now. I descended steep steps into a tomblike chamber where several outlandishly attired men and women sat deep in conversation, sipping delicately from snifters of blood.

"Rh negative," said one of them disgustedly, "not exactly my favorite."

"Let me have a sniff—pe-ugh! Touch of the AIDS virus in that one; oh, do send it back, my dear Travis."

"Whatever for? I think it lends it a certain je ne sais quoi," said Travis, "that ever-tantalizing bouquet de la mort."

Two other creatures looked up from a game of cards; their faces had the pallid phosphorescence of the dead; their eyes glittered like cut glass, scintillant and emotionless.

A slightly corpulent man, sumptuosly clothed in velvet and satin, waved languidly at me. "Heavens," he said, "what a surprise! We don't get many Red Indians here."

"Get him out of here," one of the cardsharps hissed. He was attired like one of the Spanish black robes.

"Yeah, dude," said a young man, of the type Julia had described to me as punk. "Or card him at least." He cackled at some incomprehensible joke.

"Whatever for? He's obviously one of us. Either that, or he's in desperate need of the services of an orthodontist," said the man in the velvet.

"We don't know him," said the other cardplayer, a woman, whose hair stood on end and fanned out like the tail of a peacock, and who wore a full-length cloak of some thick, black material.

"Perhaps we should ask him who he is. See here, old thing—very, very old, I'm afraid—I'm Sebastian Melmoth, your humble host. And you are—?"

"I am Nezahualcóyotl," I said, "the Voice of the Hummingbird. I'm looking for a certain person. He calls himself Hortator."

"Oh, I see. Well, you really mustn't get to the point quite so fast; it's not very dignified, you know. Let a century or two go by first."

"I have let five centuries go by."

"Perhaps you'd care for one of our sanguinary cocktails?"

"I've already supped tonight, thank you."

"And might I ask you what clan you belong to?"

"I know nothing of clans. If you won't tell me the whereabouts of Hortator, please direct me to someone who can."

"Are you an anarch?" asked the woman with the peacock hair. I could only look at her in confusion.

The other card player rose and sniffed at me. "Unusual bloodline," he said. "Not a pedigree I'm familiar with."

"Now look here," said Sebastian Melmoth, "he's obviously a vampire. But he doesn't seem to have the foggiest notion about how to behave like one. Tell me, Nezzy old chap, if you were in fact to find Hortator, what would you do?"

"I shall kill him."

The others began to laugh at me. I felt like some peasant on his first trip to Tenochtitlán. "Why do you mock me?" I said.

"Well!" said Sebastian Melmoth, "that's simply not done anymore. Not without the consent of the Prince. Who doesn't even know who you are, so I don't see why he would grant your request."

It was then that I heard his voice. "Kill me?" The voice had deepened with the centuries, but I still recognized it. There he stood, towering over Melmoth, in the full regalia of a Mexica warrior, the jaguar-skin cloak, the helmet fashioned from a jaguar's head, the quetzal plumes, the earrings of gold and jade. Behind him there hung a life-sized painting of the white men's Xipe Totec, the god nailed to a tree; a soldier was hammering a stake through his heart; a beautiful woman watched with tears in her eyes.

"Kill me?" he repeated. "Why, Nezahualcóyotl?"

"Because you tried to kill me!"

"That was a foolish thing. I admit it. I placed too much credence in the Spaniard's superstitions. I know now that you're not that simple to kill. In fact, you look very well for someone who hasn't had a drop of blood in half a millennium."

"You are part of the old things, the things that should have died when the world ended. I understand now why I have been preserved by the gods. It is so that I can take you with me, you impious creature who twice refused the honor of a sacrificial death. I have been sent to put an end to your anomalous existence so that no part of the Old World will taint the New."

"Did your god tell you this, old man?"

Suddenly I realized that I had heard no voices from the gods since awakening inside the glass box in the Los Angeles Museum. There was no more certainty in me. There was only ambiguity and confusion. My grand revelations no longer had divine authority. Perhaps it was true that they were the hallucinations of a madman. Perhaps if I had my votive objects I could summon back the voice of the hummingbird—the sacred blood-cup, the drum, the gold-tipped thorns for piercing my own flesh.

"Huitzilopochtli!" I cried out, despairing.

"You fool," said Hortator. "No god brought you to this place. There is no divine plan. It was I who told Julia Epstein where to dig. It was I who chose the moment to bring you back out of the earth. It was I, not Huitzilopochtli, who summoned you hither!"

"Why?" I said.

"Oh, don't imagine that I want to renew some monstrous cosmic struggle between you and me. It's much simpler than that. Buried with you. In the chamber at the heart of the pyramid. There were certain artifacts, were they not? Magical artifacts that will enhance my power. Your coming back to life along with the items I need is something of an inconvenience, but I'm sure you won't last long. Because you simply don't understand how things work in this new world, this age of vampires."

Then it was that the memory of the apocalypse returned to me, bursting all at once through the wall I had erected to shield myself from its pain. I could not bear these creatures of their future, with their petty rules and their ignorance of the great cycles of the cosmos. I turned and strode away, taking the steps two at a time until I reached the Alexandrian Club, where Julia was sitting nervously at a corner table.

"Where did I come from?" I screamed at her. "How did you come to possess my body? And where are the artifacts I was buried with?" I had to have them. I had to try to summon Huitzilopochtli. Surely I would hear his voice again if I went through the ritual of the sacred blood-cup.

"Quiet now," she said, "you're making a scene."

"I have to know!"

"Yes. Yes. But not here. It's dangerous for me."

We drove into the darkness. Los Angeles sparkled with man-made stars. A thousand strange new odors lanced the air. Frenzied copulations. Murderers and thieves skulking through the back streets. And the blood music, singing to me from every mortal inhabitant of the city. From within the topless towers of stone came the pounding of a million hearts, the roar of a million bloodstreams. Oh, one could be a glutton in this city, if one were a creature such as I. No wonder they had congregated here.

"I told you," said Julia. "Things are different now."

"What did Hortator mean when he said that he had summoned me back from the dead—by telling you where to dig?"

"Oh, he was being melodramatic. But he did drop a few hints."

"Before or after he made love to you?"

"You're not jealous, are you?"

"Of course not." I was silent for a while. The woman had a way of baldly confronting me with the truth. I didn't like it. I loathed the very idea of a city crammed with vampires, living by complex rules, observing silly hierarchies. But could I do? The car raced over the bridge once more; Tenochtitlán too was a city of many bridges, a floating city. Los Angeles was like a bloated, savage parody of my vanished kingdom.

Julia said, "I'll tell you, if you like. We have a series of weekly lectures at the museum. Hispanic studies, you know. Hortator came to a few of them. He would ask penetrating questions. Then he started telling me things. There was a big earthquake in Mexico City, you know. The Velasquez Building was leveled to the ground. He told me—convinced me—that there was a major find hidden beneath it. A secret room, he told me. Next to a secret passageway. He told me he'd seen it in a dream. I laughed when he drew me a map. Well, that was the thing, you see. We had been using sonar to excavate those tunnels. And the computer scan matched his drawing. To the centimeter."

"And you found me there."

"You were lying in a massive obsidian sarcophagus. You had a stake through your heart. I assumed—foolish me— that because of that, you were quite, quite dead—too many Dracula films, I suppose—so that it would be safe to put you on exhibit."

•

Memories of the apocalypse.

The king in all his splendor. This time not on the crest of a grassy hill, watching a pretended battle, but atop a pyramid of stone, looking down on the conquistadores as they swept through the city in a river of blood and fire. Man and beast conjoined now, the man-things glittering in their silvery skins, the beasts whinnying and pawing the pathways paved with the dead. Arms and legs flying in the air as the canonballs smashed through stone and adobe and human flesh.

And I beside him, I the mouthpiece of the god of the Mexica, aghast and powerless, raging. "You didn't have to play dead for them. They're just mortals. You're treated them like gods."

"They are gods," said Moctezuma. "There was nothing I could do."

Hortator had poisoned his mind. He had fed Moctezuma a diet of his own bad dreams. Told him that the Spaniard was indeed Quetzalcoatl.

I looked into the eyes of my king; and I saw such sadness, such desolation that I could not bear it. It must be a terrible destiny to be the one chosen to preside over the end of the universe. Was there no way to turn back the sun? No. Beside us as we sat, each one wrapped in his private melancholia, my deputy priests were grimly carrying on the day's duties, plucking out the hearts of victims who waited in an endless queue that stretched all the way down the thousand steps and into the conflagration in the market square.

"Don't tell me that you accepted the word of this manbeast as the word of a god!" I cried.

"Wasn't it?" the king said. "In truth. I felt a certain. Wrongness about it all."

"Then let me call on Hummingbird to turn back the tide of time!"

"What difference does it make now?"

"Majesty," I said, "when the king himself no longer believes in the old truths, how can the earth sustain itself?"

"Perhaps I've been a little. Distracted," said the king. He was wavering.

I knew that I could not stand idle. I left the king's side, I entered the sacred chamber behind the altar, whose walls were caked with the blood of ten thousand human sacrifices. I paused only to suck the juices from a fresh, still palpitating heart that one of the priests handed me. The soldiers were hacking off the limbs of the still convulsing victims, casting down the arms and legs, as has always been the custom, for the poor to dine on. The sight of the city's daily routine being carried out even now, on the brink of utter annihilation, would have moved me to tears, except that I had shed none in a thousand years. The priests worked quickly and efficiently, up to their elbows in coagulating gore. I hardly looked at them; I chucked the drained heart onto a golden platter before an image of Hummingbird, then entered the secret passageway behind the altar that led downward, downward to the hidden chamber where lay my sarcophagus and the tools of my art.

In the tunnel, the sounds of death were muffled. Canon like the distant whisper of thunder in the rain forest. The screams of the dying faint, like the cries of jungle birds. The

clash of metal on stone like the patter of rain on foliage. I
took the steep steps two at a time. Soon I was in the heart of
the pyramid.

When I reached the chamber, I found that the seal was
broken. Not with the magic words, but shattered with gun-
powder. Several of the man-beasts were already there, ran-
sacking the place, gathering up the treasures into sacks. "How
dare you?" I screamed. The man-beasts rushed at me. I summoned up my inner strength. I struck out blindly with both
fists, and two of the Spaniards slammed against the stone
walls. One of them died on the spot; the second more slowly,
a little string of brain oozing down from his helmet. The third
man-beast gaped, turned tail, started to run. Then his greed
got the better of him and he returned to gather up one of the
sacks of gold. He glanced at me; I was draining his dead
friend's blood into the sacred blood-cup so that I could call on
Hummingbird.

I closed my eyes. I called on the name of my god.
Huitzilopotchtli.

I felt myself sinking into the well of unconsciousness that
was the presence of my god. I heard the familiar buzzing in
my left ear that presaged the coming of Huitzilopotchtli. I
smiled.

My child.

Came the whisper of the Hummingbird's wings, the tiny
voice from the heart of the flames. I thrilled to its dark music. I allowed it to wash over me like the currents of the sea.
I relinquished my being. The presence of the divine was more
fulfilling even than the taste of blood, than the memory of
women.

My child.

Abruptly, the trance was broken. I was jolted into consciousness. Even now, telling the story to Julia five hundred
years later, the memory will not come back as a woven fabric; it is in tatters.

Hortator stands before me, no longer in the attire of the
Unblemished Youth, but wrapped in a metal skin from head
to toe, like one of the conquistadores. With him are a dozen
of the white-skinned creatures. He has delivered to his mas-
ters an entire world, an entire civilization.

"I know what you are now," he cries, "creature of Satan. They've told me everything." Several more of the Spaniards come in behind him, brandishing their swords and their flaming torches and their muskets. Seeing their dead comrades they cry out, back away; but Hortator laughs. "I know what you are now, and the Jesuits have told me what I must do to kill you."

Confused, uncomprehending, I lash out—

He dodges my blow, leaps across the sarcophagus, seizes the drum of Xipe Totec. And begins to pound on it, a slow relentless rhythm. I scream. He pounds. I lunge. He leaps, each leap drawing more celerity from the power of the drum. He flies along the walls, he twists, he turns, he is a whirlwind, a tempest—

Huitzilopotchtli! I cry out.

No answer. I reached into the profoundest darkness of the well within. Where was my god? Then I saw Hortator bearing down on me, brandishing a sharpened wooden stake.

As though from infinitely far away I seem to see the stake rive my stony flesh, rip apart my ribcage, pierce my heart.

Huitzilopotchtli!

Huitzilopotchtli!

Then, and only then, the god responds. The pyramids above us start to tremble. Cracks appear in the ceiling. Rocks start to rain down.

"Flee!" cries Hortator. I hear, through the fog of pain, their footsteps, metal clanking on stone. I hear some of them cry out as the cave-in crushes them.

I clutch at the wooden stake. But it is too late. I feel its leaden weight within me, feel it still the sluggish pump that is my heart, I feel the blood slow from a spurt to an ooze. I feel my heart muscle tighten around the unyielding wood like a vagina. I feel violated. I feel powerless for the first time since my changing. Then, all at once, I am spiraling downward toward the long sleep of ultimate forgetting.

•

And now, another underground passageway, another secret chamber. Five hundred years in the future, in a world

I did not belong in. I stood with Julia Epstein among the shelves and shelves of artifacts of my people, all labeled, boxed, marked in white paint in the strange curlicuish script of the man-beasts.

Crate after crate I ripped open. "What is it you're looking for?" said Julia. "This is valuable stuff—you can't just throw it around like it belonged to you."

"It does belong to me."

"Half a millennium ago. But they're priceless antiquities now. And they haven't been appraised by the insurance company yet, so—"

I saw a tattered quetzal-feather robe that had once belonged to King Moctezuma's grandfather. I saw my sacred blood-cup, chipped now. I lifted it from its box.

"Careful with that thing! It dates back to Olmec times."

"I know. I made it."

She was silent for a moment. "The drum!" I said. "There was a drum. Fashioned from human skin."

"I've seen that," she said, "in Hortator's apartment."

So that was how he had made it out of the collapsing tunnels. With the power of celerity conferred by the drum of Xipe Totec! I was furious now. He had no right to my ritual objects. I was more determined than ever to exact revenge. Perhaps he thought I would be a useless anachronism, but I would teach him not to usurp my magical tools. They had told me at the Vampire Club about new laws that forbade the killing of vampires without permission from some prince. But what did I know of princes? What did I care? I was more ancient than any prince.

But even as I spoke, we heard the sound of shattering glass, and the high-pitched wail that I now knew to be an alarm that would eventually summon the museum's security. Then came a distant thumping sound, uneven, like a fibrillating heart. I knew that sound well. The hollow pounding contained in it the scream of a dying man.

"Hortator!"

"Why do you have to go on fighting him?" Julia said. "Don't you realize that the war between you two has no meaning any more?"

"Julia, I must have a little of your blood."

She closed her eyes, craned her neck, bared it to me as a warrior bares his heart for the sacrifice. "I need the blood," I said, "so I can summon forth the voice of the Hummingbird."

"There's no voice," she whispered. "It's in your mind. The right brain speaking to the left. A hallucination of godhead. Don't you understand that people don't see visions and hear voices anymore? You come from the age of gods; we live in the age of consciousness; it's not the god who commands us anymore, it's we ourselves, our ego, our individual being. People like you, people who still hear the voices of gods. They put them insane asylums now."

What was she telling me? It made no sense. How could humans exist without prophets to transmit the commands of the gods? How lonely it must be for them in this future. To be like little islands of consciousness, not to be linked to the great cycle of the cosmos. To be not part of one great self but merely little selves, with little, meaningless lives. I could not, would not live that way. I took her in my arms; I made a tiny incision in her neck with my little fingernail; I drew a thimbleful of blood into the sacred cup; deeply I drank, and as I drank I prayed: Huitzilopotchtli. Huitzilopotchtli. Do not forsake me now.

Hortator burst into the chamber. The alarms were screeching. "The rest of the treasures of the room have now been brought to Los Angeles," he said "That's why I told Julia where you could be found. I need the other ritual objects. I need the powers they can bestow on me. As for you. You're just a historical oddity."

But I could feel the strength of Huitzilopotchti course through my flesh.

As Julia, faint from her bleeding, sat, dazed, on my old sarcophagus, still in its wooden crate, Hortator and I battled. He threw me against the wall; I lacerated his face with my fingernails; he whirled about me, pounding his drum, my drum. Each of us drew on his dark powers. A mortal would not have seen us battling at all. He would have felt now a tremor, now a flash of light, now a ripple of darkness. I leaped onto the ceiling, I sped along the walls, defying the earth's pull with speed; but Hortator was equally swift. His fangs glistened in the man-made light. We fought hand to hand on the lid of the sarcophagus where Julia still lay. We tussled on the concrete floor of the storeroom, and still the siren wailed.

"I'll really kill you this time," Hortator shouted. "The black robes told me a stake through the heart would kill you. I know better now."

And still I had not heard the voice of the hummingbird. It was beginning to dawn on me that there was something to what Julia said; that perhaps this was no longer an age of gods. The last time the god had spoken, had he not said, Do you not understand that he who rises to godhead, who creates a world, a people, a destiny, plants inevitably within his creation the seeds of his own destruction? I did not understand then, but I understood it now. My existence showed to ordinary men that there was something beyond mortality; but beyond my own immortality there was also a kind of entropy. In being granted the ability to see the grand scheme of the universe, to live for centuries and know the higher purposes of mankind, I had also learned that all, even the most sublime, is vanity. I was full of despair. How could I belong to this future? How could I live amongst dozens of creatures like myself, arcane hierarchies all selfishly struggling for domination over one another? I knew that Hortator would hound me to my death. I could not live in a world where I could not hear the voice of my god.

We had battled for what seemed like days, but I knew that only seconds had passed; so quick were our movements that time itself had seemed to stand still. He had me pinned to the ground. I felt not only his weight but the weight of this whole bizarre new universe. And with a free hand he continued to drum, frenzied now, his eyes maddened, his lips frothing. I waited for him to drain me of all my blood, to desiccate me, to consign me to the well of oblivion for ever.

Then, at that moment, the siren ceased. Hortator relaxed his hold on me. A shadow had fallen over us. I smelled the presence of another kindred. I could feel the concentrated power, a puissance that matched my own.

"Prince," Hortator whispered. He stepped back from me, then fell to the floor in supplication. I could not see this Prince, so thoroughly had he cloaked himself in magical darkness. But I knew him in the shadow that suffused the air.

"Oh, Nezahualcóyotl," said the prince, whose voice was as reverberant as a god's, "what am I to do with you? You have arrived in this city, yet you do not even come to pay homage to me as is our custom; and already you've created all sorts of controversy. The Vampire Club talks of nothing else but you. You're an anomaly; you challenge our most basic assumptions about our people's history."

I said, "I did not mean to offend you. My quarrel with Hortator is an ancient one, and not your affair; and I see now that the things we quarrel about have become irrelevant. I have no real desire to live. Let Hortator take my ritual objects and grow in power; and let me return to the earth."

"It is true," said the prince, "that I have the authority to grant you death. But how can I? You are older than I; you are so old that even the concept of the masquerade is foreign to you; it is I who should bow to you, but I cannot. There can only be one prince. Nezahualcóyotl, you must find your own destiny in some other place. Or else there will always be some who will look to you for leaderships, anarchs who will revere your disregard of our rules of civilization and who will claim that your greater age gives you greater authority. Nezahualcóyotl. You must leave. I cannot command you. I, a prince, must ask it of you as a favor."

And now the security guards were entering the room. It was just as it was in Tenochtitlán, the enemy storming the secret chamber just as my world was disintegrating all around me. The prince did something—used his powers of hypnosis perhaps—for the guards did not seem to see me, Hortator, or the rippling darkness that was the prince of Los Angeles.

"Are you all right, Ms. Epstein?" said one of them.

Julia was struggling to get up. "I—must have passed out," she said. "Something—someone—perhaps a prowler—"

"No one here now, ma'am. But they've made quite a mess."

"Are you sure you don't want me to get a doctor?" said another guard.

"I'm fine, thanks."

"Let's see if we can find him lurking around somewhere," said the first guard, and they trooped away. Astonished, I looked up. I thought I glimpsed something—a swirl of shadow—vortices within vortices—the eyes of a ancient creature, world-weary, ruthless, yet somehow also tinged with compassion. I knew that I he was right. I could not stay in Los Angeles. I knew nothing of the feuding factions of the vampire world, the warring clans, the masquerade; I belonged to a simpler time.

"I will go," I said softly.

Then Julia said, "And I will go with you."

I said, "You don't know what you're saying. You think it's some romantic thing, that there's glamour in being undead. Look at us; look at how we have relived, again and again, ancient quarrels that the world has forgotten; the vampires that rule the world are but shadows, and I am less than a shadow of their shadow."

Julia said, "Only because you have not loved."

She came toward me. In her eyes there shone the crystalline coldness of eternity. I had not wanted to transform her into one of my kind. I had sought only to use enough blood to sustain me, to let me see my visions. She had not yet become a vampire; what I saw in her eyes was the yearning. "It's a historian's dream," she said, "to pass through the ages of man like the pages of a book. To perceive the great big arc of history. It's not just that I love you. Even if I didn't, I could learn, in eternity, to love."

Hortator hissed, "Only the prince can grant the right to sire new kindred!"

But the prince said only, "Peace, peace, Hortator; will your anger never be slaked?" And then—and I could feel him fading from our presence as he spoke—he said, "Do what you wish, Nezahualcóyotl. Be glad. We will not meet again."

•

I have returned to Tenochtitlán. It is a gargantuan madhouse of twenty million souls, but it is still called by the name of my vanished tribe, the Mexica. My official title is Meso-American Studies Advisor to the Los Angeles Museum Field Research Unit, Mexico City. Julia and I have a charming apartment; one side overlooks one of the few areas of greenery in the city, the other one of the worst slums.

Julia tells me that a philosopher named Jaynes has written a book called *The Origin of Consciousness in the Breakdown of the Bicameral Mind*. It is a book that explains how, in the ancient world, men did not possess consciousness of self at all, but acted blindly, in response to voices and images projected by the right side of the brain, which they perceived to be the direct commands of gods, kings, and priests.

It is a strange world indeed, where people see no visions, and where a book has to be written explaining away the gods in terms of ganglia and synapses. I do not like it. I do not like the fact that I have been cut off forever from the divine; that I am no longer a prophet, but merely one vampire among many.

Yet the city does have its charms. Its nightlife is thriving and decadent; its music colorful; its alleyways quaint and full of titillating danger. And then there are the people. The descendants of my own people and the Spaniards who overcame them. Julia and I often make time to enjoy the inhabitants of our new home.

There are many poor people here. They pour in from the country, seeking out a better life; often they end up working as virtual slaves in huge factories that pump out cheap goods for their richer neighbors to the north. Sometimes they become gangsters or beggars. Sometimes they find a charitable person to take them in, as domestics, perhaps, or live-in prostitutes.

But sometimes, ah, sometimes, they vanish without a trace.

Tagging the Moon

I was there the night they shot Bobby Donahue. I saw him cartwheel through the air from the top edge of the overpass down toward the screaming traffic. But I never saw him hit the pavement. Nobody did. Not me, not the police, not even the dudes in the Fox 11 news chopper. I never saw him die.

And that's how I know that everything Bobby told me, and I saw, is true ... the visions ... the revelations ... the aliens from another world.

It's hard to be a has-been at twenty-four, but that's what I was back in the summer of '92. I lived under an overpass with a half-dozen homies. On the first Tuesday of the month I sold my blood; Saturdays I sold my sister. My sister was sullen and pockmarked and usually fetched less than what Dr. Sayeed paid for a pint of my extra rare blood type. But hey, I was doing her a favor compared to the shit they made her do at the home.

I wasn't a basehead no more, but I could still put away a fifth of Jim Beam all by myself, and that's what I liked to do Sundays. That, or sit leaning against the monuments at Forest Lawn, far from the roar over the freeway, or kicking it in the old hood, up toward Sylmar, where I had like family, which I never spoke to, and friends, which I did.

And then there were the kids—the ones that looked up to me—the ones who had heard the stories. Half the stories were bullshit but they had enough truth in them that I had a hard time denying them. I'd known Bobby Donahue since he was five years old, which was when they moved to the trailer park off of Hubbard, maybe ten years ago. But he was like maybe fourteen when he started to hang with the other kids on the corner of Jackman. He was a dreamy kid who always read books and always understood what people were talking about on television. I don't know why he got into tagging. Maybe it was because his father blew off to Arizona and his mom became the neighborhood slut. Maybe it was because he stopped going to school, said it bored him. Maybe it was because his brother shot himself in the head with a .38. Shit, I don't know, but I ended up father, mother, and brother to him, even though I only saw him maybe once every two or three weekends ... whenever they weren't detaining him overnight or switching his social worker on him.

Bobby was obsessed with tagging. You'd be walking down the street together past that waist-high picket fence, just kicking it and talking about some dope bitch you saw last night, and then, glancing back, you see that every one of them pickets had a name, and that name was *NOVA,* which means an exploding star, with a rainbow-colored starburst over the *O.* And you'd be thinking, how the fuck'd *that* get there? Bobby was quick. Anything with a white surface wide enough to fit him seem to call out to him. He tagged with Mean Streaks, markers, spray cans, acrylics, pastels, crayons, finger paint, and at least once with his own blood.

Which is why I don't go back to the old 'hood that much no more.

Bobby's favorite saying was, "One day, I'm a tag the fucking *moon.* You'll fucking see then, everyone's gonna see me up."

I can still see him now, that last week. He was kind of small for his age. He had squinty dark green eyes and a mass of dirty brown hair, and he dressed like a cholo, in them oversize pants. He smelled of leather and tobacco. He was going to be sixteen soon, the magic age when driving becomes legal and crime stops paying, but he still had the look that gets you into movies for half price. He totally hated the idea of turning sixteen, and he was hanging out with me a lot, riding the RTD over the Hill and meeting me, as though by accident, next to my favorite dumpster or somewhere in Forest Lawn, gazing at the tombs of the rich and famous.

Or just in Hollywood somewhere, browsing at the Cahuenga newsstand. "Yo, buy my ass a burger, dude ... I ain't eaten in like days."

"Why not?" I'm putting down this copy of *Fat Leather Chicks* that I've been leafing through, wondering if they'll throw him out for loitering by the porn. "Don't you have a home to go to no more?"

"Shit no. Dad's in detox and Mom's at some big old battered women's shelter. Come on, just one burger, I'll totally pay you back."

"Yeah, right." I'm still all flush from selling blood to Dr. Sayeed. So we walk down to the McDonald's on Hollywood Boulevard and he eats more than just one burger: he gets three Big Macs plus two orders of fries, and I'm all watching him, wondering where it can all go.

"Tag the moon yet?" I ask him in the interval between a Big Mac and a gulp of Coke.

"Working on it," he says. And he sounds like he means it.

He usually has something on his mind when he comes all the way into Hollywood to find me, but I know that he's going to take his own sweet time getting to the point. So I wait. He tells me he's been tagging all over. "In one night," he says, "I hit up Van Nuys, Pacoima, Sun Valley, Studio City, and Reseda. You know that ten-story building with the big Marilyn Monroe all the way down one side? I'm up on Marilyn's left tit, dude, I hid in the bathroom of some law office until after the closed and then I like climbed out along the ledge and I hung there with my legs wrapped around a flagpole, fucking *hung* there, and I wrote *Nova* all the way around her nipple. Wore out three Mean Streaks doing it, too," he adds. "I'll have to punk the stationery store for some more."

"Let me buy them for you, dude. It's a shame for you to get busted stealing markers." I knew what jail was like; Bobby didn't.

"You'd do that for me? Thanks, Todd." He looked at me with the kind of hero-worship I was getting less and less of these days.

"We didn't even have Mean Streaks in my day," I said. "Just spray cans and shit. No high technology."

"I love it when you old guys talk about them Stone Age times." The thing about that is, he was only half joking. To be twenty-four years old, in the minds of the kids Bobby Donahue hung out with, was to be a relic of an ancient civilization. "But you're the best," he said. "Last night I saw you still up on the 'F' on the roof of the Wells Fargo bank on Victory. That's been there almost all my life. None of my friends know how you did it. And nobody's fucking been able to wipe it off. And all them freeway signs. The piece you threw on the back of *Van Nuys Bvd—3/4 mile* ... you must of fucking had wings to get up there without getting caught."

He wolfed down another burger.

"Maybe we all had wings in them Stone Age days," I said, laughing.

Then Bobby's all, "You're probably wondering why I came looking for you all the way down in Hollywood. Dude, I been looking for you half the night. It's important."

"Okay." Out of the corner of my eye, up at the corner, I could see two kids stealing a car. They were too new at this to know that the seedy man with the WILL WORK FOR FOOD sign around his neck was an undercover cop. Life's a bitch. "What's your point?" I said.

"It's the aliens, dude. I been seeing them again. And like, now they want to meet you."

•

Okay, so maybe Bobby wasn't, like, all there. He had visions. He didn't need shrooming ... his whole life was one long acid trip flashback. Once, he was maybe eight or nine, he was running for his life with four truant officers on his back, ready to slap the plastic ties around his wrists, and I saw him from the apartment window—I still had parents back then—and he was sprinting through traffic with his eyes closed, dodging the cars as they snarled and rammed one another to avoid him ... but with the chaos raging around him he's all calm ... concentrated ... compacted into himself. He darted, he danced, he spun, beautiful as a pinball.

I ran down the stairs to let him into my building and he ran past me and I stopped the police at the door, I'm all, "Yeah, he's my brother, he's on C track, he ain't supposed to be in school until February ..." Lying comes easy to me. Then like, I turn around and see him and he asks me, "The aliens. Are they gone yet?"

"Police, Bobby. They were police."

"No, not *them,* Todd ... the *others!* They were in the boys' restroom when I was trying to pee. That's why I ditched."

•

Years later, I'm telling the story of this to Dr. Margaret Yao, who's some kind of therapist and who's writing a book about taggers. She's my friend, she thinks, though it's fucking transparent the way she tries to pump me for anecdotes she can use in her book.

"And what was Bobby Donahue doing when he had this ... ah ... extraterrestrial visitation?" she says, lighting her second joint from the butt end of her first.

"He was throwing a piece. On the bathroom wall."

"You mean putting up graffiti?" She notes my choice of words in the section of her notebook marked "special jargon."

"Well," I tell her, "piecing ain't the same as tagging. It's more complicated. It's when you do like, a whole picture ... kind of like *art.*"

She scribbles in her notebook. "But what I'm getting at," she says, "is this. The visitations from aliens ... they are associated with the graffiti somehow ... aren't they? So maybe it's his alienation speaking." She becomes all excited now. She pours me some of her special brew, Tsing Dao she calls it, some kind of Chinese beer. I love the way the Chinese characters curve around the beer can, the way the brushstrokes swell up and die away, like miniature waves. I wish I could write Chinese. Chinese is a tagger's dopeass dream language. I'm all watching the drops of condensation on the beer can and the way they distort the strokes of the calligraphy. I don't really hear Margaret when she launches into them theories of hers. She weaves them twenty-syllable words around each other like the way I used to write *Pricer* on the freeway signs, with the letters winding in and out of each other like snakes making love.

"Are you listening to me?" Margaret says. "Aliens and alienation. I mean, here's this kid, grows up on a diet of sci-fi, neglected, has a desperate need to throw up his ego-symbol all over town ... the UFO angle's a natural. In the middle ages, he would've been seeing saints and angels. Like Joan of Arc did."

"Yeah," I say. "Can you lend me five bucks?"

She stops and looks at me like I'm a sort of a thing in a museum, which I guess, to her, I am. Every night she goes home to a one-bedroom in Tarzana, pool, jacuzzi, New Age music piped into the lobby. Shit.

She's all, "Are you a little short?"

"I'd love to buy like, a blanket. November's coming. There ain't no central heating in the overpass hotel. I saw a blanket in the dumpster Saturday, but it was on some Mexican dude's turf."

She goes on staring at me and I think she's getting, you know, *wet* over what I'm saying. I'm so horny I could fuck a hole in a toilet stall wall. She takes a five-dollar bill out of her purse and folds it and purses her lips, and she's all, "But tell me more about Bobby Donahue. He seems such a *character,* I mean, so full of the energy and rage of the streets."

"He's gone now," I said.

"Dead?" She tsk-tsked with the earnest sympathy they all seem to have, those Chinese women who went to Berkeley who live in Tarzana who are writing books about us who think they love us but who never ever know us.

"I didn't say *dead,* I said *gone.*"

"So you're into denial," she said. I tried to grab for the five bucks but it was just out of reach. Then she flicked it onto my lap.

•

So I'm all, "They want to meet me," as we deposit the trash and walk out onto Hollywood Boulevard, me in my year-old unwashed jeans and him in his cholo pants, ten sizes too big and freshly jacked from the swap meet. "You shrooming or something?"

Bobby skips from star to star alongside the street to the hip-hop beat of a sidewalk ghetto blaster. I walk as quick as I can but I don't know, I feel weak and old; maybe it's because I've been sapped of all that blood, maybe it's just I'm over the hill for being a street kid, just not up to it no more. I barely catch up to his ass when he's off again and yeah, when I glance over my shoulder there's the *Nova*-starburst up on the window of a B. Dalton, blocking the Rush Limbaugh dump display.

We turned down a side alley, a dead end, behind Cherokee. Where the alley met the boulevard there wasn't that much, just the usual gang initials, and, here and there, a name crossed out. But further in, here and there became a jumble, then a jungle ... letters and logos crisscrossing one another, melding into one great abstract swath of colors ... and full-scale pieces too ... there was a bad ass picture of the Rodney King beating, with Darrell Gates hovering over it in black robes and leathery wings and the eyes of a demon ... there was a dance of death, the old man with the sickle leading a capering procession of skaters, surfers, taggers, and gangbangers across a lurid cityscape silhouetted against vermilion flames ... there was a life-size Elvis in a *Hamlet* costume, with a guitar in one hand and a skull in the other ... there was a '57 Chevy pointing ass up from a sand dune circled by cactus ... we saw all these things in the light from distant neon signs. And the names were everywhere, a whole history of tagging ... names like, *Squirt, Tryer, Phaks, Silem, Carne,* kind of like the Vietnam Memorial, because like, half the taggers who were up were like, dead now, or maybe worse than dead, drowning in their own addictions, like me.

I saw myself up, real high, in the hardest to reach ass corner of the whole wall. *Pricer,* it still read, in the curlicue lettering style I invented which is now one of the most popular styles. Smog and acid rain had dulled the colors, but I still felt the tug of my own past self, and I wondered if I'd ever be free again.

I barely looked away and when I looked back up in the corner I saw *Nova* too, scrawled above me, and I saw the shadow of Bobby Donahue skittering down the wall ... and I heard him laugh. Then he was right by me, smiling. "Jesus," I said, "you make me nervous, how you do that shit."

Bobby said, "It's like the story of the eagle and the robin; the eagle said he could fly the highest, but the robin rode on his back and like, when the eagle was so high he could barely flap his wings no more, the robin soared up a inch or two and won the bet."

"Where'd you hear that?" I knew his parents would never have told him a story, let alone his social worker or someone like that.

"The aliens told me," he said. And he pointed to the wall at the end of the blind alley, where there's a dope-ass piece, maybe eight feet square, showing the L.A. riots, like, a view from a news chopper ... and like, I see this black Porsche parked against the dead end, flush against the dumpster, with a homeless dude asleep against the wheel. The windows are all black and the license plate is black and it don't have no letters or numbers on it. It's a scary thing, because no way could this car have been driven into this position, stretched across the alley with each bumper a half inch or less from the walls; it was like the car had dropped into place out of the night sky. Still, there wasn't nothing *alien* about it. It was just a car.

I'm all, "Yeah. It's a car."

The door opens and there are two men: Laurel and Hardy—a tall man and a fat man. The fat man's all wearing surfer pants and a neon tank top and pink oversized shades. The tall man's dressed like an undertaker. But they look human to me, even if they aren't a matched set.

Bobby motions and I follow him. He's all eager; he doesn't have that I-don't-give-a-shit look that he usually does. He says, "Hey, I want you to meet my homie, Todd. He writes *Pricer*. You've heard of him."

"We certainly have," says the fat one, folding away his shades to reveal a second pair of eyeglasses underneath. "You're something of a legend, I understand."

"A *legend?* Hardly. I guess old Bobby been exaggerating, as usual."

"It's not through Bobby that we've learned of you," says the undertaker dude, who even *talks* like an undertaker, with a low-pitched, raspy, nervous-making voice. "It was through, ah, *other* channels."

"Fuck, Todd, they been watching us! All the time we thought we were alone, streaking our way from wall to wall, hanging from ledges, clinging to ducts, they were there too ... watching ... like, you know, guardian angels or something. Or like the dads we never had."

"So, they're undercovers?"

"No. Like I told you. They're aliens. They're fucking from another world. They came here in a fucking spaceship. And they're here to visit *us*. No 'take me to your leader' bullshit. They came here for *us* ... because they're taggers too."

I glance from one to the other. The fat one's jowls are quivering. The undertaker one says, "He expresses himself forcefully, although he somewhat oversimplifies the situation. My companion and I have been traveling for some time now; eons, to be precise. Your friend calls us taggers, which is true only in the sense that it pleases us to leave behind us, on those worlds as yet unsullied by the presence of life, on those dead surfaces which cry out for the tumult of living souls ... small traces of our being ... signatures, if you will ... tiny pieces of DNA that will, after eons to come, evolve to self-awareness and proclaim to those who follow us that we were here first."

There's a long silence. Bobby's all smiling, happy, expecting me to totally accept at face value the idea that these two geeks in a fancy car are not two geeks at all but like, the Creator, God. I don't know about Bobby but I've been on the street long enough to know what a rat smells like, and I'm real surprised at Bobby. I'm all wondering what drugs they've given him. Or worse, telling him they're God, maybe they've given him religion. And I'm thinking, Bobby, Bobby, what have they done to you? Ain't it enough that your parents didn't love you, that you didn't have no money and were born on the wrong side of town, so now the one thing that you really own, the thing inside of you that's you and no one else, has got to get sucked into some shit-ass cult that brainwashes taggers? I guess he realizes that I'm angry with him, with all of them. And so he cranks into his motormouth mode, which is what happens when he gets nervous, and he's all talking about me, about the legend I supposedly am ... the tall tales the young taggers tell themselves when they're overnighting at juvenile detention waiting for parents who don't want to come pick them up. "Let me tell you what Todd done one time," he says, and the so-called aliens both relax a little, smile, even, "the night before his sixteenth birthday ... there's a wall that runs along the edge of California, next to a road called Oceanside, and on the street side it's a low wall you can lean against, but on the beach side it like falls straight down, a sheer drop, all the way down ... sand in some parts, rock in others, concrete where they've built a concession stand or a shithouse. So it's like midnight, and it's a full moon, and Todd takes off there in this truck he stole, and he climbs over the wall and then ... clinging to the wall like Spiderman ... high above the sea ... he writes on the bricks in white spray paint, over and over and over, brick by brick by brick, until you can see *Pricer* slowly forming on that wall, see it from way over on the pier, and it's all glimmering in the moonlight, and he's there, like Spidey, breaking all the fucking laws of gravity, for the longest time, scurrying up and down and fucking *breaking* that name out of the brick, and it's the most beautiful thing I ever saw—"

"You never saw it," I said, "and anyways, you were probably like five years old at the time—"

•

"—and anyways," I'm all telling this to Dr. Yao so she can toss me a miserable few bucks so I can buy myself some smokes, "it wasn't true. I had a rope ladder. It's just a myth."

But she writes it all down religiously, adding, "Myth, Todd, is perhaps the most profound truth of them all."

She can say that all she wants, because she makes more money by asking an hour's worth of dumb questions than I've ever made in a week, except when I was running drugs, of course, but that don't fucking count.

•

— "and anyways it *is* true, and I saw it and it is a true memory, cuz that was the first time I ever run away from home, and I took the RTD all the way to Santa Monica because I heard they have better child protection agents there." Five years old and running away from home, I thought. But the aliens just kind of tsk-tsked and went along with his bullshit. "I know," Bobby said, "because of that full moon ... and looking up at it ... and down the wall at the name that was materializing out of the dark brick wall ... and thinking ... the wall is cool, but one day I'm a write on the fucking *moon.*"

The fat alien was all moaning and almost like having an orgasm right there in the alley over what Bobby was telling them. I had him pegged for a pervert. Hey, maybe the night wouldn't be wasted after all. Maybe I could sell him on a date with my sister, half now, half on delivery.

•

— "Plus," I tell Dr. Yao, "he didn't say that, at one minute past midnight, my birthday, they came to the wall and hauled my ass in and threw the book at me ... not just the vandalism but the GTA, with that stolen truck ... that's the reason I stopped tagging and became the, uh, legend."

"You were imprisoned?" Her upper lip trembles. I'd go at her right then if I could, but I know she'd only push that button underneath her desk and then that'd be the end of my probation.

"Yeah," I said, and then, because I know it titillates them and gets them all wet, "and well ... you know how it is in prison ... when you're young and ...like, maybe kind of, uh, slender ... not butt-ugly like some of the other dudes...."

"Oh, my God," she said, a tear forming in one eye. "They didn't ... *rape* you?"

I knew she'd be good for more than five bucks this time.

•

So, I'm all, "Well, Bobby, you are a genius when it comes to tagging, but about life, dude, you're fucking dumb." I can say all this because our friends aren't really paying attention to us; they're roaming up and down the alley and making notes on the different pieces, taking pictures even. "A fat dude and a thin dude and a Porsche, that don't make E.T. in a starship."

"You're wrong, Todd," says Bobby. "Look at what it says on the rear of the car. Will you just look?"

"It says 'Porsche.'"

"Bitch!" he whispers. "Porsche, right. *P-r-o-s-c-h-e* don't spell Porsche."

"So I'm dyslexic." I'm getting ready to punch him one because I don't like to be reminded that I don't read too good. "Ain't my fault. What's your point?"

"It's a fake, you fool. They're trying to blend in, but they copy us damn near perfect, but little things slip by … they're careless. They don't dot their i's and cross their t's. Hey like, when the fat one comes back, take a good look at his hands. You won't need to read for that."

The fat one waddled back into view at that moment. He was stuffing his camera back into a jacket pocket. He had six fingers on his right hand. *That* scared me.

The sixth finger, the one beyond the pinky, wasn't even a real finger at all, but a kind of claw. I thought I saw scales. "Don't be afraid," said the fat alien. I wondered if he'd read my mind. "We're not going to do anything to you. We're only going to watch. If you please us … and I know you will … there could be rewards … wealth … journeys beyond your wildest imaginings … sexual fulfilment. Our fingers are in many pies."

"I only got two things in life I really have a hard-on for," Bobby said. "And one of them's only like, a fantasy."

"And they are?" said the undertaker alien.

"I want to tag the moon. And I want to die."

•

I still remember the first time Bobby tried to commit suicide; he's about twelve and there's a drive-by on his street and four people get killed; one of them's Smiley, who never smiled. After Smiley's funeral, Bobby's at his house and he's all trying to hold his breath until he turns blue, but his stepdad beats him, so he has to breathe so he can cry.

Dr. Yao tells me about the value of human life, the tragedy of throwing it away; and I'm all, "Fuck you, Margaret, how can you talk about value and shit, you're the ones who put a price tag on everything," and she says, "I'm not talking money, I'm talking intangible values ... *higher* values ..." and I'm all, "When you're like me and Bobby, there *ain't* no value higher than money. A kid'll rape you cause his dick needs a quenching. He'll fucking *kill* you for a pack of smokes. They don't teach you that in Tarzana, but you'd learn it on the street pretty damn fast. To be worth something you have to be worth something *to* somebody."

Dr. Yao mutters something about nihilism, and I tell her, "But when you're up on that wall, and the whole world knows you exist and you have a name and your name cries out over the chaos of the city ... that's when, at least, you're somebody. For a while. Before they drag you away and bury your ass forever behind some prison wall."

She likes that. I think she's finally gonna let me do her.

•

What the two aliens have in mind is more than just sitting back and watching, though. They sort of want to participate. They want Bobby to go on the wildest tagging spree of his life, and they want to record all of it. And like, they want me along too, although maybe it's because Bobby's insisting on it. I'm like the crusty old commentator who's seen it all a million times ... they want my ancient wisdom. After all, I have a lofty vantage point. I'm twenty-four years old and I've done time. I can't decide if the aliens are making a documentary of some kind or whether they're just whacking off on our adrenalin.

Bobby'll be sixteen soon and then it better all be over. Or else they'll catch him and try him as an adult and send him to a *real* jail where they'll buttfuck all the dreaming out of him forever.

So like, we all pile into the Porsche that's not a Porsche. Inside it's all different ... a lot bigger, for one thing, because, the fat one tells me, space is all spindled up and twisting across itself like the strands of the writing we do; there's rooms within rooms and chambers within chambers. There's a room that turns into any place in the universe. There's a room with creatures preserved in columns of clear bubbly fluid. There's control panels and whirling lights and all that sci-fi stuff you see in movies. But you get the feeling that it's not what's really there at all, that it's like a virtual reality projection or something, because sometimes the images are weirdly superimposed or blur at the edges ... and you feel it's all there only to prove to me and Bobby that these dudes are from another world ... and that to them the place looks a whole lot different, or maybe doesn't *look* at all.

And sometimes it's just a little sports car jamming down the road, too small for four people. "Where to?" says the fat dude, and Bobby's all, I don't know, testing them, I guess, "Maybe like, the top of the Capitol Records tower." And in a moment the Porsche's lifting off and we're up above Hollywood, and I look down and I can see it all: the lights, the filth, the pimps, the tourists, the burger wrappers fluttering in the Santa Ana wind like sagebrush in the desert ... the stars above, where the aliens come from, you can barely make out through the layers of smog, but the stars in the sidewalk are bright enough to substitute for them ... we rise up and no one sees us, or if they do they don't think there's any wizardry to it; after all, this is Hollywood, where all cars fly. We thread down Hollywood and sometimes we duck into side streets. A homeless man peers at us from inside a dumpster. Maybe, living closer to the hard real world, he can still see the wonder in a car that flies and has aliens in it.

We soar up to the Capitol needle and Bobby hangs from the window by a bungee cord and writes, *Nova Nova Nova Nova Nova,* in a frieze around the topmost edges of the building. We veer up toward the Griffith Observatory and Bobby tags the dome with a thousand-colored starburst. We zoom down to the Hollywood sign and now it has *Nova Nova Nova* painted along the side of each massive letter. We skim along Mulholland drive and Bobby hits up the side of the Santa

Monica mountains, burning *Nova* into the brush with some kind of disintegrator beam. We head south and Bobby's up on every one of those towering Jap banks that own our city. We go toward the sea and Bobby tags the beach from high overhead with a kind of laser gun pencil device that fuses the sand into a hundred glassy repetitions of *Nova Nova Nova Nova* and a hundred starbursts. The aliens love it. They've stuck a transmitter in Bobby's brain and they're getting off on his joy, and even I can feel it because I know what it's like to shout your name in man-tall letters from the tops of buildings and the heights of overpasses ... I know what it's like to make the whole city that never fucking listens and never fucking cares sit up and stare me in the face and pay attention and know that I exist.

Tonight, they're *all* sitting up all right. The undertaker alien flicks a switch and we see a TV screen image hovering in the air. The airwaves are full of us. It's a gang, they're saying. A mega-gang that's decided to hit up every part of the city all at once. There's an expert on tagging on CBS now, explaining that NOVA is the initials of the New Order of Victorious Armies, some kind of neo-Nazi group ... yeah, right, that really cracks us up ... NBC says that as many as five hundred taggers are on the move ... a phone hotline is flashing on the screen ... they've preempted *Murphy Brown.* That's how fucking important we've become, two worthless street kids from beside the San Fernando railway tracks.

They give us anything we want, these aliens. Me and Bobby, we've both downed a couple of forty-ouncers by about three in the morning, and we're pissing out of the window onto the deserted streets. The experts on the TV are all explaining the different gang initials now, and there's like this psychiatrist who's all talking about alienated youth and street violence and all those other things they don't know shit about.

There's cop cars out patrolling now. They're looking for us. But the aliens cloak the flying Porsche in a cloud of pseudo-smog, and we don't show up on radar either, and anyway we're just too fast for them.

But by four in the morning Bobby's all sick of this shit. He's all, "This ain't tagging, there ain't no excitement to it, it's just high technology, there ain't no *mystery* ...no *danger.*

We just go someplace, I hit it up, we push buttons, and then we escape. Fuck this, I'm a go home now."

The aliens look at each other. The fat dude says to me, "I don't understand. I thought we were giving him ... you know, the maximum adrenalin high. What can we do?" The undertaker takes a handful of pills out of the glove compartment, I don't know, some kind of uppers I guess. Bobby just stares at them.

"You don't get it," I tell the aliens. "You tell me that you do this kind of thing yourselves, that you write your names all over like *planets* and shit, you write your names in little strings of amino acids and *we're* nothing but your signature crawling over what would have been a dead world ... but you don't seem to see that writing *big* isn't what makes it important. You've let Bobby write all over L.A. and you've let him stir up the city and upset a lot of people and there's black and whites all over town chasing us, but that ain't what it's about at all."

Right now, understand, we are parked on top of the Beverly Center, right next to the big Hard Rock Café sign, which flashes on and off and alternately makes Bobby's face white as a ghost and shadowy as death. The aliens confer with each other in whispers, in some foreign language ... sounds kind of like Japanese ... and then the tall one says to me, not at all jokingly, "So illuminate us, wise one."

So I knew something about these two aliens: they looked up to me, like the kids who used to cluster around me on the corner of Jackman and Hubbard all them years, repeating the stories about me until even I couldn't recognize them any more. At twenty-four, I was a has-been. I had passed through the fire and been burned alive and lived, kind of, even though it was only a kind of half-living. So maybe like, these aliens *were* a couple billion years old. They still hadn't gotten to the has-been stage. They couldn't see beyond themselves yet. And so I had something to teach them.

And that, to me, is a wonder in itself, and it's a fact that starts to bring me out of the death I'm in, the death I've sentenced myself to. And like, this is what I say to them: "The sociologists, the analysts, they all think the kids do this because their world's a terrible place ... their daddies beat them and their homies kill them and they're stoned out of their minds and hanging themselves every five minutes ... but that's not true. They don't do it *because* of those things ... they do it *in spite of* them. They're like the corpse that thrusts its undead arm out through the soil and grabs you by the leg as you're walking through the graveyard. They're dead, all the way dead, dead inside, and still they can't let go of life."

"So what are we to do?" says the undertaker, while Bobby twitches his bony fingers, waiting.

"You let him go, dude," I say. "You follow him at a distance, but you don't chauffeur him to where he wants to write, and you don't pluck him away when he's done."

"But," says the fat one, "what about the authorities? The LAPD's out in force by now. They think there's an army out there, a *Nova* gang. What if they catch Bobby?"

"He's already thought of that," I say.

•

Sometimes my sister comes back from a trick, and she don't give me all the money. She buys flowers and she lays them on a grave at Forest Lawn. It ain't Bobby's grave, but she says it's the thought that counts.

She don't talk to me that much anymore; I guess she thinks I killed him.

•

It's 4:30 in the morning and the jet-black Porsche lands on a knoll in Forest Lawn lightly, like a baseball cap in the wind. Bobby slips out. He knows his way around here; we've spent more than enough time among the dead people, getting stoned together, thinking about our friends who've been shot and can't afford a resting place like this, considering our own deaths too, wondering how soon they'll be. The moon is full and the grass is silver-black, and there's monument after monument ... it's a peaceful place, the stones all clean and orderly, nothing like the 'hood.

252 • TAGGING THE MOON: FAIRY TALES FROM L.A.

There's like, this humungous Grecian temple thing that looms up out of the grass, I think it's a memorial to some movie mogul. As me and the aliens watch, Bobby shimmies up an Ionian column and puts up *Nova* with a Mean Streak and a few deft flicks of his bony wrist. We see him on a dozen TV screens inside the Porsche that's a spaceship, and we even hear him breathing, amplified, Dolby surround-sound, muttering to himself like, "Fuck you for being dead, fuck you," and now, suddenly, we hear the chopper way overhead and see the search beams criss-crossing in the dark, and there's Bobby, hung on a cross of light ... and we hear sirens. And alarms. Black and whites around here somewhere. We don't see them yet. They're just around the bend of the hill probably.

"Come on, dudes," I say, "pull up, grab him," and the Porsche peels out through the grass but Bobby doesn't get in the car, instead he starts sprinting downhill, in the direction of the freeway.

We follow, and the cop cars follow but they don't go on the grass because like, this is Forest Lawn ... this is a place for *rich* dead people ... no tire tracks on *these* people's grass or it's lawsuit city ... we see Bobby run ... a tiny stick-figure now, leaping over gravemarkers, pausing to tag on the brow of a marble angel with outstretched arms, then running again ... closeup of his face hanging in the air in front of me and his face is so composed, so serene, it scares me.

"The indexes are way up," says the fat alien. "This is going to be a fabulous recording after all."

"I told you," I said. "Just leave him be and you'll get everything you want."

We follow him. He hops a wall and hits the pavement running. We follow. The cop cars follow. They're on Glendale, diverting traffic. The chopper's not police, it's fucking news. Bobby dodges the search beams. And suddenly he's gone.

"Where the—" says the undertaker alien.

"The overpass," I say.

•

There's no traffic at all on this stretch of the freeway because they've diverted everything to the 5 or the 101. There's one particular overpass where they all jumble into the 134. There's like fourteen lanes converging and diverging and above them is a row of bright green signs with big white names and numbers on them ... my guess is that we'll see Bobby there. We hurdle the blockade and we blend into the convoy of police cars that surrounds the overpass. Bobby's on his hands and knees, hugging the signs, and he has a can of green paint in one hand and a can of white in the other and he's writing, over and over, *Nova, Nova, Nova,* and the starburst, two-handed, covering the old legends with the green while writing his tagger name with the white.

They're shouting to him over the PA system. They say give yourself up, throw down your weapons, all that bullshit. There's reporters with video cameras. The Santa Ana's howling and through it there's the thrum of the helicopter. There's snipers with rifles trained on Bobby. An ambulance is pulling up. Me and the aliens, we get out of the Porsche. No one sees us because we are still cloaked in smog. We look up at where Bobby's writing.

On the signs, there's no more route numbers, no more *Burbank*, no more *Pasadena*, no more *Ventura, Los Angeles, Golden State Freeway* ... no, all the signs read *Nova, Nova, Nova* ... all roads lead to Nova. And he's all standing on top of the sign that once said *Pasadena Freeway,* balanced on the thin edge of the sign, his arms raised toward the moon ... and even that spells *Nova,* the *N* a twisted ribbon of steel, the *O* the moon, the *V* himself with his arms up, the *A* scrawled across the concrete in black paint ... he's made the whole city part of his name ... even the moon itself ... he's made himself bigger than the world.

"What's he trying to say?" the fat alien says.

And I'm all, "He's telling us who he is. The only way he knows how. Living in spite of himself. Like I told you."

I guess they gave up trying to divert the traffic because somehow it's started up again, there's eighteen-wheelers and buses and a few passenger cars now, filling the freeway except for the island of cop cars right beneath where Bobby's standing.

In the moonlight, Bobby Donahue smiles. His thin pale body's all wrapped in the moon's radiance and even from down here I see that his eyes are shining. He's all standing there, poised in the moment of childhood's end, between innocence and disillusion, and he has a grace and a beauty that no one but another tagger can understand; he's fulfilled, he's in balance. For the first time since he burst out screaming into the world of pain, he loves himself. He is free.

And then they shoot him down.

•

Today Margaret Yao actually has a copy of the *National Enquirer*. I don't know how she's managed to pay for it at the checkout without dying of embarrassment. Maybe she went in disguise.

The headline reads: *NEW EVIDENCE OF LIFE ON MOON*.

The photo, computer-enhanced and obviously retouched, shows what looks like a word, scratched in letters a hundred miles long in the lunar dust … *Nova*.

•

Bobby Donahue never hits the ground. My sister says I killed him and doesn't talk to me. She always liked him, even in junior high.

•

… "But," Dr. Yao says, "you're telling me that … when people finally get to the moon to investigate … they might even find, I don't know, fragmentary DNA segments … something that could one day evolve into…"

I tell her I don't want to sleep under the overpass anymore. I ask her if her bed in Tarzana's big enough for two. She smiles wryly. She is in love, I think; I just don't know if it's me, or merely what I stand for.

•

I sat scrunched up in the back seat as the aliens' car sped over the sleeping city. I said, "Where is he? What have you done to him?"

And they said, "Given him every honor due to him."

I watched the comet streaking, only it wasn't a comet because it burned a swath through the smog itself on its way up toward the moon.

And I said, "I don't get it. If you guys are such galactic big shots, why do you even bother to come here?"

And they said, "You might call it something like, revisiting the scene of the crime ... now and then we like to observe our handiwork."

"But ... if you really are these badass aliens from another world ... why don't you just swoop down out of the sky in your true forms, do the whole 'take me to your leader' thing? Why do you hang out with white trash like us? Why do you try to look like humans, even down to our cars? Don't you have anything better to do than to imitate us?"

The fat alien laughed for the first time. I felt they were making fun of me, treating me like a little kid. That was strange, since only an hour before they'd acted like I was the dope-ass OG motherfucking guru grandmaster and like I knew all the secrets of the universe.

The tall alien patted me on the back and said, "You have it all backwards, Todd; we're not imitating you at all. *Au contraire.* It's just that—"

The fat alien said, "We made you in our image."

They they left me on the hillside, freezing my butt off in the Santa Ana wind, and soared way way up in the direction of the sunrise.

The Other City of Angels
A note from the author

A few years ago, a Thai publisher printed an edition of one of my novels with a photo I took as the cover. For some strange reason, this book went on the Thai bestseller list, and my editor attributed it to the photo.

She kept asking me about other photographs I'd done, and as I began showing her more and more of my portfolio—pictures done for my own and my friends' amusement—she one day hinted at the idea of an exhibition. I was flabbergasted at first—after all, I hardly considered myself a fledging Richard Avedon!—but she persisted, and eventually my first gallery show, "The Other City of Angels," opened at a bookstore-coffeehouse-art gallery in Bangkok.

Why the "other" city of angels? Simple enough. I live part of the year in Bangkok, part in Los Angeles. We in the U.S. are used to referring to Los Angeles and the "City of Angels," but Bangkok is also called the City of Angels by its inhabitants, because the first two words of its full name (which starts Krung Thep Phra Mahanakorn Amorn Ratanakosin and goes on for another paragraph) also mean "City of Angels." I wanted the audience in Bangkok to see a view of the "other" city of angels—through the eyes of one of their own.

These photos, therefore, are really another fairy tale of Los Angeles... another way of looking at this bewildering, mythic, gaudy, unmanageable city. I include them in this edition of my *L.A. Fairy Tales* as a little bonus... another little piece of myself.

The Author

S.P. Somtow was born in Bangkok and educated at Eton and Cambridge; his first career was as a composer and his works have been widely performed, televised and broadcast around the world—his most recent composition was the full-length ballet *Kaki,* recently given a Royal Command Performance in Bangkok with dancers from the Bolshoi, Ballet Rambert, and Company of Performing Arts.

As an author, he has published some forty books and hundreds of short stories, articles, and poems. They include classics of science fiction and fantasy such as *Starship & Haiku* and *The Riverrun Trilogy,* novels of dark fantasy such as *Moon Dance, Vampire Junction,* and *Darker Angels,* and mainstream novels like the historical fiction *The Shattered Horse* and the semiautobiographical memoir *Jasmine Nights.*

He has also directed two films, appeared as a guest commentator on the Sci-Fi Channel and the Learning Channel, and recently had a photographic exhibition, *The Other City of Angels.* For information about S.P. Somtow, visit his web site, **http://www.primenet.com/~somtow**.

S.P. Somtow divides his time between Los Angeles and Bangkok.